OUT OF MY DREAMS

A NOVEL BY

Mary Lou Irace

Dear Joanne,
Dream on ...
love,
Marylou

D1501708

Out of My Dreams Copyright © 2016 by Mary Lou Irace

All rights reserved. Printed in the United States of America. No part of this book may be used or reproduced in any manner whatsoever without written permission except in the case of brief quotations embodied in critical articles or reviews.

This book is a work of fiction. Names, characters, businesses, organizations, places, events, and incidents either are the product of the author's imagination or are used fictitiously. Any resemblance to actual persons, living or dead, events, or locales is entirely coincidental.

For information: www.facebook.com/MaryLouIraceAuthor

Cover Photo: melisphotography (melis/shutterstock.com)
Author Photo: Sally Foley Photography

ISBN: 978-1523753819
1523753811

First Edition: April 2016

10 9 8 7 6 5 4 3 2 1

CONTENTS

To Rick

For sharing all my dreams.

CHAPTER

1

Tara Fitzpatrick watched in disbelief as the horrific images flashed across her television screen. She had been at work when it happened, and the national news and cable outlets were providing continuous coverage, keeping the public in the loop of information. Now that she was back home in her apartment, the impact of what occurred only seven blocks away overwhelmed her. Tara wondered: What if I had been walking or running by there when that maniac detonated those bombs?

It was by pure chance, luck, or fate that Tara was spared. She had passed directly in front of the Pitten Building only two hours before the historical ten-story structure was split in half by an explosion and burned to the ground. As she reflected about how fortunate she had been, Tara's heart ached for the hundreds of people who died or were severely injured at the hands of a madman.

The news was reporting that a forty-four-year-old man named Leonard Hopkins was responsible for the carnage. Security cameras across the street had captured the image of a man, exiting the building and holding a large canvas bag, minutes before the blast. The police apprehended him at his sister's house in the next town, where he surrendered without incident. According to investigators, he originally planned to kill himself inside the building, but he changed his mind at the last minute. A rambling suicide note was recovered from his apartment, detailing his anger and frustration at being fired from the job he had held for more than twelve years.

The former disgruntled employee of Silver Industries had planted several homemade bombs in some of the utility closets in the building. Hopkins gained entry into the complex by disguising himself as a food delivery worker and was simply waved through by an uninterested security guard.

Hopkins carefully set the crudely made devices to detonate at precisely 11 a.m. on May 11, 1999. This was one year to the day and hour he was fired from his lower-level administrative position for insubordination and threats to his supervisor. Tara pondered that in his ignorance and malice, he was astute enough to realize that on a Tuesday morning, the building would be filled with people.

Tara had spoken to her father earlier that day and assured him that she was safe and had arrived at work before the tragedy occurred. She had also received a frantic phone call from her best friend Leslie, who knew Tara passed by the building to catch the train to work into Manhattan every day. Tara stared at the TV while the news anchor reported that the massive explosion had been heard from miles away and that firefighters were still working to extinguish the inferno.

As Tara sat alone in her home, she realized she was shaking and had started to cry. Despite the fact that everything was under control now, she knew the devastation from this terrible incident had only just begun.

Tara sat down on her couch and closed her eyes. She whispered quietly, "God, please help all of them. And Mom? Thanks for watching out for me. Again."

Tara had become somewhat of a loner in recent years, not by choice; things just evolved that way. At the age of twenty-eight, she lived an anonymous life in the city, where everyone left her alone, and once she walked out on the street she just blended in with the crowd. Even if she dressed differently or acted strangely, no one noticed. Tara liked that. Actually, she loved that. She never cared what people thought of her, not realizing that everyone thought the world of her. Each day she woke up grateful to be alive and just did what she had to do.

Growing up in a suburban town near the beach in central New Jersey, she had wonderful memories, but the northern cities of Harbor Point and New York City always held her heart. The noise, the sea of bodies — especially on a weekday morning — all walking to their destinations, the massive structures that seemed to corral the herd of not-quite-awake humans into one giant huddle were all so comforting and safe to one who was truly a metropolitan girl.

Harbor Point, New Jersey, was the place Tara always wanted to call home. Located on the river across from New York City, it was the best of both worlds for Tara because of its urban setting with a small-town vibe. Trendy shops, restaurants, hotels, and businesses were all within a five-mile radius. Shortly after her graduation from college, Tara found a small one-bedroom with a little help from one of her father's high school buddies. She worked in Manhattan, but she adored coming home to the cozy apartment in her quiet, quaint, neighborhood.

Tara wasn't trying to live such a narrow existence. With each passing year, she seemed to retreat further into a world that only consisted of books, scientific journals, software, her relatives, and Leslie. New situations frightened her, or she was simply disinterested. She often felt her life was spinning forward and she was just along for the ride. Monday would start a new week at work, and then suddenly it was Friday. One month rolled into the next, and Tara never felt like she had anything significant to show for it. Sure, she had tremendous passion for her job, but no one special to share a romantic passion with in her everyday life. Most of her friends and cousins were married and had at least one kid; some had several kids and houses and, according to her father's standards: real, adult lives. It's not that Tara didn't want marriage and a family; they just hadn't happened yet.

Those pieces hadn't come together because her social life had become virtually non-existent. Leslie was married to a great guy named Rob Gordon, and they had an adorable baby, Buck. Since Leslie was still breastfeeding, she rarely left the suburbs of Morris

County, and Tara lost her party wingman. Other friends who used to be willing to hit the bar and club scene on a Friday night were now too exhausted or couldn't get a babysitter, or even afford a babysitter. At this stage of her own life, Tara would rather stay home most nights and watch a movie, read a book, or go visit her father.

She felt like there weren't many opportunities to meet nice, single guys. Even Tara's job restricted her prospects with acceptable candidates of the opposite sex. She worked alongside all men who were, as she put it nicely, tech geeks who were more interested in machines than in women.

Graduating with a degree in Computer Science from Rutgers University, Tara felt comfortable in the realm of technology. She had always loved computers as a child, asking her parents to buy her all the latest gadgets, games, and devices. Being a tactile person, she loved fixing things and had an overdeveloped brain for the mechanical and physical objects in her world. Friends and family members would call her when something was broken or jammed, and Tara could usually fix it or tell them what to do to make it work again. As a research analyst in a large law firm in midtown Manhattan, her current job involved collecting, processing, and reviewing data and research so it could be stored for information in litigation. She loved her job because she was always learning new things and it never got old or boring. Only her love life was boring. Tara worked with a great group of guys, but there was no one she was attracted to.

As for the lawyers who worked there, most were older and married, and any of the single ones she had met were not her type.

One younger associate had asked her out the year before and took Tara for an expensive dinner and Broadway show. But when he expected her to go home with him later that night and Tara politely declined, she never heard from him again. Then there was the bowling date with the thirty-six year old attorney who asked Tara what she thought of atheism as a viable religion, while extolling the virtues of prostitution in a capitalist society. Then there was the public defender who wanted to bring his mother along on their date because she was in town and didn't think Tara would mind. She did.

So eventually, Tara gave up trying to find Mr. Right at work and decided she would just stick to working with all the Mr. Wrongs in the technology department. It was just easier that way.

When Tara looked in the mirror, she wasn't aware that there was anything special looking back. Considering herself very average in the looks department, she didn't put a lot of time or effort in her daily appearance. She loved all things feminine, but she also had a tomboy side. Football, baseball, and hockey turned her on as much as seeing some hunk of a guy. Occasionally, Tara would put on a special outfit or dress at work, but no one seemed to notice. Leslie would yell at Tara all the time to look sexier at work so guys could see her figure better than they could in those baggy slacks and oversized shirts. She would hound Tara to use make-up to highlight her bright blue eyes, and nag her to leave her dark hair down more instead of twisting it up in a messy bun. But Tara concluded that when there was no reason to do it and no one to see it, why bother?

The sudden death of her mother from a heart attack when Tara was eight years old changed her. Over the years, she only confided in a tight circle of people, and she had only short-term romances with a couple of boyfriends. Tara realized her world was getting smaller and smaller, but it was infinitely easier to manage a few, already established relationships than to make the effort to start any new ones.

Besides, Tara often surmised lately, *I would have no idea where to begin.*

CHAPTER
2

The most logical explanation Tara could come up with that morning was that she needed to see it with her own eyes. She couldn't stand watching it on TV any more, and it was on the cover of every newspaper in the tri-state area. Tara felt compelled to go there, maybe because she had escaped being a victim herself. At least that's what she reasoned, knowing it would not be easy to see.

It had been an early Sunday morning, and Tara had decided to take a run down to see the Pitten Building. A long-distance runner since high school, she continued to hit the pavement almost every day. Running in Harbor Point was one of her great pleasures because she could be one with all the places she loved so much: the scenic track along the river, Madison Park, and the marina.

Walking out of her apartment, she looked up at the sky amid the towering buildings. Something still lingered in the air, but it wasn't the usual smog. Tara shook her head in disbelief that this had happened here, at the hands of some unstable lunatic.

"Unbelievable..." she muttered angrily as she began a five-mile run down the barely inhabited sidewalk outside her building.

As she approached the site of the former Pitten Building, Tara was hit with the pungent smell of burning plastic. She could feel stuff under her feet that didn't belong there. She could hear machines roaring, drills buzzing, and men calling out instructions to one another. The entire area was off limits except for rescue workers, firemen, and police.

When she got as close as they were permitting the public, and could see the still smoldering pile, she gasped at the horror before her. It completely took the breath out of her for a moment as she realized how unprepared she was to see this in all of its tragic reality. One of the most beautiful landmarks in Harbor Point was gone. Completely destroyed. All that remained was an enormous gray pile of brick and debris. It looked like the pictures she had seen in history books of bombed cities in Europe during World War II. Tara tried to wrap her brain around what she was seeing, but it wouldn't compute.

She thought about the people buried in that pile, the ones who never got out, who never went home that night. Hundreds of innocent lives were lost, and countless others were injured or maimed from the blast. The retrieval of bodies was now paramount, and the focus had changed from a rescue mission to recovery mode.

Tara wiped the tears from her eyes with her shirtsleeve and forced herself to watch emergency workers moving debris. The hardest to see was when they found someone or a part of someone. She eventually had to turn away from seeing the sadness on the faces of these selfless people who worked to find those who were lost.

Later that evening, Tara entered the bathroom in her apartment to perform her usual bedtime ritual. Splashing water on her face, she washed off her make-up and brushed her teeth. Suddenly, Tara froze, overcome by the feeling that she was not alone. Yet she was alone in her apartment with a deadbolt on her front door along with two chain locks. Tara turned around quickly, certain that she would catch someone standing behind her. Looking at her reflection in the mirror above the sink, she was filled with a sense of dread and panic as her heart raced and her head pounded.

"What the hell?" She said out loud, hoping the sound of her voice would scare away whatever imaginary boogeyman was there. Tara's body began to shake. She broke out in a sweat, and her breathing became labored. Gripping the sink, she sat down on the toilet, feeling like she was about to pass out. She felt trapped, despite the wide-open door. After a few minutes, she managed to stand up and make it out to her bed, where she slowly lay down.

Tara noticed that as soon as she left the bathroom she began to feel better, or at least somewhat more normal. She lay there, spread-eagled, staring up at the ceiling, trying to figure out what had just happened. Running through a checklist in her mind, Tara determined that she didn't feel unusually stressed out, was eating properly most of the time, and was working out on a regular basis. She turned her head and stared at the picture on the nightstand. It was a family picture of Tara and her parents, taken at the Point Pleasant Beach boardwalk when she was six years old. Tara loved it because her mother seemed to be looking directly at her, smiling and happy. And healthy.

Shit.

Was I having a heart attack just now? Tara feared she was going to die young like her mother and she began to sweat again. *Oh my God, that's it! I'm having heart issues! It's in my genetic make-up!* She concluded. Now a different kind of panic set in, yet at least she had some explanation for why a sensible, levelheaded, twenty-eight-year-old woman would lose her mind for no good reason.

Once she calmed down, Tara swung her legs over the side of the bed and sat up. Steadying herself, she stood and walked into the kitchen for a glass of water. Taking her laptop, she sat on the couch and searched for *heart attack symptoms.* She discovered that she matched up with a couple of things on the list but had no chest pain or limb weakness, and that it was common to confuse having a heart attack with having a panic attack.

"Oh, great. Now I'm going psycho. And I'm talking to myself way too much. I need to go buy a goldfish," she mumbled.

Tara was beginning to realize that she was too young to be acting so old and wondered if living alone was beginning to take a toll on her mental health.

Jesus, Tara. You so need to get a life.

It was late, and she couldn't call Leslie, so she picked up the novel she had started and tried to relax until she felt comfortable enough to go to sleep. Tara decided to blame a hormonal imbalance, her period, or a vitamin deficiency for her curious episode.

She woke the next morning after a restless sleep. Tara was almost afraid to go back into her bathroom for fear of a repeat of the previous night. As she proceeded with caution and stepped into the small space, everything seemed fine, like it was just a momentary lapse in her sanity. Tara shook her head and laughed at herself.

No rational, stable human being should be afraid of her bathroom, Tara.

After taking a shower and getting some coffee and oatmeal into her system, Tara was ready to face her day. Deciding not to bother Leslie with her tales of terror at this hour of the morning, Tara walked out the door and headed to work. Her curious episode was dismissed from her mind.

Until it happened again that night. No sweating or breathing problems, just that overwhelming sense of doom and despair. Simultaneously, another curious thing started. Whenever Tara began to blow dry her hair, the image of a little girl popped into her head. And only when she was in the bathroom.

What is with this damn bathroom? she wondered.

Annoyance now replaced fear, and Tara needed to come up with some logical explanation for this ridiculousness. Looking into the mirror, she firmly stated out loud: "Ok, I know I'm definitely not having a heart attack because I'd be dead by now. It has become habitual thinking, and I have to mentally command my brain to stop the pattern. I graduated summa cum laude from college, for God's sake. I can and will do this."

Tara came to the conclusion that maybe she just had way too much time to think, especially with all the turmoil surrounding the bombing. That, and she was watching way too much TV and reading newspapers. The psychologists in the media were talking about posttraumatic stress and the effects it would have on people. *Of course*, she decided, *that's what all this is.* She would just have to learn how to get over it.

But in addition to the bathroom sensations, there came the dreams; the dreams that started the following night: two reoccurring, alternate dreams. The first was of a man standing on a football or soccer field, and he never spoke, never moved, and Tara never saw his face. She opened her eyes the next morning, knowing she had a dream, but it had no significance to her, so she just dismissed it. Perhaps it was something she had seen or heard that day, and it had wormed its way into her subconscious mind.

The following night, she had a different dream where a man stood in an auditorium or theater watching something on a stage. Once again: no words, no movement, no face.

Between the dreams and the bathroom shenanigans, *every single night,* Tara thought she might seriously be losing her mind. Something wasn't right about it, and she hated when things were out of her control.

When Tara finally asked Leslie on the phone for her advice a few days later, Leslie replied: "It must be your brain instructing you to have the same dream and thoughts each night, like power of suggestion or something weird like that. I mean really, Tara, all that info you have to deal with at work every day — maybe your head is on total overload by the time you go to bed. Try drinking warm milk or taking a hot bath before you go to sleep; maybe that will help you relax."

"But what do you think it means?" Tara questioned.

"I have no idea what it means! Dreams are usually crazy and make no sense in my experience. I think you are just stressed out from work," Leslie answered.

"Yeah, maybe you're right."

"Or maybe it's something else; something *bigger*," Leslie said as she made her voice sound serious.

"What do you mean?" asked Tara.

"Well, maybe it's pent-up frustration."

"Frustration?"

"Yes."

"Frustration over what?"

"You know."

"No, I don't."

There was silence on Leslie's end. Then she started to giggle.

"Oh, shut up, you ass!" Tara yelled. Then they both began laughing.

"I'm just saying, Tara. It's been a long time. Maybe a good one-night stand with one of the geeks or creeps from your office would fix you right up. I mean a girl has needs…"

"I'm hanging up now!" Tara shouted into the phone. "Thanks for the useless advice."

Tara hung up on Leslie but not because she was mad at her. She just wanted to make a point that what she needed right now wasn't a hook-up. What she needed were answers to her many questions. That's when Tara decided she needed some real, solid advice. This required someone who could listen and fix all of it. Reassurance and counsel of the highest order in a person's life: a.k.a. Daddy.

Dialing his number, she concluded: *He won't think I'm schizophrenic or deranged. He loves me — I'm his flesh and blood, and he would never judge me. Besides, if I am going crazy, it would be his fault. He raised me.*

"Dad?"

"Hey honey! What's up?"

"Are you around this weekend?"

"Always for you. Everything ok?"

"Yes. I just need to see you. That's all."

CHAPTER

3

The following Saturday, Tara took the train home to see her father. She decided that a change of scenery would do her good; maybe sleeping in her old bed would break the streak of madness she was experiencing. Being in her childhood home surrounded by stuffed animals, trophies, and teenage paraphernalia would make her remember happy things. Tara had become weary with all these things she had no explanation for. After the curious events that continued to occur in her apartment and in her dreams this past week, she just needed to be back in her house.

There was no one on earth Tara loved and trusted more than her Dad, not even Leslie. It was a tight father-daughter bond, and Tara often wondered if the reason he never remarried was because of her. When Tara had asked him recently if he was seeing anyone special, he just winked at her and replied, "They're all special, sweetie; but when you have a permanent hole in your heart they are just not special enough to fill it. Only your mother could do that. But don't you worry, I'm never desperate for company, be it female or fellow." Tara decided that her father did a fine job of filling his life with good people, and since she had moved to Harbor Point a few years ago, he worked, hung out with his buddies, and went on the occasional date. It was all he wanted her to know; it was all she needed to know.

Tara was the only child of Ann and James Fitzpatrick. The couple had tried for more children and was shocked to discover Ann could conceive only Tara. All the Fitzpatrick and O'Connell families had multiple children, as they were from good, solid, Irish Catholic heritage. Jimmy Fitzpatrick never made it known to his wife that he was disappointed in their failure to produce more offspring. A naturally happy man, he was simply grateful for what he had and would never complain. A loving wife and one healthy child was more than one man could ask for. If this were God's plan for them, Jimmy would never be so selfish as to question it.

Jimmy Fitzpatrick lived in the same small house since Tara was born. A tall man who each year was losing more of his graying hair, Jimmy lived a quiet life since his wife passed away so many years ago. Whereas Tara didn't mind being alone most of the time, Jimmy loved to have people him around constantly. He had a posse of good friends to go fishing and drinking with on a regular basis. A plumber by trade, Jimmy had made a nice life for his family and always gave back to the people in his community, particularly his parish and the priests and nuns who lived there.

As the train pulled away from the station, Tara spotted her father walking toward her.

"Hey, little girl!" he said as he drew her into his welcoming arms.

"Hey, Daddy," she said, giving him a huge hug in return. He grabbed her overnight bag and pointed to the parking lot.

"How was the ride? Crowded?" Jimmy asked.

"No, not too bad for a Saturday, actually," she answered.

"Want to get something to eat downtown?"

"Sounds good. I'm starving!"

They put her bag in the trunk of the car and walked from the station lot to a nearby diner. The day was unusually warm, and the air conditioning felt good in the restaurant.

"So, how are things at work?" he asked as they settled into a booth.

"The job is good; tons of new stuff every day. Keeps me busy." Tara answered as she began to study the menu. Jimmy was completely in the dark about what Tara did for a living, since he could barely manage a cell phone, let alone a computer. In fact, he didn't even own one and still wrote out his checks and shopped in person. "I don't trust the Internet," he would tell Tara, and she would just laugh at him.

"Well, I just thank God you're employed. Lots of people are out of work."

Tara nodded in agreement. After catching up on the family and town gossip, Tara decided to bring up the subject of the dreams. "Um,

Dad, I need to talk to you about something. Something that's been bothering me lately."

The young waitress suddenly appeared to take their order. Tara wanted blueberry pancakes and coffee. Jimmy ordered a western omelet, white toast, and coffee.

"You look tired, Tara."

"I haven't been sleeping well lately," she sighed, looking up at his face. "That's one of the reasons I needed to come home this weekend; I need your advice on something."

"Ok, cookie — shoot," he said as the waitress placed a coffee pot and mugs on the table.

"Daddy, I've been having these dreams at night, and I'm weirding out a little bit about them."

Jimmy stirred cream and two sugars into his coffee. "What kind of dreams?"

"A kind of reoccurring dream where some random guy just stands and stares at a football field and another where I think the same guy stands in the back of a theater looking at something in front of him," Tara said as she fixed her own coffee.

Jimmy waited for the rest of the story and was surprised when she stopped speaking.

"That's it? That's the whole dream?" he asked.

"Well, yes."

"And this is keeping you up at night? I'm sorry, honey, I just don't get it. Exactly what is the problem?"

"The problem, Daddy, is that I keep having one of these dreams every night. The exact same dream. Either the guy is on the field or in the theater — every, single night. Don't you think that's a little strange?" she asked, exasperated.

"I don't really know. I guess it's possible to have reoccurring dreams like that. Why is it bothering you so much? It seems harmless enough to me," he said as he sipped his coffee.

"If I just had it once, yes. But I keep having the same two dreams; I don't know of anyone who dreams like that. And, Dad, I don't normally have dreams so it's really unusual for me."

"Are you sure you're not too stressed out at work? Maybe you need to take a day off. Why don't you come home for a long weekend? We can get a couple of your cousins together and do something fun for a change. We could take the boat out on the river or go to the beach now that the weather is getting nice; before the BENNYS get here for the summer." He scowled. Locals loved the time before Memorial Day and after Labor Day when traffic thinned, the crowds disappeared, and they reclaimed their beaches and territory from the invading tourists.

"Daddy, there's more weirdness than just the dreams. Almost every time I go into the bathroom in my apartment, I get the feeling that someone is in there with me, and I have this overwhelming sense of, well, despair. It's like a sense of hopelessness that I can't shake until I am out of there for a few minutes. It's hard to explain." She sighed in frustration. Tara decided to leave out the part about the image of the girl while drying her hair. She considered that far too peculiar to ever bring up.

"How long has this been going on?"

Tara thought back for a moment. Then it registered.

"It started on Sunday, I think. Yes, that's right. It was the day after I came back from seeing the Pitten Building," she answered. Then she quickly realized he would not be happy with her answer. But she couldn't lie — he would see right through her. *He is going to be so pissed at me.*

"Jesus, Mary, and Joseph, Tara, no wonder!" Jimmy grit his teeth and was shaking his head in disbelief. "I told you to stay away from all that crap down there. Not only because of the sight of that tragedy, but because of the shit that must be lying around on the ground. You could have gotten yourself hurt!"

Tara rolled her eyes. Now he would go on some parental rant. She would probably need to remind him of her age.

"You are lucky you are only having dreams and not horrible nightmares from seeing that place. For Christ's sake, Tara, what made you go down there?"

"I don't know why I went down there, Daddy, curiosity I guess; anger too. It still really pisses me off that a psychopath did this to all those innocent people." Jimmy raised a bushy eyebrow when she used the *p* word.

Tara's father wasn't an educated man in the degree sense of the word, but he did have a lot of depth for a plumber.

"You know what I think?"

"What, Pops?"

"I think all this bombing stuff has your mind in overdrive, especially when you try to go to sleep at night. Hell, everyone is in mourning and outraged over this. So it's only natural for you to be preoccupied with thoughts of doom and gloom. I sure as hell hope they lock that bastard away forever and let him rot in jail. But anyway, there are certain things you need to do. Let's start with you staying away from there from now on. Do you hear me, Tara?" He stated firmly, pointing his finger at her.

"Yes, Dad. But I thought I could buy the rescue workers some coffee or water and leave it there this week..."

"No, Tara. Find some other way to help. Like praying or donating money to the victims' families. I don't want you down there until they clear that site. Understand?"

"Yes, Daddy." Tara said, reluctantly.

"Also, I think you spend too much time alone. Too much time to think is never a good thing in my experience. Maybe you need a new hobby or better yet, some nice young man to take your mind off all this," he said as he raised the mug to his lips with a raised eyebrow.

Tara wasn't going to acknowledge that, so she ignored the suggestion. "So you don't think I'm just weird or crazy or have some kind of tumor pressing on a part of my brain that would cause a person to have strange, looping dreams?"

Jimmy let out one of his deep laughs that shook his growing beer belly. "No, I don't think that, little girl. You're too smart and pretty for your own good."

"But that's how I feel lately. I don't ever remember being so unsettled. I usually am able to keep it all together. It feels like I'm in another world most of the time."

"Well, honey, we always said you had that thing from your mother's side of the family that allows you to connect to the other side," he said, matter-of-factly.

Tara looked at him, stunned. "Excuse me? What *thing?*"

The waitress brought their food and placed it in front of them. "Can I get you anything else; more coffee?"

"No darlin', we're good for now, thanks." Jimmy answered with a smile. A huge plate of food was before him, and he was a happy, hungry man.

"Daddy! What are you talking about? I'm twenty-eight years old. I've never heard about some thing on Mom's side. What does that mean?" Tara glared at him, ignoring the stack of pancakes before her.

Jimmy swallowed a large forkful of omelet first. Wiping his mouth with his napkin, he began to explain. "When you were little, around two years old, you started to do something that was, well unusual."

"And you wait until now to enlighten me, Dad? What the hell?!"

"Please Tara, your language, huh?"

"Sorry."

"Ok, so when you were a baby, before you could actually talk, you used to look up out of nowhere, and just jabber and carry on a conversation with someone who wasn't there. You would look up at the ceiling, like there was someone hovering over you and talk to him or her. Darnedest thing I ever saw! Your mother and I would look at each other and crack up and shake our heads. We used to say you were talking to ghosts or long-dead relatives. I swear, Tara, you had some strange connection to someone somewhere!"

Tara looked at him, annoyed. "And you and my mother thought this was funny? Why have you never told me this? I mean, really, it is very odd for a toddler to talk to thin air, right? Did you ever have me examined by a doctor or shrink or someone?"

Jimmy dismissed her barrage of questions, waving his hand. "Little kids do and say all kinds of strange things. We just chalked it up to your imagination. Or that O'Connell thing."

"Why have you never told me this?"

"To be completely honest, I had forgotten about it until now." Then he had a look of recognition on his face. "Wait. There was one other thing I just remembered!"

"Please feel free to pile on even more lunacy, Daddy Dearest." Tara said sarcastically.

"This was really freaky. Before your mother died, like months before, we would wake up in the middle of the night and find you standing next to our bed, just staring at your mother. You would simply stand there, quietly watching her sleep. When we asked you what was wrong, you said you came down to check on her, to make sure she was still breathing." With that, Jimmy pushed the memory away and picked up a heaping forkful of his food.

"And you and Mom didn't think that was strange?" she asked completely baffled.

"Oh, yeah we did, but like I said kids do and say the darnedest things sometimes, so we just let it go. But now that I look back, it was almost as if you had a premonition or sixth sense that something was going to happen to your mother, as if you had to make sure she was all right because you knew something was going to happen."

They both stopped eating and looked at each other, the sadness of her death shared once again between them. Their waitress interrupted by asking, "Do you two need anything?" Tara quietly laughed at how ironic the question was and shook her head.

"Tara, please stop talking and eat," Jimmy pointed to her plate.

Slicing into her pancakes, Tara asked, "So Father, any other schizophrenic moments from the childhood of Tara Fitzpatrick that you can remember or would like to share?"

"No, I think that just about does it. At least nothing else that stands out in this old, feeble brain," he answered.

Tara smiled at him. She wondered if someday she would ever meet a guy who would accept her and understand her like he did. It was unconditional, connected, long lasting, unbreakable stuff: family stuff.

"Ok, Dad. Now you need to expound on this family *thing* you alluded to."

"Good to hear your college education paid off: nice vocabulary, because I have no idea what you just said!" He laughed.

"What is it, and does anyone else in our family have it — or am I the only lucky one?"

"Well as I said, this thing comes from your mother's side, not mine, thank God. And I think your Aunt Noreen has it. But listen, honey, I don't think this is anything to get crazy about. It's really not a big deal. It's like a sixth sense about things — I understand that a lot of people say they have it."

"Yeah, people who are *nuts*."

He reached across the table and took her hand. "You are far from nuts, honey."

"Yeah, well. I guess now I will have to investigate this mysterious secret, Father, with my mother's family, since you have no useful information or answers for me. Thanks. Now I really feel like a freak."

"All families are unique. Ours is no different. Why don't you call your aunt? I'm sure she'd love to hear from you, anyway. I know she was worried about you being in the city with all that's happened." Jimmy said through a mouthful of food.

Tara shook her head. "Enough of this supernatural shit. Oops, sorry, Daddy."

"Tara," he said, deepening his voice while giving her one of his disapproving, parental looks.

"You do realize, Dad, that I am almost thirty years old. I think I've earned the right to curse now and then." Tara liked saying curse words; she thought they just felt cathartic sometimes.

"Oh no, my child you are wrong. You only earn that right when you become a parent yourself. So unless you have a secret baby and husband stashed away somewhere you can't use curse words in front of me," he proclaimed with a wink.

Oh, no. Here it comes. Again.

"And on that note — met any nice lads in that big city lately?" Jimmy asked while taking another slug of coffee.

Tara wondered if her father and Leslie compared notes on the subject of her love life — or lack of it.

"Nope. Still single. Apparently, perpetually so. But I promise that you will be the first one to know if anyone materializes."

Jimmy just smiled again at his beautiful daughter. One day she would let someone else in, someone besides himself. He just hoped and prayed it would be in his lifetime.

CHAPTER

4

On Wednesday evening, after Tara got home from work and running, she called her cousin Maura and had a long conversation about Aunt Noreen's *thing*. Maura was Noreen's oldest daughter, and Tara figured if anyone had the information she needed, it would be Maura and not any of her four younger brothers. Tara trusted Maura not to say anything to the rest of the family, nor to think she was going insane.

"Did you inherit any of this crock of crap?" Tara inquired after Maura confirmed that she and a few others in the O'Connell clan knew of Aunt Noreen's gift and that it was present in the ancestors preceding her. But no one really talked about it because it was too unusual.

"No, none of us did that I know of; at least no one has had the balls to admit it. But maybe it skips a generation, like having twins. What the hell do I know?" she laughed.

"Well, all I do know is that in the twenty-eight years I've been on this earth, no one has ever talked about this family secret. I know because it's super bizarre and I would have definitely remembered it; and all of us would have been making fun of our parents — you know we would have, Maura!" Tara exclaimed.

"True, but how many times did we sit around with the old fogies? We were off doing something we weren't allowed to do and stayed as far away from the adults as possible. So if it was discussed, we were never around to hear it or even care about it. Besides, from what little I know, it wasn't like, a major talent or anything. It was more like intuition and sensing, not like reading minds or predicting the future. I mean, Jesus, Tara, most women, especially if you are a mother, can do the same things."

"From what I hear, I guess. Speaking of kids, how are yours? And Carl — please tell him I said hello and that I'm ready to beat his ass in bubble hockey at your Fourth of July party." Tara said. All of Tara's cousins who were married (which only excluded her and two others in that generation) had picked really nice spouses and they all had a great time together, excluding Gilbert, the husband of her cousin, Megan. Tara thought he lacked the fun gene, but everyone tried to be nice and include him because they loved Megan.

"Everyone is good, thanks, just crazy; they're all over the place. I'm the human taxicab: just wait until you have kids. You'll see," Maura answered.

"From your mouth to God's ears."

"When you least expect it, kid. So have I sufficiently answered all your questions on this topic?" Maura asked.

"Yeah, thanks. But, listen — do me a favor. If you don't mind, I'd rather you kept this conversation just between us for now. I don't need a thousand phone calls and emails proclaiming me the new wack-a-doodle in the family. Jeez, why do I have to be the lucky one?" Tara whined.

Maura giggled. "Don't worry. Your secret's safe with me. And for what it's worth, I know we are a crazy bunch, but I don't think you are in particular. Just think, maybe it'll turn out to be a useful thing after all."

Tara doubted her cousin's prediction; after all, Maura didn't claim to have any special insights. Those just seemed to be reserved for Tara.

Lucky me.

Tara went home to her father's house that weekend to pay a long over-due visit to her Aunt Noreen who lived in the same town. She made her father come with her.

"Sure, why not. Been a while since I've seen the old bird."

Tara smiled because Aunt Noreen wasn't much older than he was, and he insisted that she was old even when he had first started dating Tara's mother. Jimmy and Noreen enjoyed teasing each other and had a good relationship, so Tara felt OK bringing him along for the inquisition.

Noreen Leary was a widow, having lost her husband to lung cancer a few years before. She was a smart, attractive woman, who in her youth had a full mane of the most gorgeous, auburn hair and long, muscled legs from her dancing days. A member of the chorus line in many successful productions in New York, she could sing as well as dance. Jimmy always told his wife Ann that Noreen had the nicest "gams" in town, and she would dutifully swat his behind with a kitchen towel and he would run laughing from the room. Jimmy and Noreen were two people who had married their true loves and never thought about repeating those vows. The bond they shared with their spouses was special and lasting, uncommon in many of the other marriages of their peers.

Tara loved going to her aunt's house, and she had wonderful childhood memories of parties and holidays there in the small bungalow. It always smelled like vanilla cookies, and the living room walls were covered with framed posters of the shows from her Broadway years. When they were all kids, Noreen would play the upright piano in her living room, and all the cousins would dance around and sing at the top of their lungs. Aunt Noreen and Uncle Billy would never yell at them to be quiet. Their house was party central to the O'Connell clan.

Tara rushed in to greet her aunt with a big hug and kiss. Noreen held on tight, and Tara knew why. Jimmy carried the bag of doughnuts and a cardboard tray with three large cups of coffee into the kitchen. Noreen had a weakness for crullers, so she was thrilled to not only see her niece, but also the bag of treats.

"Aunt Noreen, you look like a million bucks, as usual! I love your hair and that blouse!" Tara fussed.

"Oh, sweetie, you always make me feel so good! How are you? What's new? Come in and sit down. Oh, and hello to you too, James." She pretended to sound aloof.

"Hey Noreen — what's shakin'? You look well — for a senior citizen," Jimmy joked.

"Shut your yapper, old man and sit down," she smiled. The two loved to get their digs in on each other.

Tara sat down and proceeded to recite how work was going well, how the city was turned upside down, how she wanted to lose five pounds before the summer, how freaked out she was with all of the problems in the world, and so on. She was like a little girl when she was with her family: she felt loved, protected, and safe when she was with them.

"Take a breath, Tara!" Jimmy instructed.

"Now you just shush, Jimmy Fitzpatrick! I love this kid's enthusiasm! Just let her speak for God's sake!" Noreen laughed as she took out plates, napkins, and spoons.

"Sorry. I haven't seen you for a while, Aunt Noreen, but things have been crazy!"

"I know honey. I don't know how you stay all alone in that city especially with all that has happened. You don't live anywhere near that, right?" she asked, concerned.

"No, but it's not that far. I went down to see it. You can't imagine," Tara said, shaking her head.

"My neighbor down the street lost her son — such a terrible thing. Poor child was only twenty-four years old! His parents are inconsolable, so we all have been trying to help out: bringing meals and doing the yardwork," Noreen said sadly.

"That's good of you, Noreen, I'm sure it's greatly appreciated," Jimmy said as he reached into the bag of doughnuts.

"So, aside from us having this nice visit, is there something else that brought you all the way home this weekend, Tara?" Noreen asked, innocently.

Maura had a BIG mouth.

"Um, yes. I need to ask you about something my father told me recently. That some sort of strange thing apparently exists on the O'Connell side of the family, which by the way most of us have never heard about. And frankly, Aunt Noreen, I am just a little disturbed because I may be the grand prize winner who got this...this *thing*!"

"Tara, relax," Jimmy said through a mouthful of jelly doughnut. "Noreen, I guess I never mentioned your ability to my daughter, and she is concerned that she may have inherited it."

"Oh, dear," said Noreen in a hushed tone. "It never ceases to rattle you when you discover it. Isn't that right?"

"Duh!" Tara responded.

"Sweetheart, tell me what's been going on. I need to hear specifically what your experience has been. Perhaps, then, I will be able to help you understand it."

Tara proceeded to tell her aunt about her visit to the Pitten Building site, the subsequent dreams that followed, and the feeling of dread that she experienced in her bathroom. She also relayed the information her father had given her about the incidents from her childhood. Noreen watched as Tara spoke and did not seem surprised or confused. In fact, Noreen just nodded her head in recognition of Tara's strange revelations.

"So I don't know if all this means something, or if it's due to the power of suggestion in my head, or what, and I was hoping that you could shed some light on the subject since you know of such things, according to my father, which I only was told just recently even though I've been on this earth for the past twenty-eight years!" Tara then stuck her tongue out at Jimmy.

"My goodness, that's a mouthful!" Noreen said.

"Her brain is like the computers she works with," Jimmy said, "always running and with no punctuation unless you put it in yourself!"

"Ha! That from the man who would have rotary phones if they were still in existence!" Tara pointed at him, teasing.

"Can you believe how fresh these kids are to their parents, Noreen?"

Ignoring Jimmy's question, Noreen leaned forward in her chair and looked directly into Tara's eyes. "I can see that this is causing you some distress, but you must not fret too much about it. And, for the record, you are not insane."

"Then what is it? How do you explain this? Can you please explain this? Is it my imagination or what?" Tara's eyes filled with tears as she pleaded for answers from a person she trusted to tell her the truth.

"Well Tara, here's the deal: I am no expert on this subject, and I genuinely believe that many times there is no explanation for things the human heart and mind can hold. I do think that there are many situations and occurrences in this life that cannot be explained or measured in easy terms. Therefore, certain people can see and feel things that others simply cannot or will not. This would include the ability to connect with people who have died and passed into whatever is after this life."

"Wait a minute Noreen. Are you saying that Tara is some kind of *psychic*?" asked Jimmy.

"I really can't answer that. All I know is that for many generations before me, certain members of our family, mostly the females, have inherited an ability to experience certain things: feelings, sensations, and knowledge that others can't. Why is this? I don't know. What is it? I can't answer that either. And like you said, we can't read people's minds or summon spirits back from the dead. But we do have some kind of a sixth sense that allows us to experience things that are unusual. That's the best explanation I can offer you." She sat there looking at Noreen. On the one hand, Tara was grateful that there was no grand revelation here, yet disappointed there was no real explanation either.

"I guess the main thing I am asking is what this all means — why is this happening to me, and is it significant in any way?" Tara questioned.

"All I can tell you is that in my experience, you will eventually be able to figure it out. Often, it just takes some time. Just pay attention to the signs." Noreen offered in response.

"So tell me, Aunt Noreen, what kind of things have happened to you over the years? I think I need a point of comparison here."

"Well, it doesn't happen all that often for me. It began when I was about twelve; that's when I remember the first incident. I was sitting in a sweetshop in Jersey City with my mother and two of my brothers, and there was a little girl and her parents sitting in the booth behind us. I was happily eating a chocolate ice cream sundae when I was suddenly overcome with sadness and began crying. When my mother asked me what was wrong, I told her that the little girl next to us was very, very sick, and I felt bad. "How do you know she is sick?" my older brother asked, and I said that I just knew she was. In an effort to prove me wrong because he thought I was just trying to get attention, he leaned over the seat and flat out asked the parents if their daughter was sick. The father got up from the booth and asked if he could speak to my mother in private. They walked over to the other side of the shop, and he asked her how did they know the little girl was sick since they had just come from the hospital where they were told their five-year-old child had an inoperable brain tumor and only had about six months to live. They told her if she was a good girl at the doctor's she could have ice cream after. Having received the worst possible news a parent could hear, they would not disappoint their baby and brought her there for a sundae. My mother told the father what I had said, and he just nodded and went back to his family. Needless to say, my brother Patrick got a good spanking for being so rude, and I had a long talk with my mother about the gift that was apparently now passed on to me. Over the years, similar oddities would happen to me that were out of the ordinary, that never had a simple, logical explanation. All I can tell you is that it is a feeling that comes over you — a knowing — about things. Often it comes out of nowhere, but it is a certainty that whatever it is, is true. You just have to trust that it's real because you may have the ability that most people do not have and sometimes things will happen that at first, you will have no explanation for. But as I said before, in time, usually you will figure it out."

Tara leaned back in her chair and let out an exhausted breath in frustration. Tara preferred concrete explanations for things, like a math problem or scientific theory. This was too intangible for her to comprehend, and it annoyed her more than anything. Tara didn't ask for this, and she didn't want it either.

"I can see that you are not happy with the fact that I have no real answers for you, dear."

Tara laughed at her aunt being able to read her mind.

"But take my advice: don't make such a big deal out of this. I honestly don't know if it is a blessing or a curse. It is what it is, and it's just a small part of who we are, Tara."

"I guess. But I'm still hoping it's just a hormonal glitch due to approaching thirty and that it will just pass, like when you have gas." They all giggled at Tara's attempt to lighten the mood.

"Maybe so, but my advice is to just embrace whatever it is, as I did, but keep it to yourself because most people will not understand it or believe you. Unless they know you, they will find you and your gift just plain odd," warned Noreen.

"Kind of like having an extra toe. You know it's there, but you should keep it hidden so as not to turn people off." Tara said.

All three of them had a good chuckle, and Jimmy mirrored his daughter's remark by adding, "You hit the proverbial toenail on the head, sweetheart. That seems to be the long and the short of it."

"Ok, Pops, it's time to head out. I have a haircut appointment, and I want to run to a few stores while I'm here. Aunt Noreen, it was so great to see you." Tara stood and hugged her.

"Oh, you too, my sweet girl. Call me anytime you need me. And please be careful in that city, ok?"

"Will do. I probably won't see you again until Maura's Fourth of July party," Tara said.

"See you then, cutie pie. God Bless."

"Thanks again, Noreen," Jimmy said with a wink.

As Tara sat on the train the next day heading back into the city, she thought about what Noreen had told her. It was so mystifying that she decided she would try to put all this ridiculousness out of her mind and get on with her life. Tara realized she was too much in her own head lately, and she was beginning to see it was consuming her every thought.

I need to make some changes.

CHAPTER

5

Rolling over in bed, Tara pushed the covers off and groaned. It was a gray, cloudy Monday morning, making it more difficult to start the week. She rose slowly and took a shower, feeling the hot water wake up her body and mind. Trying to think of all the good things in her life, Tara realized that she felt unsettled and restless. She was still having the two dreams, but not every night. There were no more panic attacks in her bathroom, just that lingering feeling of uneasiness.

Always one who was brought up to be grateful for things like good health and having food and a roof over her head, Tara felt a stab of guilt for simply wanting, what — more? Hell, just wanting anything at this point. She was beginning to feel weary at twenty-eight and maybe because of all the things that were happening to her, she wanted peace. *That, and a little excitement wouldn't hurt.*

All Tara could see were the cracks in her life, all the gaping holes that needed to be filled. Most times lately it was as if she were standing on the edge of a cliff, not sure whether to jump off or to run back to safety. It wasn't as if she could make an appointment with a doctor and get a diagnosis of what was bothering her. This was an abstract, intangible nemesis now, and Tara was used to the world of the finite and concrete.

Tara was tired of thinking about it. Actually, she was just plain tired of herself. It was time to start focusing on other people who really needed help, like those who were still recovering from the injuries sustained in the bombing at the Pitten Building. Tara decided to talk to a few of the lawyers at her firm about setting up a fund to help with their impending medical bills. Maybe she could make a difference in their lives and bring them some form of comfort.

At work, Tara started a handwritten list and kept it in her pocket. It was titled "How To Reboot My Life," and she added to it as she thought of things throughout the day. Tara was a list maker from the time she first learned to write. She loved lists; they forced her to take action, and God knows she needed some kind of action.

To Do List

1. Do something for the victims of the bombing (talk to Legal)
2. Stop depending on Leslie and Rob for my social life
3. Get a social life
4. Cultivate some new friendships with single people

5. Improve my wardrobe (thus, getting Leslie off my back)
6. Find some new hobbies
7. Go to a new place in the city every Saturday or Sunday
8. Go back to attending Sunday Mass (a few prayers can't hurt)
9. Do some volunteer work down at St. Andrews Food Pantry
10. Start living my life instead of watching my life pass me by

There was no particular order in which they needed to be completed; she just aspired to accomplish everything on it. Tara knew her life was too insular, and she had been asleep for far too long. She had come to the conclusion that she needed people, and hopefully, there were some folks out there who needed her, too.

Tara's boss asked her to search for some information one of the attorneys needed for a case. The lawyer was representing a family suing a doctor for malpractice. Their son was left brain-damaged after a botched operation. While searching for support web sites, she came across one article that was particularly interesting to her. Written by a surgeon examining near-death experiences and the brain, it focused on those in the medical community who gave the subject some credence. One prominent physician acknowledged that although there was no scientific proof that this phenomenon was real, he believed that the human brain was capable of so much more than could ever be measured. How else, he reasoned, could humans since the beginning of time have created such wonderful masterpieces of art, music, literature, architecture, inventions, etc.? He not only was intrigued by the magnificence of the human mind,

OUT OF MY DREAMS

but also that of the human heart. As a scientist, he understood the mechanics of the muscle that pumped blood throughout the body, but he was also amazed at its ability to feel, to love, and to ache. His theory postulated that it can be studied, but never fully explained.

Tara stared at the computer screen. *Ok*, she thought, *here is a competent, medical expert who doesn't discount the possibility that things exist in this world that can't always be explained. My aunt and I and whoever else has had strange experiences are not totally bonkers. Here it is in black and white in a respected medical journal that some phenomenon is in the realm of the unknown, and society must simply accept that fact.*

She knew the dreams she was having meant something, she just had no idea what. In fact, in all the years Tara's mother had been gone, Tara never dreamed about her. Not once. She wondered why then, was she continually dreaming of some random guy?

"Tara, go to lunch," her boss yelled from the other room.

"All right, George. I'll finish that research when I get back."

"Good. That pain in the ass Henderson keeps hounding me," he growled. Tara loved working for George Patterson. One of the nerds, for sure, but a lovable one who had a terrific wife. Alma Patterson sent in a constant flow of home-baked cookies and brownies for the staff, including cakes on their birthdays.

Taking her cell phone and bagged lunch, Tara walked out of her building. The sun had come out and it had turned it to a beautiful spring afternoon. She sat in the courtyard that was adjacent to the old, stone structure that housed the law offices of Carran, McCabe, and Tucker. Pulling out a peanut butter and jelly sandwich, she decided to call Leslie.

"Les, hey. Listen, I just had a thought while I was at work."

"Hold on a minute. I need to turn the TV down." Leslie spoke quietly to Buck while she adjusted the volume.

"How's my favorite child in all the world?" Tara asked.

"This kid's going to need a hearing aid by the time he's fifteen. Okay, what's up?" she asked.

"So here's my question. I was just reading this article for work and it made me think of my mother. Which then made me think that in all the years since she died, I've never, not one single time, had a dream about her. Yet I still continue to dream about some random dude I don't even know. Why is that? What does that mean?" Tara asked through a mouthful of sandwich.

"You're still having them?" Leslie sounded surprised. Tara hadn't mentioned it to her for a while now. "I thought you were all done with that stuff."

"Um, no. I just stopped telling you because the dreams don't come every night like they did in the beginning, but I still have them. I guess I didn't want you to think I was some whack job."

"Well, you are a little bit whacked, Tara. Maybe nuts."

"Love you, too. But seriously, why do you think that is — about the dream stuff and my mother?"

Leslie let out a loud sigh. "I still have no answers for you — I'm sorry. Why don't you look that up on the Internet?"

"Yeah, I probably should, right?" Tara snickered.

"Listen, don't laugh. Think about it: The Internet is non-judgmental and free of fees and it has more information than any therapist, doctor, lawyer, or school. All joking aside, besides me, the Internet is your best friend and with whom you spend the most time," Leslie joked, but she was actually serious. Tara should spend more time with a nice guy, not her computer. She was always connected, only it was to the wrong thing.

"Well, thanks for nothing. Some best friend you are."

"No problem. Always happy to help. By the way, have you heard from Keith?" Leslie asked.

"Oh god, no," Tara groaned as she pulled an apple from her lunch bag. "I think he got the message when I never called him back," she said, relieved. "But I think Dennis was pissed at me."

Tara's cousin Dennis had set her up recently on a blind date with an accountant named Keith who lived in his building. She was ready to go home after the first ten minutes when he called her Terry. *For Christ's sake, the guy couldn't even remember my name?* Tara thought. She questioned his ability to figure out people's taxes if he couldn't even get his date's name right.

"I wonder if he found his way home that night."

"You are so mean. And judgmental." Leslie laughed.

"Hey, zero chemistry. Never will be."

"Whatever you say, dear. I'm going to ask Rob again if he knows someone."

"Spare me. Now I really feel like a charity case. Besides, I can't go on any more blind dates. Too much drama, and they never work out for me."

"I think you need to find some single people in the city you can go out clubbing with!" Leslie said excitedly.

"Yes, because that is so my scene. Now *you* are the one who's nuts!" Tara laughed.

"Come here next weekend. The three of us can hang out, eat, drink a few beers, just do nothing."

"Wow. Third wheeling. Sounds fun," Tara said caustically.

"Well, desperate times, my friend."

"I'm not desperate, yet. But I may be if I meet one more guy like Keith," Tara said.

CHAPTER

6

Tara spread the newspaper out on her kitchen table. The front page was once again dominated by the story of the Pitten Building bombing. Investigators had pieced together the timeline and details from that day and had filed a report with federal authorities. Tara was included in the majority of people who initially assumed it was the act of either homegrown or international terrorists. The idea that a single individual could wreak such havoc and destruction was frightening, Tara thought, as she read the article.

Leonard Hopkins entered the building, and over the course of a week, planted his bombs in the utility closets under the removable ceiling tiles. Each day, he went to a different floor in the ten-story building, and would come and go within a fifteen-minute timeframe. It was not at all suspicious for food delivery workers to be seen throughout the building, so no one questioned him. Hopkins had originally planned to commit suicide in front of his former boss, but he could not find him that morning. As fate would have it, the supervisor stayed home that day due to the stomach flu, but Hopkins was unaware of this and had already set the timers to go off at 11:00 a.m. When the bombs went off, they blew off the side of the building that faced the river. Anyone on the east side was killed instantly. Several employees were able to escape, if they were lucky enough to be on the opposite end of the floor from the utility closet. Many were trapped under blown-out walls and sheet rock or in elevators. The fifth bomb, the one that finally brought down the rest of the building in flames, had a faulty timer and detonated at noon.

The Pitten Building was a historic landmark, sitting at the edge of the river, with only a few small businesses surrounding it. Several of them had also been destroyed or suffered blown-out windows with smoke and water damage, and anyone who had been passing by the building at the time of the blast was severely injured or killed. Tara shuddered reading this, because it could have been her. The train into Manhattan was two blocks away from the Pitten Building, and Tara had been forced to find an alternate route to get to work over the past few weeks. The destruction would have been so much worse had the Pitten Building stood in the center of the city. Still, 326 people had died that day, and those injured numbered in the hundreds. Tara thought sadly about the one person she knew who died in the building and the pain his family must be experiencing.

"The bastard who did this..." Tara muttered.

The disaster site cleanup progressed each day with the constant presence of recovery personnel, police, and investigators. Trucks were transporting debris to a nearby empty hanger at Newark airport so it could be sifted and separated for clues, personal items, and sadly, body parts. The newspaper reported the process would take months to complete.

Tara closed the newspaper in frustration. *Months! Months to get answers. And a lifetime of wondering: why?*

Later that week, Tara was on the train waiting for her stop in Lofton, a lovely town nestled in Morris County. Braving the mass exodus from the city on a Friday afternoon in early June, Tara was headed to Leslie's for the weekend. It was Buck's birthday, and the prince was turning one, and Leslie was frantic and needed help with everything. Tara was lugging large shopping bags filled with trucks, blocks, and other age-appropriate toys she knew he would like. His party was going to be a huge event, and Leslie had been stressing out over every detail for weeks.

Leslie kept calling Tara every couple of days asking advice on everything from the flavor of the cake filling to balloon color to her outfit for the big day.

"I'm out of my frigging mind here — HELP ME!" Leslie screamed into the phone last week.

"Calm down! My ear, for God's sake!" complained Tara. "If this is what motherhood does to a sane, rational, intelligent woman, then I am never having kids!"

"You have NO idea of the pressure I am under to pull off this milestone event. Between my mother and Rob's mother — I swear, they are making me crazy!" Leslie wailed.

"I'm sure it will be a party of epic proportions. Just relax and take deep breaths. I will be there to help you, and we will get everything done. Don't worry."

"You are a lifesaver; thanks for agreeing to come early to rescue me. I can promise there will be plenty of alcohol and cake to repay you. Wait till you see the size of the cake my in-laws ordered. It's obscene."

"I'm surprised you gave up control of the cake to Rob's parents. I'm kind of proud of you."

"Yeah, well I had to let them do something. Rob kept hounding me that they wanted to contribute so I just gave them a few demands, I mean suggestions."

They both were laughing. Leslie was always in charge, especially for her son's first birthday party.

"How's my man Rob holding up under your dictatorship?" asked Tara.

"Oh please! He is so pissed with me right now over this party. But, hell, all he has to do is write out a few checks. I'm the one who has to do everything to pull this thing off in spectacular fashion."

"Ah, domestic bliss!"

"Shut up. Just get your ass here on Friday. *I need you.*"

Tara relaxed in her seat on the train and closed her eyes. She thought back to the early years when she met the best friend she could ever hope to have. She felt lucky, blessed to have Leslie in her life.

Tara and Leslie had become best friends easily and quickly. They both shared the same, razor-sharp sense of humor and only had to look at each other to know what the other was thinking. Tara could still remember the first day of kindergarten when Leslie walked up to Tara and told her she liked her shoes. After school that day, Leslie went over to Tara's house and her mother served them oatmeal cookies and pink lemonade. Since Tara was an only child, Leslie became her surrogate sister. The Fitzpatricks would take Leslie on most of their vacations so Tara had someone to hang out with, and Leslie loved it because Mr. and Mrs. Fitz (as she lovingly referred to them) spoiled her rotten and made her feel special. Leslie came from a family of six kids and hated sharing and hand-me-downs. When she was at Tara's, she could actually have a say and be heard. Mrs. Fitz taught Leslie how to knit (a perfect, vertical-honeycomb pattern), make killer mashed potatoes (using the perfect ratio of milk to butter), and roast a whole chicken (low and slow). She called Leslie her Irish/Italian daughter because she had blond hair and dark brown eyes.

On the night Mrs. Fitz passed away, Leslie lay in Tara's bed and curled her tiny frame around Tara, and they both cried for a long time. And when they finally stopped, Leslie told Tara that her mom actually was called up to heaven because God just wanted to have the world's best mashed potatoes and there was only one person who could make them. That made Tara smile for the first time that horrible day, and ever since then, Leslie has always been able to tell Tara the thing that she most needed to hear at the worst possible times.

Physically, two people couldn't have been more different. Tara was tall, thin, and athletic, and she had unusual, blue-violet eyes, and raven hair. Leslie was petite, standing just about five feet tall, curvy, with light hair and dark eyes, and as far as coordination was concerned, Tara told Leslie she had none. Leslie was more outgoing, and Tara often benefited from the relationships that came easily to her. Leslie was a cheerleader in high school, so that helped Tara's social life. Tara was the better student, especially in math and science, and that was a huge advantage for Leslie.

Tara evoked the memory of how vastly opposite the Fitzpatrick/Mancino ethnic backgrounds were, particularly when it came to Sunday dinner. At the Fitzpatrick's Irish house, dinner was just the three of them, unless they had company, and the meal consisted of roast beef or chicken, a starch, one or two vegetable dishes, dinner rolls, and dessert (usually cake, pie, or pudding with whipped cream). Dinner was always at five, and as soon as the meal was finished, the table was cleared and the dishes were washed. If the weather was nice and it wasn't too dark outside, Tara was permitted to play or go and ride her bike.

At the Mancino's Italian house, Sunday dinner began early morning with Leslie's mom making *gravy* (which was an odd thing to call tomato sauce) and *braciole* (which was a strange thing to call stuffed steak), meatballs, and sweet and hot sausage. The family ate in the dining room rather than the kitchen, and it felt like a crowd because there were Mr. and Mrs. Mancino, their six kids, and often their kid's friends, and other relatives. There were bowls of macaroni and long loaves of Italian bread, freshly grated parmesan cheese, and always a huge salad. Salad was rarely an option with dinner at the Fitzpatrick's house. There was a lot of yelling and loud arguing at the Mancinos, but not in a mean way. Tara concluded that in such a large family, you had to yell or no one could have possibly heard you!

At Leslie's house, everyone sat down to start "dinner" at noon, and just never left the table until way after dark. The food just kept coming with the main meal, then nuts and candies, then fruit, then several desserts, then after-dinner liquors and coffee or espresso for the adults. Tara recalled how she would push herself away from the table at the end of the night, feeling like a stuffed pig.

Tara and Leslie were friends for life, even deciding to go to the same college so they could experience their newfound independence together. When Rob came into Leslie's life, Tara read him the riot act that if he ever hurt her friend she would stab him (yes, she used those exact words). Rob always understood and accepted the depth of the friendship. They were as close as sisters, and they had been through everything together.

Rob was waiting for Tara at the train station. After giving him a quick hug, she handed him some of the bags she had hauled off the platform.

"Shit, Tara. What did you do — clean out Toys-R-Us?" he laughed.

"That's my boy! We have to spoil him on his first birthday!" Tara said with affection.

"You and the rest of the universe. Thank God you're here. Your friend has gone bat-shit crazy, and she needs you to calm her down," Rob said, shaking his head.

"Where are all her other friends?" Tara called them the Matrons of Morris County.

"Get real, Tara. You know she only wants you when she gets like this," he grinned at her.

"Yeah, I know." Tara smiled back.

Tara walked in the front door just as Leslie came storming down the stairs.

"Where the hell have you two been? What took so damn long?"

Tara and Rob looked at each other in disbelief.

"Leslie, it's FRIDAY. And it's RUSH HOUR! You know the traffic is insane!" He walked away, frustrated, shaking his head. Rob put Tara's stuff in the guest room down the hall. Leslie grabbed Tara and hugged her.

"Thank God, you're here! We are so getting hammered after this party is over tomorrow," Leslie said, shaking her head as she turned to lead Tara into the kitchen.

Looking around, Tara asked, "Where's Buck?" Then she spotted him in the adjacent family room, safely tucked in his playpen smiling at the sound of her voice.

"Come here you little chunk-a-monk, so Aunt Tara can take a bite out of you!" She cooed as she lifted him up to kiss and squeeze him. "Are you excited for your party tomorrow, birthday boy! Your poor stressed-out mother is about to lose it!"

"For God's sake, Tara, put him down. I need help here. Rob, can you please watch him?" Leslie barked.

Taking the baby, he said, "You will so owe me when this party is over, Leslie. And I will expect payment in the form of sexy lingerie *and* a new golf club."

"Yeah, buddy, don't worry. Just do as I ask from now until tomorrow. Then, after the last person leaves, well, we'll see about you," she smirked. With that, Leslie grabbed her car keys and dragged Tara by the arm out of the house.

After running all over town picking up food for the party, decorations, helium-filled balloons, party signs for the lawn, a piñata in the shape of a bear that would, of course, reflect the theme of Buck's party, and, finally, pizza for dinner, everything seemed to be ready for the big extravaganza.

The celebration was, consequently, a rousing success. Leslie pulled off not only a great party, complete with a sunny, warm June day, but she succeeded in having both her mother and her mother-in-law gush with praise for her efforts. The families were happy, the guests were happy, Buck was happy, and poor Rob was relieved it was finally over. He sure as hell would make Leslie own up to her payback.

Much later that evening, after all the extra food was put away the mess cleaned up, and after everyone had left, Tara and Leslie took full glasses of wine and sat in lounge chairs on the deck. Raising her glass to Tara's and clinking it in a gesture of thanks, Leslie yawned and took a huge swig of merlot.

"You are the best. Thank you in a million ways for all of this." Leslie said.

"No sweat. It really was a fun party. Everyone was having a good time, and they all raved about the food," Tara answered, also taking a sip of her wine.

Leslie, her mother, and two of her sisters made all of the food and appetizers. It was a true Italian feast, with an overabundance of everything. The cake consisted of three tiers: chocolate, red velvet, and vanilla, and Leslie's aunt and cousin made trays of wonderful cookies and biscotti.

"And what was most important was to see how happy my Buckwheat was seeing all those toys!" Tara closed her eyes and smiled at the memory of him sticking his pudgy little fist in the cake, much to Rob and his family's horror. The Mancinos had to explain that it was a family tradition at a first birthday, never needing to be repeated at subsequent birthdays. The Gordon family was great, but a little uptight sometimes, and they frowned at Leslie's loud, sometimes overbearing relatives.

"Excuse me. Did you just call my son Buckwheat?" Leslie feigned being offended, grasping her hand to her heart.

"I sure did. That may be my new name for him." Tara hated the name Leslie had chosen for her son because it rhymed with a certain curse word, and she feared he would be teased when he got to middle school. "I warned you not to name him that, but you refused to listen. I can't help myself," she laughed, the obvious result of too much beer and wine.

"Bitch." Leslie giggled, now feeling the effects of too much alcohol also. "I'm so happy this is over — you have no idea."

"Well, you done good, Mama," Tara said, patting Leslie's hand.

They both sat in silence looking up at a sky full of stars on a beautiful night. Summer was almost here, and the air was fresh, the just-cut grass smelled heavenly, and it was blessedly quiet for the first time that day.

"So enough about me and all this epic drama that will be forever referred to as Buck's Big Adventure. What's new? Let's hear all about you now, my best friend in all the world." Leslie said.

"Are you drunk?" Tara leaned over to peer at her.

"No, just enjoying the peace and quiet out here. Please, I need to talk about you for a change. And I apologize for the last week."

"Make that the last two months!" Tara shrieked.

"Ok. I know. But seriously, what's been happening?"

"Nothing new, really." Tara let out a yawn. "Still trying to make some changes. Get my life back on track."

"I didn't realize it had come off the rails," Leslie said, surprised.

Tara gazed down at her glass. "Yeah, well, I feel like it has. See, Les, you sit here in this beautiful house in a great little town with the perfect husband and the perfect child living the perfect life. And then I look at myself, at my life, and I feel like I'm so behind the eight ball. I mean, I feel like my life hasn't really started yet, and I'm almost thirty. Time is passing me by, and I don't have much to show for it."

"Tara, first of all, nobody's life is perfect. Especially mine. Rob and I fight all the time. Sure, we make up, but we still argue a lot over stuff like money and the amount of sex he requires when I'm dead tired. Oh, and then there's the amount of time he spends at work, and how our respective families annoy us. And the baby — as much as I adore him — sucks the life out of me. I'm sleep deprived, I need to lose about ten pounds of baby weight, and I have stretch marks and cellulite, whereas I used to look hot, and my brain is going to mush from a lack of intellectual stimulation. And if that wasn't bad enough, I had to list my occupation as "housewife" on our last tax return. I have a teaching degree, for Christ's sake! If that's what you consider perfect, then perfection is highly overrated."

They looked at each other and giggled.

"Oh, so the grass is always greener, right?" Tara smiled.

Leslie sipped her wine. "That's correct, my friend."

"So nothing's perfect. I get it. But I just feel like I'm standing on the dock waiting for the ship to come in, and it never does. I'm waiting for something, but I don't know what it is. I'm always waiting for *it,* but I don't know what *it* is, exactly. It's like I need to force myself to jump into something new or challenging or unexpected. But instead of moving forward, I'm just stuck."

"Tara, I'm going to suggest something here." The wine was making Leslie brave. "As your best friend — someone who has known you practically your whole life. Someone who will always have your back."

"What's that?" Tara sat up in her chair and looked at her.

"Please don't bite my head off, but maybe this would be a good time for you to go and talk to a therapist or someone. I mean you never really spoke with anyone after your mom's death," Leslie said.

"I did speak with someone. YOU — remember? And my Dad. The two people I trust most in this entire world. And I got through it in one piece."

"Thanks for the vote of confidence, but I just provided support, not real advice on how to cope with heavy shit like a parent's death when you are eight years old. Maybe it takes time, like years, for issues to surface, unresolved issues you may have been suppressing. Maybe that's why you had, or are still having, those dreams and other stuff. Maybe it is all tied in with your mom's death that you never properly or fully grieved for. Jeez, Tara, I never even saw you cry at her funeral." Leslie's eyes were filled with tears.

Tara stared at her. "Well thank you, Dr. Freud. What makes you think I haven't dealt with my mother's death? I mean, really, it's only been *twenty frigging years!* I'm fine, always have been," Tara said defensively.

As a child, Tara learned from her parents that she shouldn't wear her heart on her sleeve for all to see. "No one needs to see on the outside what is going on in the inside. People don't like to see another one's sadness. It's how we handle things in our family," she remembered her mother telling her. Tara didn't cry at the funeral because she wanted her mother to be proud that she had the emotional fortitude to stay strong for her. It was a heavy burden for a young child to carry then, and maybe it still was twenty years later.

"I just think it wouldn't be horrible for you to talk to a professional about losing your mother, especially since you were so young. That has to leave you with some kind of baggage that you carry into other parts of your life. It's not a character flaw Tara, so don't get defensive with me. It's human to have scars, and we are all human, and we all hurt sometimes. That's all I'm saying. I would never criticize or judge you. I love you. And I know you feel free to tell me stuff I sometimes don't want to hear. That's why we are best friends. Isn't that right?"

Tara realized she was lucky enough to have someone who cared so much about her and knew her well enough to tell her the painful truth of the matter. "You know something, Les? If you were anyone else I would have told you to go to hell. And maybe you are right, you witch," she reluctantly laughed. "Maybe I do need to go and talk to someone. Someone who can help me put the pieces in order and get unstuck. But to tell you the honest truth, I'm hesitant about sharing my personal, private stuff with a complete stranger. I don't know if I can."

"Listen, you don't have to make a decision tonight; just think about it. But I know the key is to find the right person to talk to, and then it can work. One of my friends was talking a while back when we were all at the playground about some therapist she used to see years ago whose office is in the city. Why don't I get her name and number so at least you would have it. Then when you're ready, you can go and see her — take your time about the whole idea. I realize it would be a huge step for you."

Tara took a sip of her wine and looked up at the night sky. Maybe her mother was watching her at that very moment. Maybe this was a sign that the time was right — that she needed to do this.

Pay attention to the signs, Tara thought.

"Ok Leslie. Maybe it is time. Get me her name and number."

CHAPTER

7

Tara noticed her palms were beginning to sweat. She had rushed over after work to make a five-thirty appointment. Struggling to relax, she sat down and flipped through a magazine. Tara hated doctor's offices, and this one was so much worse because she would have to discuss her feelings rather than physical ailments. She didn't like talking about herself; she would always ask the questions when talking to someone. It was a classic tactic of evasion, and Tara was the master.

Tara was the only person in the waiting room aside from the receptionist. Wondering if there was some secret door the patients left through after their appointments were finished to maintain confidentiality, she was happy that at least she didn't have to sit there and make eye contact with anyone else.

The appointment had taken two weeks to get, and Tara had almost cancelled a couple of times since making it. She didn't breathe a word of her decision to seek therapy to anyone but Leslie, and she certainly would not tell her father. He would freak if he knew she had decided to see a shrink. James Fitzpatrick was from the generation who believed that problems were best kept and solved within the family. Plus, it would make him feel as though he had failed as a parent by not being able to help his daughter with what had been troubling her. As was the case with most aspects of her life, she would limit whom she confided in.

Although Tara was anxious, she knew she was doing the right thing. Too many conflicting emotions were pulling at her, and she was constantly on edge. Since she couldn't explain her own feelings to herself she concluded that maybe someone else, someone who spent years studying this stuff in school, could help her sort everything out. This was a huge step, but one she was now ready to take.

The door finally opened, and the receptionist stepped out.

"Dr. Saxon will see you now, Ms. Fitzpatrick. Please come with me," she said with a warm smile.

Tara rose apprehensively from her chair and followed the receptionist down a short hallway to another room. The walls were painted a soft yellow, and there were two upholstered chairs facing each other in the center of the room. Off to the side stood a large, modern desk and a water cooler in the corner. Tara was relieved to see that there was no couch in the room. She had been having visions of lying on a couch with electrodes hooked to her head.

Sitting at the desk was a petite woman with short, gray hair and purple glasses perched on the edge of her nose. Tara was surprised because this was exactly how she had pictured her to look, minus the purple specs that gave her a youthful, approachable appearance. Dr. Saxon stood and came around from behind the desk.

"Welcome, Tara," she said as she extended her small hand, "I'm Wendy Saxon. Please have a seat." She gestured to the overstuffed chairs, while holding a clipboard that held several of the forms Tara had completed when she first arrived. Tara glanced quickly at the diplomas that hung on the wall behind the desk and the two picture frames that held the images of her family before she moved to take her seat.

Tara had done a thorough background check on this woman. Dr. Saxon was born in Brooklyn, and Tara learned that she had also attended Rutgers University as an undergraduate earning a degree in psychology. Both her masters and doctoral degrees in clinical psychology were from Columbia University, where she was also employed as an adjunct professor. She had written four books and published countless articles, was an avid runner as Tara was, had a husband who was also a clinical psychologist like herself, and had two married sons. Tara reasoned that a woman as accomplished as Dr. Saxon had to know what she was talking about and, therefore, was legitimate.

"Tara, let's begin by having you relax, close your eyes, and take a deep breath, letting it out very slowly," she directed, her voice calming and soothing. It was obvious that Tara was extremely nervous.

After repeating this exercise several times, Dr. Saxon said, "Now, Tara open your eyes. I'm going to talk for a bit about me, about what I do, about what we can do here in this room. I would like you to sit, relax, and just listen to me while I speak. Does that sound good?" she asked, looking at Tara with a smile.

Tara nodded her head in agreement. Not having to talk about herself right away was a huge relief, and she began to calm down and settle in to the big, comfortable chair.

"I realize coming here today is intimidating. Talking to a complete stranger about complicated issues in one's life is a scary process. Believe me, I understand that. But I want you to know that this office, this room, is a safe place. By safe I mean that whatever you tell me, whatever is discussed between you as my patient and me as your doctor stays between us and only us. When you come into this room and we close that door, we enter into a professional, private relationship where our mutual goal is to get answers to the problems that are preventing you from living a full, happy life. We will discuss how you feel about the events and issues in your world and explore the ways in which they have affected your past and present. We can then set a course for you to cope with them in the future. We will not solve the problems of the world, but we will strive to solve your problems and to get to the essence of who you are and what is troubling you at this stage of your life. At times it may be difficult for you, and you might discover things about yourself that you struggle to accept. But in doing so, you will find the answers to the questions you have been asking and thus, be able to gain perspective and clarity."

Tara watched as Dr. Saxon spoke, feeling more comfortable and secure by the minute. Dr. Saxon was honest and confident, and Tara began to draw strength from the words she was hearing. Hell, Tara was even starting to feel hopeful and excited at the prospect of this deep introspection into her life.

"I want you to learn to trust me, to trust the process, and this takes patience and time. I will follow your lead regarding that progression, and I will never push you further than you are willing to go. We will work as a team, understanding that I am your doctor and I am here only to help you — not to lecture and never to judge. You, in turn, need to agree to be my patient and that means that when you enter this room you will try your very best to be open and honest with your feelings and your stories and that you will let me do my job. I can't guarantee miracles. I can, however, assure you that I will try my professional best to help you bring about the positive changes you seek to make in your life, and we will approach that process with dignity, mutual respect, and professionalism. Agreed?"

Tara relaxed and smiled. She hoped this would work and that the two would have a successful, working relationship.

"Very well, then. Let's begin."

The first hour-long session was spent giving Dr. Saxon details of her life: Tara's background, health history, education, and family composition. Dr. Saxon wrote down the information in her notes trying to get a historical portrait of Tara Fitzpatrick. They talked about their mutual love affair with Rutgers University, and that topic was a great icebreaker. They discussed favorite places both on and off campus and the joys and struggles of navigating a large university.

Dr. Saxon explained that this first session was basically for the purpose of introduction and intake. Taking off her purple-framed eyeglasses, the doctor looked at Tara's face. She saw a lovely young woman who was basically happy, yet conflicted. When Tara had talked about her family history and said that her mother had died when she was a young girl, Dr. Saxon had a pretty good idea of the kind of problems they would be dealing with. But the beauty of this job was that the therapy was as unique as the patient, and no two people ever had the same story. As she did with all her new patients, she was eager to delve into the mind and world of Tara Fitzpatrick and believed the two of them would be a good match in the therapeutic sense. Sometimes, not too often, she would have a patient who she felt she was not the right fit for. Dr. Saxon didn't get that feeling about Tara.

"That will be all for today, Tara. What do you think? Not so terrible, right?" she smiled.

"No, Dr. Saxon. Not so bad at all. Thank you for making this easier than I thought it would be. I'm looking forward to working with you." Tara stood up, relieved to have completed this first session.

"Does this time and day work well for you then?"

"Yes, it's perfect," answered Tara.

"Good. Let's meet once every week for now, and we can make adjustments as we move ahead, ok?"

"Sounds great. Thank you again, Doctor."

Dr. Saxon walked her to the door and opened it. "Have a great week, Tara."

"You also."

Leaving with an appointment card for the following week in her hand, Tara thought, "This I can do." She walked to the subway with a new attitude, believing that this was a proactive attempt to get some clarity in her life. It was a step forward and not back, and Tara was ready.

When she got home to her apartment, Tara called Leslie.

"So, how did it go?" Leslie asked.

Tara took a sip of wine. "I'm just having a much needed drink."

"That bad?"

"No, it's a celebration kind of drink. I'm really proud of myself for going through with it. And she's really nice and has this soothing voice and way about her. I think it will be ok after all."

"Told you."

"Les?"

"What?"

"You really are a good friend. Do you know that?"

"Back at you, girl."

Tara opened up to Dr. Saxon in ways she never thought possible. At first she found some parts of therapy difficult, but she was learning to identify and isolate the conflicts in her life and address the barriers she had put in place to protect herself.

OUT OF MY DREAMS

One of her major breakthroughs was when she discovered why she had let so few people into her life after her mother died. She now understood that the aftermath of her mother's death and the failure to grieve sufficiently had caused her to fear losing any more people in her life. The less she had, the less there was to lose. Fear of abandonment was paralyzing her ability to form attachments with others and, thus, resulted in her unconscious choice to limit new relationships. Tara sat in amazement looking at Dr. Saxon when she had this important revelation in their third session.

"And that, Tara," she smiled, "is what we call the *AHA!* moment in this process."

Along with Dr. Saxon's skillful guidance, Tara learned that she needed to seek out more relationships with others, both friendships and romantic relationships as well. Life, and people for that matter, involved taking risks and would result in good and bad outcomes. Taking risks and not knowing what would happen was what life was all about. Tara was discovering that being human, living a human life, was never perfect. But with that imperfection came the joy of human emotion. Life had to be lived for its good and bad times, and feeling heartache and pain would be offset by feeling love and happiness.

In one of their sessions, Dr. Saxon leaned in, indicating that Tara should lean forward also. Whispering in her ear she said, "This is the secret of life, Tara. Pay attention as it comes to you. No human being since the beginning of time has lived a life unscathed. It all comes at different times, in different stages, and in various forms. The key is to accept when the bad wave hits and be ready to deal with it. Allow yourself to experience the pain of it, to let it wash over you, but eventually let it leave you with the understanding that the pain will pass and be replaced by joy. If you can learn to follow and experience that journey, you will carry the necessary skills to get through anything in life that is thrown in your path."

Tara agreed to not let fear rule her life in the future. Realizing that she could not control all the things that would happen in her life, she learned that there were better ways to cope and react to problems. Thinking of all the people who were killed in the Pitten Building gave her the strength to see that these were true victims. Tara was alive and, therefore, still in control of her world and her future. From that moment on, she vowed to stop pitying herself and her situation and make the changes she needed to make.

CHAPTER

8

July in Harbor Point was a favorite time of year for Tara. She loved summer. The haze and humidity, the sight of women in barely there outfits, the men suffering in their suits, and the hot air that felt like a welcome hug. But what she loved most were the weekends. Most people left town for the New Jersey coastline, and the restaurants in her neighborhood were less crowded. Only the diehards, those who shared her love of Harbor Point, would remain and stroll the less inhabited streets.

It was a Saturday morning, and Tara had run only about three miles due to the heat. Normally, she would put in closer to six, as she had been contemplating training for the New York marathon in November, but it was too hot, and she wanted to get an iced coffee.

As she was walking down the street toward her apartment, she came upon a small street fair with vendors, artists, and musicians. This was another one of the many things Tara loved about summer in Harbor Point. There were days when she could simply walk out of her apartment and be immersed in activity all around her. Now that she was in therapy, she was more aware of the how and why of her life and she paid attention to her surroundings trying to appreciate them. It occurred to her that even though she had been living a lonely life unconsciously, consciously she had chosen to live and work in places where it was hard to be alone. Tara got her people fix on a daily basis but in a way that she really didn't have to be in contact with any one person in particular. She was now trying to be more outgoing with people, even if they were complete strangers. Tara had even joined a book club at work that met in the public library once a week. Trying to embrace new things and new people had become her latest challenge.

Tara's strategy to attain her improved personal transformation led her to encounter an elderly man sitting under the shade of a building, catching his eye before she had time to look away. There were a few booth-type attractions set up on the street, mainly artisans and crafters. His sign was the most intriguing to her.

COME AND CHAT WITH THE AMAZING KANE

Tara read the colorful placard that sat on the table as she sipped from the long straw in her cup. The old man looked at her as Tara focused on his sign, wondering what to make of him.

"Hello," said Tara.

"Well, hello to you, young lady. I see you've been out walking or running this morning."

Tara was dressed in a fitted tank top, nylon shorts, and running shoes. "Running," she said after she swallowed a sip of coffee.

"Either you are very brave, very dedicated, or very foolish, my dear!" he laughed.

"Well, as they say, two out of three ain't bad," Tara answered.

"Wasn't that a song years ago by what was his name? Meatball, I think?" he said, scratching his head.

"Meatloaf!" Tara corrected him, giggling.

"Oh yes, that's right!"

Nodding her head toward his sign, she asked, "So what makes you so amazing, aside from your musical knowledge?"

He laughed. "Well, I can read people, not all people mind you. Only if there is someone trying to come through to them. Charles Kane at your service." He did a small bow from his seated position.

Tara looked at him cautiously. He had a kind face and a sparkle in his eyes. She guessed that he was in his mid to late seventies, and he was thin, with white hair and a short beard to match. He looked like an emaciated Santa Claus. "Well, Mr. Kane, I'm not sure I need your services right now, but I would love to sit in that chair in this nice shady place for a minute or two, if you wouldn't mind."

"Please call me Charlie. I would be delighted to simply enjoy the company of a beautiful, young Irish lass like yourself on this lovely summer day, Miss...?"

"Tara Fitzpatrick. And how did you know I was Irish?" she questioned.

"Well now, your name just confirmed what I suspected, didn't it!" he winked.

"Wow, you really are amazing!" she exclaimed.

They both laughed.

"My dear girl, aside from my mental abilities, you have the map of Ireland written on your face. Black Irish, I think they call it, isn't that right?" Charlie asked.

"That's what they tell me, but usually it includes dark hair *and* dark eyes, and mine are of the traditional Irish variety. But in an age of political correctness, something about calling oneself Black Irish just doesn't sit right." They laughed again.

"You are delightful, young lady. I take it you live here in the city and within walking, or at least running, distance of where we are now?"

"My dear, Mr. Kane, you truly are psychic!" However charming Charlie Kane seemed, Tara wasn't about to give her home address to a complete stranger. "Not too far from here, yes." Changing the subject, she asked, "So what do you use to read someone? Do you use tarot cards or read palms or what? And how much do you charge for your insight into the soul?" Tara smiled at him.

"First of all, I don't take money from anyone to do this. Secondly, I don't use cards or palms to read a person, even though those can be useful techniques. All I need is to be in the presence of someone, and if they have a person who is trying to come through, I feel a certain energy from them and surrounding them," he explained.

"If you don't take money, how can you do this?" Tara assumed this was a source of income for him because he was here on the street with the others who accepted donations for their talents or wares.

"My dear, I don't do this for a living! If I took money, I would cheapen this strange ability that I have been given. It is my responsibility to use it for good, not for profit. Also, I have found that it is a way for me to exercise, if you will, my powers of telepathy so I can stay sharp and accurate in my readings. It's like a muscle that needs to be worked so it doesn't atrophy. Besides, most people don't believe this is for real, anyway. That is until I am finished with their reading." He said with a raised eyebrow and a smirk.

Tara sat there listening intently. "So all those people on TV who get paid for private sessions and group readings are fakes?"

"No, I'm not saying that. I never needed to take money for this. I made my fortune in real estate many years ago, Miss Fitzpatrick."

"So why do you think someone such as yourself can connect to the other side, Mr. Kane? I mean it's natural for the average person to be suspicious of fortunetellers and mediums, right? I mean, it is crazy stuff." Tara was more interested in getting answers to these questions because of her own questionable family history with matters of the bizarre and unknown.

"I do not consider myself a fortune teller, although I have at times been able to sense when certain things are about to happen. I usually deal with the here and now. Life is crazy business sometimes. I think there is so much in this world that cannot be explained. For example, who can rationalize why a murderer is allowed to walk free? Or why a child is taken from his or her family by a drunk driver? Who can justify that? It's all the same thing."

Thinking back to her conversation with Aunt Noreen, Tara nodded in agreement.

"The truth of it is, I am not someone who gets a vibe from every Tom, Dick, and Harry on the street. I cannot perform on command. This ability only works when people have someone who is trying to get a message to them from the other side."

Charlie saw he had a captive audience in Tara, and he wondered if she was one of "them." He had seen that same look on her face many years before on a young man he showed a house to in Danbury who was fascinated when Charlie told him his father who had died the year before was behind him nodding his head to buy the house. The young man admitted that since his father's passing he had been seeing shadows during the day and finding things his father left around his home. The other family members thought he was crazy, and he relished the chance to speak with someone like Charlie who shared his oddity and didn't discount him.

"I will never tell anyone something bad or negative, but that is never an issue because those are not the kind of messages that come through. The energy is usually positive because that is what the surviving loved one needs — positive encouragement. There is no negative after this life, only peace and goodness. I consider myself a messenger, if you will. I am just open to those who want to use me to try and communicate between this world and whatever existence is after this. That is the best explanation I have for something I can't explain." Charlie began to fan his face with a paper plate.

"Are there people you cannot read?" Tara asked.

"If there is no one who needs to speak with them, then the answer is, yes. Sometimes I have to tell the person that whomever they want to connect with is at peace in the next life and that alone is enough to comfort them. I think that is why most people are suspicious of this process. Any fraud can tell them their deceased are fine and happy and profess they have psychic ability. It is only when you have a specific, descriptive, spot-on message to impart that people accept the fact that you are for real."

"Let me ask you, were you always this way? And was your family supportive of you, or do they just think you are strange?"

"My, so many questions! I sense that possibly you, Tara, also understand more than most. And that maybe, I have just found a kindred spirit in you. Am I correct?" Charlie asked.

"To be honest, I don't really know where I stand on the subject of being in tune with things not of this world. And I may have experienced some recent, confusing happenings. Let's just say I seem to be open to the idea that there are many questions I have had recently that I have never had before. So, to answer your question, I think I believe in being intuitive, but I don't believe that humans can be psychic."

Leaning forward in his chair, Charlie looked right into her blue eyes. "To prove a point, let me tell you what I'm getting from you right now, with your permission, of course."

Sitting back in the folding chair, she said, "Ok, I love a little scientific experimentation. Bring it on, Mr. Charles Kane!"

"Very well. If I am a quack, then nothing I say will make sense to your life. However, if I get things correct, then you can consider me legit. Ok?" he challenged.

Tara nodded in agreement as she adjusted her hair back into a high bun.

Then Charlie began to speak, "Two people were behind you when you first walked up to my table. Stepping forward first was a woman about your age with dark hair and beautiful blue eyes like yours."

"Um, excuse me Mr. Kane, stop right there. That's the oldest trick in the book. Of course that woman would be my mother, and she would resemble me! Nice try, though."

"I never said it was your mother. *You* did. May I continue without interruption, please?" Charlie asked.

"Yes, sorry."

"This woman was gently guiding you over to me, placing her hand on the small of your back. She seemed well aware of your reluctance and your curiosity. This is someone who has been following you consistently for a long time. I now assume your mother has passed. Is that correct?"

"Yes," Tara responded. This was way too generic.

Charlie Kane had seen this look countless times before. "When you were a little girl?"

Tara nodded.

"She passed suddenly, without saying goodbye, right?"

"Yes. My mother had a heart attack in her sleep when I was eight years old."

"She never wanted to leave you. She is always with you. She listens whenever you speak to her. Your mother is so proud of the woman you've become and is grateful for how you have taken care of your father for her over all these years. You were the light of her life."

Tara smiled at his words. Then she stopped him again. "Hold it right there, again, Amazing Kane! What you have just told me could apply to most people living in this city! Most psychics just tell people what they want or need to hear, and it's always nonspecific like that!"

"Did I say I was finished? Good lord, girl, you talk too much! May I please finish my thought now?" he said, exasperated.

"Yes, sorry!" She emphasized, as she slumped down into the chair.

"As I started to say before I was so rudely interrupted," he winked at her and smiled, "She wanted to thank you for looking after your father. She says to tell you she saw you take the cigarettes out of your father's coat pocket, the green plaid one that she tried to throw out on several occasions, and flush them down the toilet when you were ten years old because you were afraid he would get lung cancer and die on you too. She watched your friend and her mother blow off the Mother's Day Tea in your senior year of high school to take you down to Cape May for the afternoon so you wouldn't miss her so much. She was there the day — and excuse me for being so blunt here — you passed into womanhood when you were twelve and sat crying on the roof outside your bedroom window because you wanted to talk to her and only her about it. Your mother also wants you to know that she was the one who put the heart necklace of hers you loved so much on your dresser when your father yelled at you for going in her jewelry box, and you screamed that you couldn't have because it was locked and your father had the only key. She wanted you to wear it to your high school graduation so you would have a little piece of her heart with you on that day. And she wants you to know that just when you were falling asleep, when you felt like there was a bug on your cheek, it was her kissing you goodnight. She wants you to know that she hasn't missed a moment of your life. Not one moment."

Tara sat there stunned.

"Oh and one last thing. She said she still loves to hear you sing *Look to the Rainbow,* whatever that means."

"Oh, my God!" Tara gasped. "There is no way you could have possibly known that!"

"What?"

"That song. My mother and I loved *Finian's Rainbow.* It was a movie about a fictional town in Ireland. It starred Fred Astaire, and my mother loved him! He sang that song in the movie. We used to love to sing it together; it was our special song. No one knew that except for my Dad." Tara began to cry, but they were happy tears. Because she knew that message could have only come from her mother. And it meant that Charlie was legitimate. And Aunt Noreen was legitimate. And maybe she too, was not crazy.

"So, I'm good then?" Charlie asked.

"Yes Charlie. You are spectacular," she said as she wiped her eyes with the napkin that was wrapped around her coffee cup.

Looking back at Charlie, she smiled.

"And thus, Kane truly *is* amazing."

"Indeed. Now may I address the second energy I'm getting from you? A male energy?" he asked.

"Second energy? I don't know who that could be. My father is very much alive, so are both grandfathers and the many uncles I have." Tara look puzzled.

"It doesn't have to be a relative you know," said Charlie.

"I don't know who else it could be, then," she said curiously.

"Just give me a minute here. This one is not as clear, more confusing. A lot of activity surrounding him for some reason." Charlie appeared slightly flustered.

"What?" Tara asked. Then after a few seconds she repeated "What is it, Charlie?"

He shook his head, as if he had lost his thought.

Suddenly, a deep, male voice interrupted them. "Grandpa, are you trying to pick up pretty young girls again?"

CHAPTER

9

Tara looked up to see a handsome guy around her age holding a paper bag and a bottle of water. He was about six feet tall, dressed in cargo shorts, a red T-shirt, and flip-flops, and he was wearing a baseball cap on his head.

"It's about time you came back. I'm starving here and dying of thirst in this heat!" Charlie complained.

"Relax old man. Here you go." He handed Charlie the bag and put the bottle of water down on the small table. Charlie dug eagerly into the bag's contents.

"Sorry, did I interrupt here?" he asked as he looked at Tara.

"No, not at all. Your grandfather and I have been having a very stimulating back and forth, and I am totally charmed by him," she answered.

"Yes, well he does have that effect on people, especially the ladies. Sometimes I think he just does this to flirt with unsuspecting females," he said with a smile.

The cutest smile Tara had seen in a long time. Oh, and really nice brown eyes and blond hair that she could see underneath his cap. Oh, and muscular, too.

"Tara Fitzpatrick, this is my least favorite grandson, Evan Kane. I like his older brother much better," Charlie joked.

She stood up and turned to face Evan who tried not to look down at the long, shapely legs that held her up. But he couldn't help staring at her lovely face.

"Nice to meet you, Evan." She extended her hand. "Your grandfather is a hoot!"

He took her hand, and it felt soft and warm. "My pleasure, Tara. Yeah, we roll him out at family parties as the entertainment," he said with an affectionate smirk.

"What took you so long to come back? You were gone for an hour. I could have died here waiting for you!" Charlie said through a mouthful of bagel.

Rolling his eyes, Evan said, "Grandpa, do you have any idea how crowded it is around here? The lines everywhere are huge!" Smiling at Tara, he asked, "Why do senior citizens think they own the world and that everyone should kiss the ground they walk on?"

"I'll answer that, Tara. Because we are older, wiser, richer, and smarter than you kids, and you should show more respect than you do. Although, he is a good boy, I must admit." Charlie said as he took a big gulp of water.

Giggling, Tara said, "I know. My father goes on a rampage about how the mail comes too late, how he can't get good service in restaurants any more, and that he shouldn't have to wait in line at the grocery store! He complains they should have special checkout registers for seniors like they have handicapped parking spaces! And my two grandfathers do nothing but read grocery store circulars, compare prices, and wait anxiously for the next big canned goods or toilet paper sale!"

Evan laughed, "Yeah, he is the same way. What is it about those sales, anyway?"

"I think it brings out the ancient hunting and gathering instinct in senior citizens. And then they call their friends and relatives to brag about how much they saved and that they now have twenty cans of peas or corn niblets stored in their basement for the apocalypse!" Tara joked.

Beautiful and clever — a surprising, yet refreshing combination, Evan thought to himself.

"Don't knock it until you've tried it kids. It's a real kick!" said Charlie.

They all laughed, and then Tara glanced at her watch.

"Oh, wow. I was enjoying your company so much Charlie, I totally lost track of time! I really need to be going!" she said as she reached down to pick up her iced coffee that had melted by her feet.

"Must you really go? Things were just getting interesting," Charlie said as he raised an eyebrow and looked at his grandson. "Besides, I hadn't finished with…"

Evan interrupted him. "I'll tell you what Grandpa. Maybe if Tara will give me her phone number, you will be able to see her again." Evan smiled as he looked at Tara, who was melting now from more than the heat.

"A splendid idea. You may not be my favorite grandchild, but you are by far the smartest! You know, Tara, Evan graduated from the University of Pennsylvania and is a well paid financial wiz on Wall Street." Charlie boasted proudly.

"Ah, well, I can see why you would be so proud of him," Tara answered, not trying to act impressed by the fact that he wasn't just a good-looking guy. He had a decent brain in that head of his.

"And since Evan and I seem to share the same fascination and observations on geriatric behavior, well how could I possibly refuse?" she smiled at him.

Evan tried to contain his enthusiasm. He hadn't met such an unusual girl, well, ever. Pretty, yes, there were plenty of them in this city. Since he was young, attractive and made a lot of money, Evan was never at a loss for female companionship. But he had become bored with the same type of woman who either just wanted him for sex or for his bank account, and since he had just turned thirty, he was ready for something more, something deeper than a mindless tryst. A woman who could stimulate more than his groin, one who he could actually have an intelligent, meaningful conversation with was what he now desired. The fact that Tara seemed to be all this and gorgeous too, well that was enough to have him very interested.

Along with his grandson, Charlie had become taken with Tara, but for very different reasons. He sensed something unique in her: a fire and yet a sadness, too. More than anything, he believed her to be a lovely young woman who could be good for Evan. After all, one didn't have to be a mind reader to see that these two young people were definitely attracted to one another.

Taking the empty paper bag and a pen from Charlie's shirt pocket, Evan ripped it in two and wrote his address, cell phone number, work phone number, and email address on his half and handed the other half to Tara. She wrote her information down and handed it back to Evan.

Tara felt like she had just been handed an early Christmas present. When was the last time she had met such a cute guy who also had a sense of humor? She tucked the piece of paper into her sports bra.

Evan thought this was incredibly erotic and felt slightly aroused at the innocent gesture.

Tara turned to Charlie. "Well, Mr. Charles Kane, it has been a pleasure beyond words to spend my morning in your company. You are a gentleman for giving me a cool place to sit on this unbelievably hot day." She then leaned in and whispered in his ear. "And thank you for telling me about my Mom. You are too good to be a fake, and I believe you are the real deal in more ways than one." Then she gave him a kiss on his cheek.

Charlie both blushed and beamed at the attention from her. "I do so hope we meet again, Miss Fitzpatrick, and that my intelligent grandson will ask you on a date. If I were only forty or so years younger!" Charlie muttered, shaking his head.

"Don't worry, Grandpa. I'll keep you posted. Tara, can I walk with you? Apparently, we live in the same direction," Evan asked.

"Sure, I'd like that. Thanks again, Charlie. You truly are amazing!"

"That's what all the girls say!" He winked at Tara.

"Grandpa, I'll call you this week. Get home safely, ok?" The two men hugged briefly.

Then Tara and Evan walked down the street as Charlie watched them go.

"I predict good things for those two" Charlie said out loud to himself and chuckled. "After all, I am the Amazing Kane!"

CHAPTER

10

Tara and Evan walked side by side toward her apartment, talking, laughing, and pointing out things to each other in store windows. Evan couldn't take his eyes off Tara. Not only was she beautiful and sweet, she was also smart and funny. He felt so comfortable with her, which was strange when he first met a girl. Feeling like he didn't have to impress her, that he didn't have to work hard to get her interested, was new and refreshing. It was just easy and good, and he felt an attraction that was so strong, well, it surprised the hell out of him.

"So be honest. What did you think of my grandfather?" he asked, looking down at the ground.

Tara replied, "I thought he was amazing, just like he advertised." She looked at his face to see if she could read anything more into his question. "Why do you ask?"

"Oh, I don't know. What he does, what he can do, sometimes puts people off. Not everybody believes in that stuff, and I wouldn't want you to think he was some senile, deranged, old guy who accosted you on the street. My grandfather is a very well-educated, successful individual who just has a very peculiar ability to see and feel things that are, well, off the radar." He watched her face to get her reaction.

"For your information, Mr. Evan Kane, I believe we have more in common than just a shared interest in the habits of senior citizens. I also hail from a long line of lunatics who have the ability to connect with things out of this world. Only I just learned this recently whereas you probably have known for some time because I assume your flesh and blood communicate far better than mine." She finished her rant and then gave him a huge smile. "Someday over a bottle of wine I can tell you the whole, sordid story. Just rest assured that if you can accept my word, having just met me a short time ago, that I wasn't fazed in the least about what your grandfather can do, then I won't consider members of your family any more crazy than members of mine. Agreed?"

Wanting to kiss her right then and there on the street, Evan couldn't have asked for a better response to his concerns.

"Agreed. And I can't wait to hear about the Fitzpatrick clan. So should I apologize at least for my grandfather's matchmaking efforts back there?" he asked.

"Subtlety is not his strong suit, huh?" she laughed.

"I know you may find this hard to believe, but he really has never done anything like that before — I mean trying to set me up with someone he has just met. I think he just really took a shine to you and would like to see more of you himself. In a totally grandfatherly way of course," he added quickly.

"It's obvious he loves you very much and is extremely proud of you. Our families always want what is best for us. Or should I say, what they think is best for us. Sometimes we have no say in the matter."

"Well, I don't know about your family, but mine has wanted me married with two kids for at least the past four years or so." Evan surprised himself for revealing such candid thoughts to a complete stranger. "Thank God they all live in Connecticut and I am here so I'm not under their microscope all the time, only the occasional weekend and holiday. How about you? Does your family torture you as well?"

Suddenly, Evan realized that he assumed Tara was single. But what if she wasn't? When he was introduced to her he looked right away to see if she was wearing a ring on her finger. But she could have just as easily left her wedding or engagement ring at home because she had been out running. Or what if she already had a boyfriend?

I mean, Christ, this girl is gorgeous! There was no way she could be unattached. She was probably living with some asshole that didn't deserve her, right? A healthy dose of panic set in. *What the hell?*

Tara smiled. "I am an only child, but I come from a huge extended Irish family on both sides. My father gets the obligatory dig in about not being married at twenty-eight, but both my parents have so many siblings and I have so many cousins, the scrutiny is equally distributed among all of us. I may not have the husband and kids they wish I had, but I have a great job and I live and work here in the greatest place on earth, so some of them envy me for that alone."

Relieved to hear her confirm she was single, Evan said, "I get the same thing, just on a much smaller scale than you! My mother is always asking me "Did you meet someone nice in that city?" It drives me insane!" Evan said. "As if being thirty and unmarried was a liability!"

"Where is your family from?" he asked.

"All over New Jersey, but I grew up in Monmouth County, near the beach."

"Ah, a shore girl" he smiled.

"Let me correct you, Mr. Greenwich. Those of use who were born and bred in that area call it the beach, not the shore. That word is used by New York and North Jersey people." She mouthed the word BENNY, making a face.

Evan laughed. "You learn something new every day. By the way, besides dazzling my grandfather, what do you do for a living?"

"I'm part of a team that manages all the electronic data for a large, mid-town law firm, basically litigation support services."

He stopped walking and gaped at her. "I would have *never* taken you for a techie! You definitely do not fit the mold: too pretty for that."

"Well, thank you — I think. But I'm not a complete geek. I work with all guys so sometimes just to freak them out a little and throw off the stereotype, I'll show to the office in high heels and a short skirt," she said matter-of-factly.

Evan imagined the sight of those long legs in stilettos and a tight dress, but he pushed the image from his brain. *Not a good idea right now*, he warned himself.

Finally, they reached Tara's building.

"This is me," she said, pointing.

He took his hat off and quickly ran his hand through his hair. "Listen, Tara, I know this is kind of crazy, just having met, but are you busy tonight? I mean, you certainly wouldn't want me to incur the wrath of my grandfather by not asking you out on a date, would you?" He said it firmly but shyly at the same time.

Tara found it adorable. She thought for a moment. On the one hand, she didn't want to appear too eager, but she also felt like she didn't have to play they usual games with this guy. They were both taking a gamble and if he had the guts to ask her out so soon after just meeting her, the least she could do was to reciprocate by saying yes.

"No, I'm not busy and no, I would not want to upset my new friend, Charlie!" she answered. "What time were you thinking? I just have to get a couple of things done today, but I should be done by around five."

"That would be fine. I'd love to take you to a place my friend owns over on State Street. Casual place, but nice. Sports bar. Would you be ok with that?" he asked.

"Sounds great. We can watch the game tonight, too. Wait — you are a Yankee fan, right? I mean a smart guy like you couldn't possibly prefer any other team."

He laughed and put his hand over his heart. "Pinstripes in the blood, of course!"

"Thank God! That could have easily been a deal breaker, you know," she smiled.

"How about I come back around seven tonight. Will that give you enough time?"

"Perfect. Plenty of time."

"All right then, I'll see you later." Evan turned to leave, then stopped. Turning back to her, he said, "Tara, I'm really looking forward to tonight."

Their eyes met and held for a few moments.

"Me, too" she whispered back.

As she walked up the stairs, Tara thought: *this is too good to be true. He is handsome, smart, and nice. We seem to share a similar sense of humor, and he actually seems interested in me. God, please don't let me jinx this.* In the elevator, she closed her eyes and whispered a silent prayer to her mother, as she often did.

"Mom, please ask God to cut me a break on this one."

Evan walked the few blocks to his apartment. He couldn't stop smiling. What were the chances that on such an ordinary day, he would meet such an extraordinary girl? He had his grandfather to thank.

Maybe he really did have a gift for magic after all.

Tara opened her front door and doubled over with laughter.

"Oh, my God! Are you kidding me? Is this some kind of sign or what?" Evan said, with a huge smile on his face.

Tara's sundress and Evan's polo shirt were the exact same shade of blue, and it looked as though they had called each other prior to their date and planned to match one another. It wasn't lost on either one of them that this may indeed have been a sign that they would be compatible in more ways than one.

"This is too funny! We look like Thing 1 and 2! Your grandfather would have a field day with this!" Tara giggled.

"Well, regardless of our sartorial synchronicity, you look beautiful. These are for you." Evan handed Tara a colorful bouquet of flowers.

"Thank you. They're gorgeous! Let me just put them in water before we go. Please, come in." Tara said, walking to her kitchen to fetch a vase.

Evan closed her front door and gazed at Tara. When he met her earlier in the day, he thought she was alluring in her running gear. But now, she had transformed herself into a striking beauty in a dress that highlighted her unusual eyes and high-heeled sandals that showed off her long, tanned legs. And the hair that had been piled in a bun, was long and dark and fell in waves down her back. Evan fantasized about running his fingers through it.

Tara placed the flowers on the coffee table in her living room. "Would you like something to drink, or should we go?" she asked.

"I made a reservation, so we should probably leave. I love your place, by the way. It's so much neater than my apartment." Evan noticed that everything was organized and that her living room was filled with framed photographs.

"It's small, but I love it." Tara grabbed her purse. "I'm ready if you are."

Stepping out on the street, Evan took Tara's hand in his. He felt a jolt of electricity at the contact, one that went right to his heart and his groin. It was like he was back in high school. He was nervous and excited, yet he was so comfortable around her already. Tara was sexy without even trying to be, and she smelled light and fresh, just like the beach.

Evan's friend Jake greeted them at the front of the restaurant, giving Evan a hug. He then turned to smile at Tara. Evan had called him earlier to make a reservation, telling Jake he had just met an incredible girl.

"Tara, this is my good friend, Jake, who I have known since, well, forever! Jake, this is Tara."

Jake took her hand and kissed it. "Nice to meet you Tara. I knew you had to be something special. Evan has only ever come here with other guy friends."

Tara blushed and smiled ear to ear. "It's a great place you have here. Actually, my father and I came in about a year ago for a quick dinner. My dad is a bit old fashioned, and he warned me about coming here alone due to what he called "a too-high testosterone level!" But I loved the food and all these jumbo TV screens!"

"Well, you can come in any time, with or without this guy! I'll be sure to keep the fellas in line," Jake joked, giving Evan a gentle punch on the arm.

"I'm assuming you do have a table for us?" Evan asked, anxious to have Tara all to himself.

"Right this way!" Jake led them to a semi-private booth in the corner, the one Evan had specifically requested.

Tara and Evan ordered beer and burgers and handed the menus back to their waitress.

"So, Tara. I want to hear all about you." Evan settled back in his seat, looking directly into her blue-violet eyes. "Just start after your birth and tell me everything there is to know."

Tara stared at him dumbfounded. "Excuse me?"

"I want to know all about you. So, you go first," he answered.

"Wow. I've never been on a date where the guy didn't want to dominate the conversation with tales of how great he is to impress me. You are unusual in more ways than one, Evan Kane. Aren't you the least bit conceited or self-absorbed?" She laughed. "Unfortunately, most of the guys I've been out with are."

Evan paused and stared at her. "I find I am very interested in getting to know you, Tara. To tell you the truth, I am really excited about meeting you, and I don't ever remember being so attracted to or honest with any other girl. You are a breath of fresh air, and I don't normally feel this way."

Evan was shocked at his declaration. This was not the way most of his dates started. But he felt, probably for the first time, that no games were necessary with this charming, intelligent, and beautiful girl.

"Very well, then. I'll go first. But hang on to your chair. There are a lot of ups and downs in the life of Tara Fitzpatrick." She winked at him.

Evan thought he would have a heart attack. *My God, she takes my breath away.*

Tara told Evan about her childhood, her mother's death, her father, and her crazy, extended Irish family. She rambled on about her best friend, Leslie, and her adventures at college. She discussed her job, her love of running, her fascination with all things technical, and any and all things sports related. Evan drank his beer, listening to her, and he was amazed at the depth Tara possessed. Here was a woman who had lost her mother when she was a little girl, but she never wanted anyone to feel sorry for her. Tara told him she understood at an early age that life can change in an instant, and always tried to tell the people she cared about how much they meant to her, not just when they expected to hear it.

He sensed there were many layers to Tara and that her profound loss at an early age left the inevitable scars. Evan hoped she would someday share that pain and that she would share it with him.

Their food arrived, but the conversation never stopped.

"OK, Evan. I'm hungry. So I need to use my mouth for eating this delicious burger. You're up. Spill it. All of it. I want to know all about you, now," Tara said, smiling.

Tara realized that at the start of any new relationship it was hard to see flaws. When she opened her front door and saw him standing there, looking strong and confident, she thought she had died and gone to heaven. But she also learned that Evan wasn't just wrapped up in his own stuff. Most guys love to just talk about themselves on first dates, to show how much they know and how much they have. Evan was different. He seemed more interested in getting to know the real Tara and asked most of the questions, a tactic she had perfected to avoid letting anyone see into her too much. A guy who actually listened when you said something, rather than thinking about what he could say next that would make himself look good.

Evan was very handsome, but didn't seem to rely on his good looks and charm to get what he wanted. He had worked hard for everything he had achieved, including a full-tuition scholarship to an Ivy League institution. No one had ever handed him anything, and he wouldn't have taken it if they had tried. He took pride in being a self-made man, and he loved hard work and any kind of challenge, whether it was school or work.

Evan didn't always have it easy. Both his parents were very much alive, but his father had left them for another woman when Evan was a baby. As a consequence of his father's desertion, Evan's mother legally changed their last names back to her maiden name. Evan's older brother, his only sibling, got involved with drugs as a teenager, which took a toll on the family, particularly his mother, who had already been reeling from the betrayal of her husband. Evan was very protective of his mother and were it not for his grandfather, they would not have been able to survive those first difficult years after his father left. His brother's drug problem and subsequent rehab stints drained any money they had and his father refused to help, focusing only on his new family. Although Evan resented his father for a very long time, they had worked to repair and rebuild their relationship in recent years. Vowing never to be the kind of man his father was — one who would abandon his wife and children — Evan emulated his grandfather who was decent, loyal, and trustworthy. Tara was beginning to understand the deep connection between Evan and Charlie, and that every family had a story to tell, both good and bad.

Evan Kane worked in a large investment firm downtown, having been hired before he even graduated college. He had done quite well for himself, acquiring all the material things he always wanted. He was moving up quickly, learning all there was to know, and he was hungry for success. He had a great job, a great family, plenty of male and female friends, and a great life.

Over the past few years, most of the guys Tara went out with bored her. She couldn't wait to go home, lock the door, and put her pajamas on and read or watch TV. Her longest relationship was in her senior year of college, lasting about ten months. But then Tara discovered he was cheating on her with some sorority chick with fake boobs and a very rich, well-connected father. Tara had been in the dark where guys were concerned, but now there was a light at the end of a long, bleak tunnel. And that light was shining bright, right across the table from her.

Tara and Evan's date ended at three-thirty the following morning. Finding it extremely hard to part that night, they both didn't want to screw it up by rushing things too much.

Tara thought she would die right there on her front doorstep when he kissed her. *He felt so good, he smelled great and Jesus Christ in heaven, he could kiss!* Tara felt the kiss was filled with passion and promise. Evan let a quiet moan escape while kissing her, and Tara wanted to rip his clothes off right in front of her apartment.

Evan waited all night to kiss her. Taking her face in his hands, he started softly and when she responded by pressing herself into him, he deepened the kiss and moved his hands into her hair and then down her back and pulled her in so close they felt attached to each other. Tara responded by slowly moving her hands from his lower back up to his shoulders while letting him completely explore her mouth in those few minutes, while she explored his.

Finally, when they pulled apart, they looked at each other and smiled. Knowing their chemistry was off the charts, Evan said the inevitable. "So, ok, I will let you leave me and go in and get a few hours of sleep. But then I will be right back here at ten to take you to brunch. And then we'll just see what the day brings, but we are definitely spending it together. That is, if it's all right with you."

"More than all right. Although after that kiss, sleeping will be a complete letdown," she answered, not wanting him to go.

Evan knew he had to go, but he didn't want to leave. He had a hold of her hand and wouldn't let go. Before he left that first night, he had walked away three times, and three times he returned to take her in his arms and kiss her again.

Their second date began hours later in Manhattan. It started with brunch and ended with dinner, and in between there was walking through Central Park, shopping on Fifth Avenue, and seeing a movie. When he brought her home later that night, after what was now beginning to become entertainment for anyone walking by her apartment, Tara was surprised that he didn't ask to come up. He did, however, ask if she would be willing to go out the following night for dinner. When she said yes, he told her they were going to a place where dresses and heels and suits and ties would be required and that he would pick her up at seven thirty. Their good-bye kisses were getting longer and hotter, and both of them felt as if they were going to burst into flames with the heat that was between them. Tara realized this was so much more than pure lust; it was lust, and mutual admiration, and compatibility that come with finding someone truly special.

Evan couldn't remember a more enjoyable Monday than he did that day. His secretary, Denise asked him to please stop whistling in his office because she couldn't concentrate and asked, "What, are you in love or something? Please be quiet in there!" and he laughed at her question.

Tara spent the day thinking about what she would wear and how it was the absolute best weekend of her entire life. If she died today, she thought, she could die a happy girl. She had met the best guy she could ever hope to meet, and she prayed he felt the same way. Everything that day was better: the sun was shining, her food tasted better than ever before, and nothing could put her in a bad mood. Because tonight she would see him again.

She opened the door to a superbly dressed Evan, holding a dozen red roses. *Was this guy for real?* Tara wanted to jump him right there on her doorstep.

Evan eyes grazed approvingly over Tara in a fitted, red dress that accentuated her figure and displayed the perfect amount of cleavage. He tried not to gape at her legs in the black stiletto heels.

"You look spectacular," he said as he handed her the flowers and kissed her gently on the lips.

"Thank you, Evan. And you look very handsome tonight. Please, come in. I hope I have another vase in here. You are starting to spoil me!" she gushed.

"So, where are we going tonight?" she asked as she walked back in with the flowers arranged in a porcelain vase and placed them on a table.

"Le Bernardin," he said as he pulled her into him, kissing her and running his hands down her back.

"I love it there. I've only been there once, but it was great," she said as she nestled her head into his neck, smelling his wonderful scent that was becoming her favorite thing in the world.

"We had better get going before I change my mind and order us Chinese take-out. And I want all of New York City to see me with this unbelievably sexy girl."

Tara had died and gone straight to heaven.

Watching him as he selected a very expensive bottle of wine, Tara realized this was his attempt to really impress her. The funny thing was he didn't have to bother spending so much money to do this because she was already hooked, and it was only their third date. Tara was waiting for the proverbial shoe to drop and for him to disappear in a puff of smoke.

It was too fairy tale in a cold, cruel world, wasn't it? This didn't happen in real life, only in movies and books, and especially not to me, Tara Fitzpatrick. Right?

He filled their glasses after giving the waiter his approval on the selection of wine and handed it to Tara. Raising his glass, he said,

"Here's to the most beautiful woman in New York City from the luckiest guy in the entire world." Evan looked at her with such intensity; Tara was taken aback by it. *Could he possibly feel as much as I do right now?* Tara was so excited that they were out on a Monday night, having such an elegant dinner.

The restaurant was not as full as it would be on a Saturday night, but he didn't want to wait until the weekend to take her out to a nicer place. He had never in his past gone out on a date during the week. He was usually working late or just wanted to get home and crash on the couch after a long day. Suddenly, he felt this urgent need to be with her every moment he could, and their first two dates were casual. This night needed to be special. After they ordered, Evan relaxed back into his chair. "So remember the other day when you told me that my grandfather's psychic abilities didn't surprise you because you had something similar in your family?"

Tara nodded.

"I'm intrigued to hear your story so I know you won't go running away from me. Not many people give that psychic stuff much validity, and it takes a brave person to admit to it. I mean if you hadn't met my Grandpa like you did, I probably would have kept that little family secret hidden. By the way, did he read you?"

Tara sipped her wine and decided she would skip the part about how she was the newest visionary phenomenon in the Fitzpatrick/O'Connell clan. No need to scare him off even though he was cut from the same clairvoyant cloth. Realizing that it would be another area in which they were compatible made her smile at him.

"As a matter of fact, he did. And he was spot on about everything. I assure you that your grandfather has a genuine gift for whatever that thing is, because he told me things that no one else could have possibly known. It was really extraordinary. Charlie made me cry, but in a good way."

"I've seen him tell people things that turned their lives around. He can't do it with everyone, only certain people," Evan said.

"He did tell me that, and I think that gives him a lot of credibility because he is so honest about it. It really is, well amazing, isn't it?" Tara laughed.

"So how about your side? What lurks in the shadows of your family tree?" he smirked.

"Well my mother's sister and some great aunt as well as my great grandmother are all I know right now. You see, I just found out about this whole thing within the past few months, so I haven't really been able to investigate it properly. I'm still trying to get this hidden information from my secretive family," she joked.

"I'm curious. What caused this family secret of yours to suddenly be revealed?" he asked.

Oh, crap. Tara decided right then and there she would never lie to Evan or withhold the truth from him. So she just decided to give him an honest answer.

"Um, well, I began to have these dreams after I went down to see the Pitten Building after it was bombed. It was odd because I was having them night after night, and I started to freak out a little bit. When I told my father about it, he said I had some weird things happen to me when I was a little kid, and he and my mom thought that maybe I had inherited the O'Connell thing. I guess it's a watered-down version of what your grandfather has. So, in a nutshell, I have only had a couple of odd occurrences over the past twenty-eight years, so I don't consider myself one of the chosen."

Evan laughed.

"So now, should I be the one worrying that you will run screaming from this lovely restaurant?" Tara asked as she slowly brought the wineglass to her lips.

She looked at him with the most sensuous expression Evan had ever seen. He became instantly aroused. He swallowed and said, "Not a chance."

They both realized this was not a subject they wanted to pursue at this point. In fact, Tara found it to be a total buzz kill, and she changed the subject with his obvious blessing. Tonight was all about the romance and the newness and the discovery that magic did exist in finding yourself with someone who takes your breath away.

When they arrived back at Tara's, Evan hoped she would invite him in. Tara had decided when she opened the door hours before that he would not be leaving until the next morning.

Evan couldn't contain his excitement when she took his hand and led him into her bedroom. He was equally excited with what she was wearing under that red dress. The sight of Tara, standing there in nothing but her heels and black lace underwear, made Evan crazy with lust — crazy for her.

They spent the night exploring each other, feeling and tasting and touching. They made love several times, and their passion was intense and consuming. Evan had slept with many women in his life, but Tara was so different, and he already felt so much for her. He wanted her, wanted her body, desired to make love to her, and yet he wanted more. As he moved inside her and looked down at her face, he could barely contain the feelings that overwhelmed him.

Tara knew. She knew as she fell into the abyss with this man, this wonderful, exciting, sexy, considerate guy who she wanted more than anyone she had ever wanted before. Their connection was perfect, and she was sure that he felt the same as her. It was more than sex, more than two people satisfying a need for each other. It was new, it was deep, and it would last. Of that, they were both certain.

As they lay entwined in her bed, and the sun slowly began to make its way through her bedroom curtains, Evan spoke, "Let's both call in sick today. I've never, not once, called in sick, even when I was sick. I just know that number one: I would be too tired to function properly today; number two, I would not be able to concentrate at all; and number three, I cannot seem to get enough of you."

Releasing herself from his embrace, she moved onto her side and propped her head on her hand and looked at him. "All right then, I will call in sick. But if we are sick, we *must* stay in bed, you do realize that?"

He smiled and pulled her back under him.

CHAPTER

12

After dinner one night in late August, Tara and Evan took a walk to look at the most recent progress at the former Pitten Building. As they walked holding hands past the vast, empty space where the old building used to stand, they looked sadly at one another. Tara knew they were thinking the same thing. How solemn this place had become, how great the tragedy, how enormous the job had been to remove everything, and how so many lives were changed forever. The couple also looked at one another knowing how precious life is and how it can be changed in an instant.

Turning Tara around, Evan pulled her into him. He put his hand under her chin and lifted her face to look at his.

"I realize we've only been together a short time, but I need to say this. I love you, Tara. I am so totally in love with you. It's probably horrible to stand in this place and tell you this, but I feel like I have to tell you right now. I know it's the right time but maybe the wrong place."

"No Evan. Nothing about what you just said is wrong. It's all so right. I love you, too. I feel guilty saying this as we stand here, but I am so happy. And I think that being here of all places makes us realize how lucky we are and how much we have and how easy it is to have it all taken away."

This was one of the things Evan was learning to love about her: appreciating everyone and everything in her life. In a world where there was such misery and negativity, Tara tried to see the bigger picture and what really mattered.

"Let's go home," Tara whispered.

As Tara laid her head on Evan's chest after, he pulled her into him tightly.

"What's wrong?" she asked.

"I was just thinking about earlier today. All those people. Sometimes it's just overwhelming. A guy I knew from my previous company was killed that day, and it's one of those stories where he was just in the wrong place at the wrong time. A shitty twist of fate. He went there that morning to meet with a client, but he wasn't scheduled to go until one. He decided to have coffee with one of his old college buddies first, so he got up to the third floor at around 10:45, just before the bombs went off. And if that wasn't bad enough, his poor wife didn't even know he was there that day. When he didn't call her after lunch like he usually did, she called his office looking for him. His secretary had to tell her where he was. Can you imagine?"

"Were you close with him?" Tara asked.

"No, but he was a really good guy. Young, like us. I heard he had just gotten married a few months before he was killed."

Tara hugged him tighter, as though the idea that something like that happening to them would literally be the end of her world.

"Did you know anyone who died in there?" Evan asked.

Tara thought back to the first time she had gone down to see the site the week it happened. The memory was still vivid and disturbing, as she recalled what she saw that day.

Turning to walk back home, Tara had noticed all the photos and memorabilia people had placed on the security fences and on the sidewalk surrounding the site. There were posters and fliers, stuffed animals, candles, and flowers. Many of the notes and letters left there were written by children. She knew what these kids would face in the future, and it broke Tara's heart even more. It was bad enough when you were in school and everyone felt sorry for you because you didn't have a mom or dad. Having a mom or dad die under these circumstances carried an even heavier burden.

The ages of the victims ranged from early twenties to late forties: the prime of their lives. This was unfathomable. But there were also victims who were her father's age and even older who probably had grandchildren. The weight of this sorrow began to overwhelm Tara, and she needed to leave. It was all simply too much for any human being to bear.

At that moment, Tara looked up and was drawn to one photo in particular. She felt compelled, pulled to the flier and the face that seemed to be looking right back at her.

Recognizing the face but not being able to immediately place it anywhere, Tara was quickly racking her brain trying to remember where she knew him from: was it elementary, high school, college, or a past work life?

Then it hit her; it was a guy she knew from college. He had dated a good friend of hers when they were undergrads, and she had lived in the same dorm with Tara their freshman year and then in the same house as sorority sisters. They hadn't been in touch since they graduated, and Tara wondered what had happened to them as a couple. With that thought, Tara's question was answered when she glanced further down the flier and read his wife's name along with the names of his children.

"Jesus Christ, that's fucking spooky," she mumbled aloud so that the woman standing next to her made a face at her choice of language.

What are the chances of finding someone I know among all these hundreds of strangers?

Tara took out her cell phone. The call went straight to voice mail so she left a message: "Leslie, call me back when you get this."

After a few minutes, her cell phone rang.

"Tara, it's me. What's up? Where are you?"

"Down at the Pitten Building. Oh my God, Leslie, you have no idea how bad it is. The devastation; the destruction is so unbelievable! You don't ever want to come down here to see it. It's so much worse than they show on TV. Like a thousand times worse!"

"I have no intention of seeing it. Trust me."

"It's just this huge, burned pile of...nothing. That beautiful building is just gone," Tara said, depressed.

"Tara you should get out of there. It's probably not safe. Why are you there?"

"I don't know. But listen to this: I'm walking around down here and they have this fence of like, memorials. You know, pictures, messages, and stuff. So I'm looking at all this and I see one flier in particular, and the guy in the picture looks really familiar. So I'm thinking and looking, and it finally hits me. Turns out its Ray Monroe. Do you remember him? The guy Kim Butler was dating at Rutgers? They got married after graduation. Looks like they are, were, still married and have two kids."

"Oh God!" Leslie yelled, "He's missing? Or dead?"

"I assume dead. No one's alive in there anymore," Tara answered.

"No, I saw that they pulled someone out of there the other day, and he was alive!" Leslie corrected her.

"Um, Les, it's Sunday. There's no one still alive in that."

"Poor Kim and her kids. How old are they?"

"I don't know; little, I guess. Like Buck.

"That's so horrible. I can't even imagine what she must be going through. Hey, if your father finds out you were down there he's going to have a frigging fit and..."

Tara cut her off. "Listen, I need to get out of here. It's all too much. I'll call you back later tonight, ok?"

"Ok. Just be careful around there," Leslie cautioned.

Tara took one last look at the picture on the fence and read the heartfelt plea. He was a handsome guy who she remembered also as a really nice person.

"Yes, I do remember you, Ray."

"I did see a picture of someone I went to Rutgers with on a memorial fence down there. He dated one of my friends. They married right out of college and had a couple of kids."

"Wow, how was she after it happened?" Evan asked.

"I don't know. We lost touch after graduation, but I couldn't get the thought of them out of my head after that. As a matter of fact, it took a long time to stop thinking about them and all those poor people who were killed. Remember when I told you I had those continuous dreams after the first time I went down to look at the bombing site?"

"Yes. When I asked you if you thought my grandfather was crazy," he laughed.

Tara thought back to the months before when she had so many questions about what was happening to her. Hesitantly, she relayed the details to Evan, explaining that seeing that nightmare probably prompted all that disruption in her sleep because of the hundreds of people who perished that day.

"Maybe *he* was the guy in your dream," Evan said, matter-of-factly.

Tara sat up and looked at him like he was the Oracle at Delphi.

"Oh, my God, maybe it was him!" Tara mumbled. "I just assumed the man in the dream represented some random stranger, but that makes perfect sense! You have no idea how crazy I was over all that stuff. I feel pretty stupid that I never put two and two together. But I still have no idea what any of that means or why I kept having the dreams for so long." Tara did not want to tell Evan that she still had the occasional dream and bathroom creepers.

"Maybe you should talk to my grandfather about them. That would seem to fall into his realm of the unknown and unexplainable," he said with amusement.

"Well, actually, I talk to a therapist now instead," she said quietly, waiting for his reaction.

Evan looked at her. "You're in therapy? You never told me that."

"Why? Is that a problem for you?" she asked, now guarded and slightly defensive.

"No, I'm just surprised you never mentioned it before. That's all. It's not a judgment, Tara. Not at all," he answered.

She got out of bed and slipped his T-shirt on over her naked body. Tara needed the safety of clothes, as if it would make her feel less vulnerable.

Sitting back down on the bed, she seemed to be deep in thought trying to decide the best way to explain this without seeming like a total head case.

"When I started having these dreams every night, *every single night,* I knew that wasn't normal. As if that wasn't bad enough, each time I would go into my bathroom in my apartment, I felt like I was not alone, and I would feel overcome by a sense of, well, despair, is the only way to describe it. I talked to my father, to a couple of my relatives, and of course to Leslie about it. People who know I am a very sensible, sane person. NOT a stark, raving lunatic."

He tucked a stray piece of hair behind her ear. "You're not crazy, Tara."

She smiled with such affection at him. "Well, for a certain financial analyst, I am." Continuing, she said, "So anyway, that was why I think I connected so well with your grandfather that day. He told me some things about my mother that no one other than me could have possibly known. And my dad told me I used to talk to imaginary people above my head when I was a toddler and that certain members of my family have this unique ability and..."

"Tara, slow down."

"I'm sorry. I haven't really talked about this stuff in a while, and it drives me crazy because I still can't explain it, and I need to have an explanation for things. The whole thing really affected me at the time. It still does." She had a painful expression on her face.

"It's ok. The bombing was a horrible time for everyone. We were all affected by what happened, some more than others."

Tara continued, determined to get all of this absurdity out in the open and see to what his reaction would be. "After a few weeks, the dreams and the bathroom stuff stopped happening every night, but I continued to have them now and then. That's when Leslie suggested something that finally made sense to me."

"What was that?" he asked.

"That maybe I had never really dealt with my mother's death. That I hadn't grieved properly or sufficiently. Which I hadn't because I just wanted to forget about it and not have people feel sorry for me. But I didn't want to ever forget my mother, so I buried everything. I suppressed all those feelings. It was a weird time for an eight-year-old. I just told everyone I was fine and wanted to move on, but I really couldn't emotionally. My own mother always taught me to not wear your heart on your sleeve for everyone to see and that people don't want to see your pain and anguish because it makes them feel uncomfortable. So I pretended to be fine, but really I wasn't. Can you understand any of that?" She searched his eyes for an answer.

"Yeah, babe. I get it. Come here."

She lay back down in his arms. He held her and kissed the top of her head.

"So that was when Leslie gave me the name of this woman, and I've been seeing her for a couple of months."

"Has it helped?" he asked.

"Yes, it has. Talking to someone who doesn't know you, who doesn't have a connection to any part of your life, takes the emotion out of it. She helps me focus on certain issues without the personal relationship getting in the way. She asks all the right questions in order to get the right answers. Does that make any sense?" Tara asked.

"Perfect. Why do you think you waited so many years to go then?" he asked.

"I'm not sure, but I spent my teens and most of my twenties hiding from life. After my mom died, my father and I had to learn a new normal and we just kind of focused on moving forward rather than looking back. I was caught up in school and sports, and time just moved so quickly, and we established a routine. When I moved here after college, I became just another anonymous person, living alone, limiting my social life and just concentrating on my career and work. By taking no risks and playing it safe all the time, I rationalized I couldn't get hurt by anything or anyone."

"That's pretty heavy stuff," he concluded. "When I met you, I couldn't believe you were single. I felt like it was the luckiest day of my life," he said as he pulled her closer.

"Well, I wasn't a total hermit. Leslie and Rob would occasionally set me up or one of my cousins would call with the name of some guy they felt I just had to meet. There have even been a couple of the lawyers in my firm, but nothing ever serious. I didn't realize it, but I never allowed myself to get that close with anyone."

Tara watched Evan frown at this bit of information and quickly shifted gears. "Before you, baby Buck was the main man in my life!"

They both laughed.

"I have to meet this kid soon and see what my competition looks like," he said jokingly.

"Well you will, soon. Leslie and Rob invited us next weekend. They are anxious to finally meet you. Then after that, if you are a good boy, I'll unleash my family on you," Tara said, feeling him out on the subject of taking their relationship to the next level.

"Bring it on, baby. I love a challenge." He rolled her underneath him and began kissing her neck.

Tara stopped him and grabbed his face between her hands. "Thank you, Evan." She looked at him with deep affection.

"What for?"

"For not laughing, or judging, or running out of here. For just listening, for being interested. For just...everything. You are everything, you know? It still scares me to let go like this, to share all these emotions. I'm not used to it," she admitted.

"You don't have to be afraid. It scares me too, sometimes. I've never felt this way about anyone before. I love you. I want us to be open and honest with each other, to be intimate in every way together."

"God, how did I get so lucky?" she asked, pulling him closer.

"I really don't know. But right now, I would like to be the one to get lucky if you don't mind," he said as he moved his hands under her shirt.

"Oh, that can definitely be arranged," Tara answered as she climbed on top of him, pulling the T-shirt over her head.

CHAPTER

13

The following morning, Tara was at work and glanced at the digital clock on her desk. The time was 11:12 a.m. She thought it was odd seeing two sequential numbers like that.

She didn't give it another thought until later that night when she was getting ready for bed. Glancing at the clock on her nightstand as she pulled down the sheet and quilt from her bed, she saw it again: 11:12 p.m.

"What the hell?" she said out loud. *How weird is that?* Twice in one day she looked at the clock and saw those same numbers staring back at her.

Just a coincidence, she told herself as she climbed in to bed to read her book and watch TV.

About twenty minutes later, her cell rang. It was Evan, who had left for Boston that afternoon on business.

"Hey, you," she answered yawning.

"Wow, tired already?" he asked.

"Yes, when somebody keeps me up all night doing dirty, nasty things to me. You wear me out. But in no way is that a complaint. How was the flight?"

"Crowded. And it's already freezing cold here," he answered.

"Well, when you come back, I'll get you all hot and bothered."

"Jesus, Tara, not now, ok? I won't be able to concentrate tonight, and I have a mountain of stuff to go through before bed," he groaned.

"Ok, I'll save it. Remember: Saturday we are going to Leslie's."

"Got it. What time do you want to leave?" he asked.

"Let's leave here around two. Buck will be up from his nap by the time we get there, and he'll be ready to go with his Aunt Tara. I can't wait for you to meet him. Oh, and of course Leslie. And Rob, too."

"Sounds good. Listen, I just wanted to call and say goodnight. I need to put in at least three more hours of work," he said, already exhausted.

"No problem. I'm glad you got there safely. I hate not being able to sleep with you. Your travel schedule is seriously interfering with my love life," Tara joked.

"Unfortunately, it's only going to get worse," he warned.

Evan's firm was sending him to Boston a lot, and there was a strong chance he would be asked to go work in that office on a permanent basis. It was a subject he had carefully avoided with Tara, deciding to deal with it when the time came. He had finally met a girl he could have a future with, and he wasn't quite sure how to handle it. He didn't want her to break things off if she decided she couldn't do the long distance thing.

"I miss you. Call me tomorrow when you get a chance. I love you," she said quietly.

"Miss you too. I love you. Bye."

Tara put the phone on her nightstand and thought about how much she loved Evan. It had been so long since she had shared her everyday life with anyone outside of her father and Leslie. She turned out her light and decided a few prayers were in order.

Tara closed her eyes and quietly whispered. "Mommy, please ask God, to bless what Evan and I have found together and ask him to watch over us and help our love to grow stronger every day. Please pray that Evan will always be safe when he travels and that God will always let him return home to me. I love and miss you. And I ask the Blessed Mother to pray for all of us, especially for Daddy, Leslie, and her family, Buck, all the Fitzpatrick and O'Connell families, and, of course, my sweet Evan. Thank you God, for all the blessings you have given us. Please continue to be with us in all things, for my life here on earth is nothing without you in it. Please forgive me my sins. You know what I'm talking about there, for I am human and totally fallible. Please know if I offend you in any way, it is never done deliberately. Please keep my mother safe with you in heaven. Amen.

Then she said an Act of Contrition, the Lord's Prayer, and a Hail Mary. *Twelve years of Catholic school never leaves you.*

The next day at work, it happened again. Tara was on her computer doing research and looked up at the time: 11:12 a.m.

Ok, *so* not funny, she thought.

Then again, that night, she turned to glance at the time after she had come out of the bathroom because she wanted to watch the news, and there it was glaring at her: 11:12 p.m. *Are you kidding me?*

The next day, she walked downstairs to the small cafeteria in her building to buy a sandwich and bottle of water and decided to get a cookie because she needed something sweet. She also grabbed a magazine. Tara placed the items down on the counter while the cashier totaled up her order.

"That'll be $11.12 please," the young girl muttered, snapping the wad of gum in her mouth.

"Excuse me?" Tara asked.

"That'll be $11.12," she repeated, impatiently.

Gawking at her in disbelief, Tara handed her a twenty-dollar bill. Like a zombie, she walked back to her office and found a sunny place outside to eat. It was Indian summer in New York, and everyone was outdoors at lunch trying to regain some of his or her suntan.

She decided to call Leslie about Saturday. It was a good excuse to call because in reality, the 11:12 number business was starting to freak her out. With much unease and irritation, Tara mused: *Here we go again with the batshit, unexplainable drivel. I hate when things make no sense. First it was my bathroom, now it's the damn clock.*

"Ok, so maybe it's because you went down there again this past weekend," Leslie surmised. "Would you just stay the hell away from that place from now on! Every time you go down there, you have these weird repercussions after. JUST STAY AWAY — period, end of story!"

"But why is that? Do you think it means anything? Or is my mind just becoming fixated on that stuff again?" Tara whined.

"How the hell should I know? You have a perfectly good shrink at your disposal, which you are paying good money for. Ask her for crying out loud!" Leslie said, dumbfounded at her friend's cluelessness.

Tara hesitated for a minute. "Yeah, well I haven't even told her about the bizarre dreams and bathroom escapades, yet," she said sheepishly.

"What do you mean you haven't told her? Isn't that one of the main reasons you went to see her in the first place?" Leslie asked.

"Yes, but we started with my childhood issues and my mom's death, and I just haven't gotten around to it yet. Do you realize how fast one measly hour flies by?" Tara asked.

"I think that you need to tell her about all this hocus-pocus stuff. Maybe it's all tied together in some strange way. Let her figure it out for you."

"I know — you're right. Hell, she won't think I'm crazy or anything, right?"

They both giggled like they were back in third grade.

"Let's talk about Saturday! We can't wait to meet Prince Charming. What time are you coming?" Leslie asked.

"I thought we would leave the city at two. That way, by the time we get there, Buck should be up. Did you hear that? It almost rhymes! I still, to this day, can't believe you saddled that beautiful child with that horrendous name," Tara said, disgusted.

"Would you just put a lid on it? You are so obsessed with my son's name. You need to talk to your therapist about that, too. It is really unnatural, and frankly, disturbing."

"When that precious child was born I warned you not to name him that, but you ignored me. I am merely preparing you for what lies ahead when he goes to school so you won't be shell-shocked. Kids are cruel, you know. Buck. Fuck. Duck. Suck. Muck. Need I continue?" Tara asked.

"Good thing you are seeing a therapist because there is something seriously wrong with you. I am not kidding. Does your boyfriend like your sense of humor?"

"Of course. He thinks everything about me is adorable, as I do about him," Tara gushed.

"Yeah, just you wait until one of you burps, or worse yet farts, in front of each other for the first time. Then the honeymoon will be over. Believe me, it's not pretty," Leslie warned.

Tara almost choked on the sandwich she was eating. They both were hysterically laughing.

"You still can make me wet my pants!" Tara gasped through her choking fit.

"Yeah. Me *and* your new squeeze!" Leslie fired back.

Tara lost it again and decided it would be best to just stop eating altogether. Her best friend was on a roll now. Tara was getting dirty looks from the people around her.

"I do so love you and your atrophied brain, Leslie Mancino Gordon!"

"Thanks for pointing out my obvious housewife shortcomings, you little jerk!" Leslie said, giggling.

"Enough! What can I bring Saturday besides my sexy boyfriend?" Tara teased.

"Bring me a chocolate cheesecake and I'll allow you to name my next child."

"That's a deal. I'm going to force you to sign that in blood when I get there."

"Deal. Listen, I've got to go. I'll just see you Saturday," Leslie said.

"Talk to you later. Oh, and please, you and Rob need to go easy on Evan. I want him to stick around for a very long time," Tara pleaded.

"Don't worry. I remember what it's like to fall in love so hard it hurts."

"Thanks," Tara said, relieved.

"But just you remember — one day he will pee in front of you with the bathroom door open and leave droplets on the toilet seat and then you won't think he's so wonderful."

Fat chance of that happening, Tara thought.

CHAPTER

14

On Friday, Tara had an appointment with Dr. Saxon after work. Evan wasn't getting in from the airport until around seven-thirty, and he would go straight to her apartment. She couldn't wait to see him, but she had other pressing issues on her mind.

"All right, Tara. Please close your eyes for a moment and feel your body settle into the chair. Breathe in through your nose and slowly blow that breath out from your mouth. Relax and remember this is your time to accomplish positive goals that you have set for yourself. This is the place you want to be right now, the place you have chosen to be. You are in total control of what you will say, and I will help you to interpret those feeling and thoughts, and you will continue to move forward in your journey to discover the future for yourself, while understanding your past and present. Take another breath, release it slowly, and open your eyes."

When Tara did, she was met with a warm smile from her therapist.

"It's apparent you need to address something specific today. Am I correct?" Dr. Saxon asked.

"Yes." Tara answered quietly. "I need to talk about something that affected me months ago and something that has been happening this past week. I don't know if they are connected, but I haven't felt this unsettled in a long time."

"Let's start at the beginning then, wherever you feel comfortable."

"All right," said Tara, taking another deep breath. "First, let me ask you a question. What is your opinion on dreams? Dreams when you are sleeping, not aspirational dreams," she clarified.

"Ah, dreams! One of science's great conundrums. The age old mystery over what is real and unreal."

Tara felt relieved. This was obviously a subject Dr. Saxon had dealt with many times before by patients as confused as she was.

"Dreams are a great source of debate for both scientists and therapists, I'm afraid to say. There is no definitive answer as to why we have them and what they ultimately represent. For example, Freud theorized that dreams were the manifestation of unconscious wants and needs. Others believe that dreams are nothing more than aimless brain activity or an emotional response to daily life rather than a deeply embedded psychological need. The question of why we dream or what dreams signify runs the gamut from helping us solve problems to learning how to cope with traumatic events or stress. Dreams can reflect a fear we have during the day resulting in our brain trying to deal with it at night when we are asleep."

"So basically what I'm hearing is that you don't put much validity in dreams?" asked Tara.

Dr. Saxon corrected her, raising a single index finger. "That's not what I said. What I am saying is that there is no scientific proof for why we dream or what those dreams mean. I think what we need to do first is have you tell me about any dreams you may be having and then we can try to connect them to things that are happening in your life. Please go ahead and tell me about these most recent events, dreams or otherwise."

Tara told her in as much detail as she could about the two reoccurring dreams of the man watching the children. She also relayed how she had seen the picture of the man she knew from her past on the memorial fence at the Pitten Building.

"I literally had one of these two dreams almost every night for months. They started right after I first went down to see that massacre. My boyfriend thinks that maybe the man in the dream is this old college acquaintance. Do you think there might be a connection between the dreams and this man?"

"I won't discount that possibility. But as I said, dreams are a tricky thing and can often have several interpretations. But let me ask you this: What was your initial reaction to witnessing that scene of devastation?" the doctor asked.

"Horror, shock, anger, incredible sadness. The loss was staggering. How would people deal with this, how would families deal with such an enormous burden? Then, as I just stared at that huge pile, I wondered how the city would clean up the surrounding area. Now that I think back, that may have been an odd reaction to have in light of the fact I was standing in front of a human tomb."

"Unfortunately, there is no rule book on how to process something as horrendous as the sight you saw that day, Tara. Go easy on yourself and give yourself a break," Dr. Saxon said.

Tara gave her a weak smile.

"Are you a very organized person, Tara? I mean at home, at work — do you fare better in order or are you just as comfortable in clutter and chaos?"

Tara was a neat freak who despised mess and kept her apartment spotless and organized. The same was true of her office space and other aspects of her life. In school, she would complete work as soon as it was assigned, and finish term papers well in advance of their due date. She felt scattered and anxious when things were in disarray, even needing to purge closets and drawers when they were overrun with junk. "I prefer, rather insist, that the things in my world be where they should be and belong," Tara replied.

"Did you ever have a part of your life that you felt was disorganized, that needed to be cleaned up or fixed or made right again?" Dr. Saxon asked.

Tara thought for a moment. "Yes. I guess so."

"When was that?"

"After my mother died. Everything was a mess, and nothing made sense." Tara looked at the floor then back up at her therapist.

"Did you feel disorganization at that time or did you feel grief?" she asked.

"Both. I remember feeling like a boat that had been set adrift from its anchor. There were too many unanswered questions swimming around in my head. How would my father and I survive? How are we going to be able to function in a world without my mother? Because my mother was the glue. She held everything together. She was the person in our family who connected all the dots. Without her, I feared, who would take care of me? My father had to go out and work every day. Who would make my lunch? Who would drive me everywhere? How would every day from this day forward ever be normal again?" Tara winced at the anguish it brought back, reliving those feelings as if it happened yesterday.

"And how did you feel as a result of those fears, those feelings?" Dr. Saxon asked.

"I felt panic. Like it was so overwhelming and I couldn't have that thought in my head. I think I simply could not deal with it. As an eight-year-old child, the idea of daily life without my mother to take care of me was so inconceivable, my brain couldn't process it."

"So how did you deal with it?"

"By not dealing with it, I guess. I had no coping skills at that age to deal with anything like that. Plus, my father was so paralyzed by grief, I became really frightened."

"Why was that, Tara? What were you afraid of?"

"That he would die, too," Tara whispered quietly.

"So what did little, eight-year-old Tara decide to do then?"

"I would try to make it all better for him, for us. I would be the strong one for my father. Then he wouldn't have the extra burden of worrying about me, too. If he saw I was all right, it would be so much easier for him, and then he wouldn't have a heart attack also. I would show him and everyone else that I was fine, that I was strong. That I could deal with this. And so I pretended."

"Pretended what, Tara?"

"Pretended that I was fine. That everything was normal. That our lives hadn't just been turned upside-down. I guess I buried all those feeling and fears." The tears began to roll down her cheeks. "Jesus Christ," Tara said quietly.

"And then what, Tara?"

"And then I buried my grief, along with my mother. I never even cried at her funeral. I kept telling everyone who asked that I was fine. I buried my emotions under a heap of everyday life so I wouldn't have to deal with it. It was too messy to deal with. There was too much stuff. I see it so clearly now." Tara sat back, understanding this was a huge realization for her.

"So let me ask you: Do you see any connection now between your mother's death and those dreams?" Dr. Saxon asked.

Tara paused and laughed. With a smirk, she uttered, "Oh — you're good."

Dr. Saxon smiled back.

"So am I to assume that the dreams and feelings of despair that began after witnessing the mess at the Pitten Building were a result of the stuff I never dealt with after my mother's death? That the victims buried beneath that building represented my own experience with death and how overwhelming the situation was?" she asked.

"Well, what do you think?"

Tara wiped her eyes and blew her nose into a wad of tissues she had grabbed from the table in front of her. She was surprised how good she felt, how unburdened. "I think," she hesitated, "that witnessing that scene shocked my system. It ignited emotions in my adult self that I had buried as a child. The mess of it all seemed just as insurmountable as it had seemed to me when I was eight years old. I questioned how the aftermath of the bombing would be dealt with now, just the same as I questioned how we would deal with my mother's death all those years ago."

"It seems that what you witnessed that day set off a series of triggers for you. The pile of debris, the idea of unexpected death and sudden loss, children losing parents that day to an unforeseeable event, the fact that your college friend and her young children would now experience the same fears and upheaval you had, the idea that your father was left to deal with so much also — all these things were swirling around in your brain and in your heart. Dreams can be a result of a response to a traumatic or stressful event. A dream can also cause the brain to link together two separate traumatic events such as your mother's death and the bombing. Dreams serve to be the human mind's way of helping us cope with conflict or turmoil. When we are asleep, we are not focused on a specific thought or task. Therefore, our brain is free to make associations between seemingly random thoughts. When we sleep, the events of the day or our emotions that are in flux or conflict can be put to rest in the dream state."

OUT OF MY DREAMS

Tara listened with interest. She was fascinated by what Dr. Saxon was saying because it was science trying its best to explain what was based in no factual proof. It made her think and question, but at least it was somewhat of a logical reason to explain what was happening to her.

Dr. Saxon continued. "Dreams mirror in a sleep state the emotions we feel when we are awake. Sometimes our brains are on such overload, we dream to alleviate all those images."

"So do you think that the man in my dream was my father?" Tara asked.

"Perhaps it was. Or perhaps it was your mind linking your father and your friend's husband who perished in the building, trying to connect the two. Maybe the image of the man triggered a memory of generalized loss. The man was helpless in your dream just as your father was helpless in preventing his wife's death and in raising you without her. We could also interpret that he was standing there watching his life pass him by without your mother at his side. Do you see where I am going with this Tara? Your two dreams can have several interpretations. The human brain is such a miraculous machine. It is such a mystery that we will never be able to explain its functions, especially why and how we dream."

Feeling like some of the puzzle pieces of her life were finally coming together, she decided to go off on a tangent. What the hell, she thought, might as well go for broke while they were on the subject of the unexplainable.

"I would like your educated opinion on another subject, if I may?" Tara asked.

"Of course, what is it?"

"I realize you are a woman of science, but as part of your job, do you put any credence in the idea of being connected to the world beyond this life? Please don't think I'm insane asking this," she pleaded.

"What do you mean?" Dr. Saxon asked, confused.

"Do you think that certain people have the ability to connect with those who have passed and are able to communicate with them?" Tara laughed nervously.

"In all my years of practice, I have learned many things. One is that nothing is impossible and that all things are possible. In studying the human mind and human heart anything can be real and there are many things that can't be explained, only felt. If something is real to a patient, who am I to question it? Does that answer your question?"

Tara thought back to the day she read the article at work about the doctor who discussed the complexities of the human heart. Here was another medical professional confirming that some things in this life are just too strange or complicated to explain.

"Yes, thank you. The reason I asked you that question is because my family on my mother's side claims to possess some type of psychic gift that gives them the ability to sense things that others can't, and I think that maybe I may have inherited that ability or skill or habit — I really don't know what to call it," Tara tried to explain cautiously, trying not to sound delusional, but once it came out of her mouth she wished she could take it back. It felt unnatural and foreign to bring it up in the presence of someone she now admired and respected like Dr. Saxon.

Suddenly, Dr. Saxon's desk intercom buzzed, indicating their session was finished and that the next appointment was due to arrive.

"I'm sorry, Tara, but time is up for today. We can pick back up on this next time. You also alluded to other recent events that concerned you that we never got to today, so we will continue discussing that in our next meeting, also."

Tara slowly stood up and stretched. She felt like they were on such a roll; she hated to leave. But those were the rules.

Dr. Saxon took Tara's hand in both of hers. "Great work today, Tara. I really think we broke through a lot of walls in this session."

"Thank you, again. Now I understand why they pay you the big bucks," Tara said, teasing.

"That's right, Tara — all that money! Just putting it toward the yacht!" she laughed.

As Tara stepped out in to the still warm early evening, she felt drained but good. She never believed this therapy mumbo-jumbo would be beneficial until now, and she appreciated how much Dr. Saxon was able to help her come to her own conclusions about what all this meant. Tara was finally getting some answers, and she saw the light at the end of the tunnel of confusion that had dominated many parts of her life.

CHAPTER

15

"**E**van, I can't breathe!" Tara laughed as he picked her up off the ground in a tight hug. Then, he silenced her protests by covering her mouth with his, and she melted in to his embrace.

Holding him tightly, she whispered, "I missed you. So much."

"Me too. You have no idea." He kissed her again.

"Oh, I know how much. I can *feel* how much," she mumbled in to his mouth.

"Well then, Ms. Fitzpatrick — let's go do something about that right this minute. Then afterwards, if you are good, I'll take you out for a nice dinner."

"Don't you worry, Mr. Kane, I'll be very good."

Tara dragged him by his tie into her apartment and locked the door.

"So how did it go today?" he asked as he took a sip of beer from the frosted mug.

"Really good. Made some great progress. You know how some people think seeing a therapist is a waste of time? I think if you get a good one, like I have, it can really help."

"How so?" Evan asked.

"She helped me see that some of the problems I had been having could have been linked to my mother's death and to the bombing. I mean a lot of it is common sense, but sometimes you can't see the forest for the trees, you know?"

"Don't be so hard on yourself, honey. If I lost my mother at eight years old, I'm sure I would have ended up on the streets, doing drugs and getting in trouble. You survived pretty well I'd say; give yourself some credit," he said reaching over to take her hand.

"That's what Leslie always says. Oh, Evan — tomorrow we are going there! You get to meet Buck!" Her face lit up.

Evan frowned. "The thought of competing with anyone, baby or otherwise, for your attention doesn't thrill me, Tara."

She put her mug down mid sip. "You have *no* competition, Evan. No one does to me what you do. Never has and probably never will."

Evan smiled at her.

Tara looked across the table and was amazed that in such a short time she had fallen so deeply in love with this man. It had to be divine intervention, she thought. Or more likely, her mother had something to do with it. Tara had always felt that even though her mom was gone, she was always looking out for her over the years. Never ready to find someone before, now she was and somehow, she believed, her mother conspired to have the paths of Tara Fitzpatrick and Evan Kane collide. It was too powerful, and it had to have been orchestrated by more than pure chance. "So, tell me about your week. Successful, I hope?" Tara asked, sipping her beer.

"Yes and no," he answered, but it appeared as if he had something ominous to say.

"Give me the no first. Better to end on a good note."

Evan wrapped both of his hands around his glass. Then he looked into Tara's face, which made his heart skip a beat. Now was the time to tell her the news he had been dreading for weeks.

"I will be spending the majority of my time in Boston over the next few months. There are several projects and new accounts that I've been in charge of, and they involve a lot of client contact. Unfortunately, most of them are there in Boston."

"Ok, so we'll do what we have to. It's your job, and it's important. We will make it work, Evan. Although the idea of not seeing you during the week, well it just plain sucks," she smiled at him.

"That's not the worst of it, Tara. They may want me to transfer there permanently; in fact, I am hoping that since I am in charge of these accounts, they will just promote me to manage the whole deal. This could actually be a turning point in my career."

"Oh, Evan, that's great news! You have worked so hard for this, and you really deserve a promotion like that!" Tara was genuinely happy for his news and his success.

"But Tara, it means that I would have to move to Boston. Out of Harbor Point. More importantly, away from you." He looked at her face to gauge her reaction. Most of the girls he had dated in the past would have been pissed off. All he could see was excitement from Tara for his great opportunity, and it made him love her all the more.

"I realize that. But this is your career, and you have worked so hard for this. You can't possibly turn your back on this because it's the opportunity of a lifetime. I mean how many guys your age would be entrusted with so much responsibility? They obviously have a great deal of confidence in your ability to do this, and I am so proud of you!"

"But what about us?" he asked.

"What about us? I'm all in here, Evan. I will do what I need to do to continue to build a relationship with you. I love you. Distance will not change that. At least for me, it won't."

"I just feel this is all coming at the best possible time for me and my career and yet the worst possible time for us and our relationship."

"Why?" she asked.

"Because I feel like what we have is so good, and I don't want to lose you because I will probably have to move to Boston. I feel like we are on a certain path, and I don't want it to be interrupted."

"It will only change if we let it, Evan. For my part, I won't let it. I can promise you that. You — us — just means too much to me," Tara said, reaching out to take his hand.

"For me, too. I love you, Tara." He kissed the palm of her hand.

"Ok, so then let's just see what happens. We'll do this one day at a time and not stress out over it. You have enough on your plate right now with making this all happen. In the meantime, we can amass frequent flier miles and pay Amtrak rates, and you can run up the mileage in that fancy BMW you are so proud of. And if it turns out that you have to move there permanently, we will just deal with it then. One step at a time, ok?" She smiled at him and made him feel so good and secure in so many ways.

"Who knew such good news for me would cause such problems for us. It's just not fair," he said, sadly.

"My darling Evan, that is the story of my life."

The next morning, Tara woke up early and turned to look at Evan. He was dead asleep after a night of having their lovemaking take on a new urgency. She quietly got up so as not to disturb him and slipped on his T-shirt, smiling at the scent of it as she pulled it over her head. Their clothes were hastily discarded all over the floor when the two of them returned to her apartment after dinner, and she nearly tripped over his shoes as she walked across her bedroom.

Tara went into the bathroom and flipped on the light. Suddenly, she was overtaken by a terrible panic attack. She couldn't breathe and then she felt as though she was breathing too much. The small room felt like it was closing in on her, and she became lightheaded. Her heart was beating a hundred times per second, and she broke out in a sweat. Sitting down on the toilet seat, she put her hands over her face.

Although Tara felt like she was having a heart attack, she had felt this before, and she knew what it was. Usually, she would feel it coming on and was always able to stop it, or at least, minimize it. This one came out of the blue and surprised her.

Knowing Evan was just a few feet away from the door should have helped, but it only made her more anxious. *What if he saw me like this? What would he think? Would he run away from his crazy girlfriend?* Tara had to pull herself together. Now.

Her mind was racing, but she tried to imagine herself sitting in Dr. Saxon's office, in that comfortable chair, the place that had become her sanctuary, and she closed her eyes. Summoning her therapist's soothing, relaxing tone of voice, telling her to breathe slowly in and out, Tara was able to put herself in her happy place. This was a technique that was used in behavior modification therapy to combat and quell feelings of anxiety when they crept into the psyche.

"When you feel anxious, close your eyes and think of a memory or a place you can go back to in your mind," Dr. Saxon had instructed. Tara's happy place was sitting at the edge of the ocean, just where the waves lost their force. When the waves would just kiss the sand before being pulled back into the sea, on a hot summer day. Listening to the seagulls call overhead and the smell of salt in the thick, humid air: this was pure paradise for her.

After a few minutes, Tara began to calm down and her breathing became regulated.

Eventually, she opened her eyes and realized the panic attack had passed. Slowly she stood up and leaned in to the small mirror above the sink. She looked like hell and was a sweaty mess.

Turning on the shower, she brushed her teeth while waiting for the water to get hot. Then she peeled off the shirt and stepped into the water, hoping to wash the aftermath of this episode down the drain. As she stood under the stream of water, she wondered what had brought this maelstrom on her with such force. This bathroom was becoming its own personal house of horrors. Tara laughed at the absurdity of that thought.

"I really am crazy if I'm afraid of my own bathroom," she said under her breath as the water streamed over her body.

Suddenly, the shower door opened and standing there was a very naked, very *awake* Evan.

"What did you say, sweetheart?" he asked.

Pulling him in with her and wrapping her arms around him she answered, "Nothing you need to hear. Just get in here."

CHAPTER

16

Tara and Evan arrived at the Gordon household, armed with a cheesecake, cookies, and a coconut cream pie for Rob, his absolute favorite. (Tara had made a face when she looked at the receipt for the cookies: $11.12! *What the heck?*) Leslie would always chastise Tara for putting love handles on her husband, and Rob would mouth *THANK YOU!* behind his wife's back.

Tara nervously rang the doorbell. She wanted her closest friends in the world to like and approve of Evan. As the front door opened, they both were met with hugs, handshakes, and warm welcomes.

Leslie and Rob did everything to put Evan at ease, and he knew that Tara's friends would be nothing less than terrific, just like her. He relaxed immediately and felt accepted in their inner circle. Evan watched his girlfriend practically swoon when she snatched Buck from his father's arms and covered him with kisses as the child squealed with laughter.

"I'm going to eat you alive, Bucky! You are the best baby and cutest boy in the entire universe! Evan! This is my boy! Isn't he just like the most awesome baby you have ever seen in your life!"

Evan smiled at his enamored girlfriend.

The four adults settled in around the large kitchen island asking questions of each other, laughing (particularly at something Buck did), drinking beer, and eating the ton of snacks Leslie had assembled for them. The guys discovered they had a lot in common, especially a love of Philadelphia because Rob had also attended college there. They were accomplished businessmen, relative slobs, and avid golfers. At one point, after a few beers, Rob winked at Tara and gave her a thumbs-up when he got down on the kitchen floor to play with Buck and his monster Tonka trucks.

After a dinner of grilled filet mignon steaks, Rob took Evan downstairs to the basement to show him his latest project. Buck sat in his high chair eating small crackers and drooling from his impending teeth. Tara and Leslie began to clean up the kitchen and set out all the desserts they would indulge in next.

"So," Tara beamed, "what do you think? He's perfect, isn't he?"

Leslie laughed at her friend. "Yes, dear. He's perfect. And you are *so* gone over him, it's positively nauseating!"

"I know. I've never felt like this. I never want to be away from him. And he says he feels the same way, too. Do you think this is all too fast?"

"Jesus Christ, Tara. You guys are like, thirty years old! There are no rules at that age. When it's right, you know it. You are not two kids in high school. Although you act like it with all that mooning over each other crap." Leslie rolled her eyes. "Just enjoy it and do what feels right for the both of you."

Tara hugged Leslie. "He makes me so happy sometimes I have to pinch myself to make sure it's real."

"Looks pretty real to me. Your father will be so thrilled to meet him. Both a Yankees and a Rangers fan. You will, however, have a problem with the fact that he likes the Eagles — you realize that? Your uncles and cousins will crucify him."

"I know. Can't be helped. I'm just surprised Rob never jumped ship on any of his New York teams."

"Are you kidding me? He said he would never become a Philly sports fan. He probably was beaten up a few times for that."

They both giggled.

"Speak of the devil — when will your father meet him? I mean you've been dating for a while now. And when are you going to unleash the whole Fitzpatrick/O'Connell clan on poor Evan?" Leslie asked.

"Actually, my dad is coming into the city for brunch with us next weekend. And I guess Evan will meet everyone else at Thanksgiving. I wanted to wait a couple of months before I fed him to the wolves." She laughed.

"Don't worry. You father will love Evan. He seems like a really good guy. Well done, my friend." Leslie winked.

"My father would probably be happy with anyone I brought home at this point. I think he thought that maybe I was a lesbian," Tara said.

"He just didn't want you to be alone, that's all. He wouldn't have cared if it were a guy or girl. So how about Evan's family; when will you meet them?"

"I don't know if you remember, but I already met his grandfather. I love, love, love him! We have to pick a weekend to drive to Connecticut to meet his mother and brother. I don't know when I'll meet his father. He lives in Miami."

"Doesn't his mother live with his grandfather?" Leslie asked.

"She used to. Now she lives in a retirement community. Charlie shuffles between his home in Connecticut and a smaller apartment he still has in Harbor Point."

Tara took a huge black and white cookie out of one of the bags. Waving it at Buck, she danced over to his chair. "Look what Aunt Tara got especially for you, Buckwheat!"

Leslie made a face. "I am so getting back at you when you have your first child; you have no idea."

"Unlike you, I will carefully explore all possible names and their ramifications before I select something as crucial as a name for my offspring," Tara said, as she broke the cookie into manageable pieces for Buck to eat.

"Anyway, how is everything else? Work good?" Leslie asked as she licked powdered sugar from her finger.

"Yeah, work is fine. Had a rough time this morning, though." Tara shivered at the memory.

Leslie turned to look at her. "Why? What happened?"

"Horrible panic attack. Right there in my frigging bathroom. With Evan right outside the door. I swear my bathroom has become my personal chamber of torture. I think it may be cursed. Or haunted. Nothing good happens in there. Oh wait, scratch that. I did have a very nice shower with my boyfriend in there this morning after I calmed down." Tara smirked at Leslie.

"Ew, gross. TMI," Leslie said, gagging.

"No seriously, Leslie. It was the worst one ever. I thought I would pass out. Thank God I'm seeing Dr. Saxon or I would have totally embarrassed myself in front of Evan."

"Are you going to bring it up in your next session with her?" Leslie asked.

"Yes, I will; haven't had a panic attack in a long time. By the way, thanks for convincing me to go see her. It has really helped me, and I think it made me open up my life again. Hell, right after beginning therapy, I met Evan."

Leslie shook her head in disagreement. "Your mother sent you Evan." Like it was a statement of fact.

Tara looked back at her. "You know, I thought the same thing the other day. Isn't that funny?"

"No, not at all. You know your mother would want a say in the guy you would eventually end up with."

"Do you think I'll end up with Evan? Really?" Tara hopefully asked her best friend.

"My dearest, bestest friend. After seeing you two today, and how you are with each other, I know he is destined to be your happy ending."

Tara then proceeded to tell Leslie about the upcoming changes with Evan's job and her fears about their future.

"Hey, if it's meant to be it will survive the distance and whatever else comes up. Just hold on tight to each other and don't let anything come between what you have. It's as simple as that."

Tara smiled at Leslie. Nothing, but nothing, beats a best girlfriend. "I sure hope so."

"Hey, by the way, did you get the email about the reunion?" Leslie asked.

"Which? High school or college?"

"College. Not a university-sponsored event. Julia Walsh is having our old crowd out to her new house. It's supposed to be enormous. I think she just wants to show everyone how rich she is." Leslie rolled her eyes.

"I haven't checked my email all weekend. When is it?" Tara asked.

"End of next month. You can take the train in. I think it's on a Sunday, which sucks, but I'll drive from here, which also sucks because then you can drink and I can't, because I always have to be the designated driver. Won't it be fun to see who got fat and old?" Leslie said with a very evil look in her eye as she chuckled.

"Les, you are horrible! Although it will be kind of fun to see everyone again. Sure, count me in," Tara replied.

The guys came back up from the basement, and Evan immediately grabbed Tara in a bear hug.

"Hey Rob, remember how great new love is? Look at poor Evan. He actually missed Tara for like all of ten minutes, and he can't keep his hands off her. And she is, like gushing all over him and making me sick with all that lovey-dovey crap. I think I may puke." Leslie walked over to get the coffee, and Rob and Tara looked at each other, uttering the same observation.

"PMS."

"Shut up, you two. I don't have PMS. Just a heightened sense of nausea right now."

"Sorry, Leslie. I'll try hard to control myself." Evan laughed.

"It's ok, Evan. I don't blame you. It's my oversexed friend that I have a problem with."

With that, Rob grabbed his wife and dipped her over in a dramatic kiss. "Who says we don't still got it, baby!" Rob boasted, as Leslie pulled away from him, face flushed but happy from the attention.

"Let's go sit and eat this fattening junk. Evan, don't let her bring this stuff here anymore. I'm still trying to lose this baby weight, and I have no self-control," Leslie whined.

"You look great, Leslie. You know I love how you look now," Rob said.

"That and a dollar will get you lucky tonight, buddy."

They all laughed and sat down in the kitchen. Tara looked around at her friends and the guy she had fallen totally in love with, happy that they liked each other and had hit it off so well.

It was one more sign that told her this was meant to be. That's what her Aunt Noreen had told her. *Pay attention to the signs. They will come. You just have to watch for them.*

CHAPTER

17

"I haven't had a panic attack in months," Tara told Dr. Saxon the following week in their session. "And I have had two this week. I need to get a handle on this," she said, shaking her head.

"Can you think back to the events of this past week, before you had your first one. Did anything significant happen or something different in the normal course of your day?" Dr. Saxon inquired as she put a cup of water on the table between them.

"Not that I can think of. Wait, well maybe," Tara said, looking as though a light bulb just went off in her head. "Evan told me he would have to spend more time in Boston for his job and would possibly have to move there permanently. But it's really great news for him. He will most likely be put in charge there and assume a huge leadership role in his firm," she said, proudly.

"Well, that's good news for him, but how do you feel about that?"

"I'm thrilled for him, of course. He's worked really hard and deserves that kind of recognition. I would be a complete selfish ass if I weren't happy for him. Right?" Tara stared at Dr. Saxon.

"Your time here is for you to discuss how you feel about things in your life. You don't have to pretend you are happy with this news if you are not."

When Tara didn't respond, Dr. Saxon continued. "How would you feel if Evan moved to Boston? From what you've told me, your relationship is progressing nicely and you really seem to care a great deal for him."

"I do," Tara answered. "I've fallen in love with him, and he tells me he feels the same way, that he loves me."

"That's wonderful. So then how would you really feel if he moved four hours away?" she asked.

"I guess I would hate it, actually. We were getting into a nice routine with each other, spending just about every night between our two apartments. I would miss seeing him every day. Really, really miss him," Tara said sadly. She was finally being honest with herself about this news. As great as it was for his career, it wasn't so great for them as a couple in love who did not wish to be separated.

"Let me ask you something, Tara. How many people have you truly loved in your life besides your parents and other family members?"

"Well, there's Leslie. And Buck, and I'm super fond of Rob, her husband. I thought I was in love in college, but now when I compare it to how I feel about Evan, it doesn't even come close."

"So when do you remember having panic attacks before in your life?"

"I guess about two years after my mother died, when I was about ten years old."

"Can you recall any more specific memories surrounding that time period?"

Tara closed her eyes and paused. Then she opened them and looked directly at Dr. Saxon.

"Yes, I do remember something. The first panic attack came the day I found something. Something of my father's."

"What was that?"

"I found a pack of cigarettes in my father's coat pocket. I had been looking for loose change to use in those gumball machines they used to have in the supermarket. I reached in and pulled out the obviously used, open pack. I couldn't believe it!" Tara said in disbelief, as if the memory was just yesterday.

"What did you do then?" Dr. Saxon asked.

"At first, I tried to flush them down the toilet, but they got stuck. I pulled them out and ran in to the kitchen, threw the wet pack of cigarettes on the table and started screaming at my dad. I had never, ever, raised my voice to him. I was always too afraid. But I was pissed off. And I was scared."

"Of what, Tara?"

"That he would get cancer or die of a heart attack. I screamed and asked how could he be so selfish? Did he want to die and leave me, too? Well, you should have seen his face. He was crushed. Then I started to panic. I couldn't breathe. I broke out in a cold sweat and was shaking. I then scared the shit out of my poor father. I was hyperventilating on the kitchen floor while my father held me, telling me to calm down, pleading with me to calm down. When I finally stopped and the panic subsided, I looked up and saw tears streaming down his face. He kept repeating over and over that he was sorry, that he had only smoked a few recently and promised he would stop after seeing how upset it made me. But I didn't believe him."

"Why didn't you believe him? Did you think your father would lie to you about that?"

"I don't know. All I could see was the fear. The fear of losing him, too. I wasn't listening to the words coming from his mouth, I was just thinking of how it would affect my life, and it terrified me."

"But he assured you he would stop," Dr. Saxon said.

"Yes, but sometimes people tell you things and make promises that they can't possibly keep."

"Who made a promise to you that they didn't keep, Tara?"

She thought for a moment. "My mother."

"What did she promise you?"

"That she wouldn't die. That she would never leave me."

"When did she make you that promise?"

"When I was little, I used to wake up in the middle of the night and wander in to my parent's bedroom. I would stand next to the side where my mother slept and just watch her."

"Why?" Dr. Saxon asked.

"To make sure she was still breathing. And when I saw she was ok, I would go back to my own room and go to sleep. In the morning, she would reassure me that she wasn't going anywhere and would never, never leave me. I only recently remembered this because my father told me that I used to do that."

"What caused that to resurface?" she asked, curious.

"When I told my dad about the dreams after going to see the Pitten Building after the explosion, he told me about some gift that exists in our family, of which I had no idea about, and that certain members of our family had like a sixth sense about certain things. He surmised that maybe I did that with my mother because I had a kind of premonition about her death."

Dr. Saxon didn't seem to give this information much interest.

"Let's go back to those dreams for a moment. We discussed previously how some of the images you saw at the explosion site could be connected to events in your life. What did you think when you saw all of those pictures on the fence and personal items left on the ground that day?"

"I thought what a waste, what a terrible waste. Some nutcase-psychopath took it upon himself to ruin families and lives. All I could think about were those poor kids who would also suffer because they had their parent snatched away," Tara said, angry.

"Similar to your own situation when you were eight years old, right?"

"Yes." She answered quietly. "The hell they would go through reminded me of myself. No dad or mom to tuck them into bed at night. No parent to calm their fears when they have a nightmare. Or to take care of them when they are sick. Not having both parents there when they graduate high school, get married, or have their first baby. Gone. All gone."

"So dreams of the future were buried under all that debris, and when you buried your mother, all your future dreams you would have shared with her were gone. Is that correct?"

Tara nodded and began to cry.

"Life has a way of presenting us with symbols in the present that connect us to our past. You just have to recognize them when they do," Dr. Saxon said.

"Enlighten me here, Doctor," Tara said while wiping her eyes with a tissue.

"Well, let's start with the panic attacks. You began to have panic attacks after Evan told you he might have to move to Boston. How would you connect this to your childhood when you discovered those cigarettes in your father's pocket?"

"Oh, I get it," laughed Tara.

"Humor would not be an appropriate response here," Dr. Saxon chided.

"No, I'm not laughing that way. I am just amazed at how obvious this stuff is sometimes!"

Dr. Saxon smiled at her. "I would like to hear you say it out loud, please."

"So I'm having panic attacks because I'm afraid of losing Evan, like I was having panic attacks when I was afraid of losing my father?"

Dr. Saxon nodded. "It's called Abandonment Complex, and it's common for people, particularly children, who lose someone they love. They fear if they love anyone else, they will lose them also. In addition, I suspect that your desire to check on your mother while she was sleeping was rooted in a primal fear of losing her. It is actually a common fear for young children."

"So no gift then, huh, Doctor?"

"Who am I to say? Just giving you the scientific explanation," she smirked.

Tara concluded that Dr. Wendy Saxon was not a big believer in mediums and psychics and the like. "Then in regards to the panic attacks and this Abandonment Complex, I have neglected to allow too many people in to my life?" Tara asked.

"Let's assume that is correct. So here comes this wonderful man into your life, rather unexpectedly. You fall in love with him and he with you. This is not an everyday occurrence for Tara Fitzpatrick. And so you open your life and your heart. Now he tells you he may have to move and leave the intimacy you have come to share together. Now can you see why you would have a panic attack?"

"Duh, well now I do!"

"So how do you think you should handle the possibility of Evan's moving away? Should you bury those feelings or deal with them in a more rational way?" Dr. Saxon asked.

Tara could now see what she had been doing wrong all these years. She had to change how she would think, feel, and act toward events in her present and future. Sitting up straight in the chair, she looked directly at her doctor.

"I believe first of all, that I will be happy for his promotion and the great opportunity he will have in his career. Secondly, I will assure him, and myself, that we will not let distance come between what we have built with each other. And lastly..."

"Yes?"

"I may need to consider moving with him to Boston. Eventually. Hopefully."

"Or he may even ask you to marry him. There are all kinds of possibilities," Dr. Saxon said, smiling.

"And if he doesn't? If this distance thing ruins what we have?" Tara asked.

"Then, as with everything else in life, it wasn't meant to be and wasn't as strong as you thought it was. Tara Fitzpatrick, however, will survive and thrive no matter what, having lived through worse tragedy than a breakup with a boyfriend. And you live in a city that endured much worse than you."

They both became quiet for a moment, appreciating the magnitude of what she had just said.

"Touché," said Tara.

Closing Tara's file as she stood, Dr. Saxon said, "Good work, today. I think we are in the homestretch here."

"Thanks again; this felt really helpful. I'll see you next week."

As Tara walked home, she thought back to that day in May, a day that changed so many lives, including hers. Tara stood behind the barricades, looking at the ugliness and tragedy caused by one person against so many. That's when she was drawn to the one face she recognized: Ray Monroe. Ray who had probably kissed his wife goodbye that morning, or maybe not. Like so many other commuters, he had left the house before his family was even awake at the crack of dawn. Ray who got on the train into Harbor Point and went to do what everyone else does on a Tuesday. He just went to work. And then Tara wondered: Was he able to say goodbye once those bombs exploded in the building? Or was he one of the victims who perished instantly? What was his story? Sadness and anger had consumed Tara that first day she saw his picture and for many days after.

CHAPTER

18

It was only six in the morning, but since the heavy drapes were closed tight, it might as well have been midnight. Evan hated living out of a hotel room, even though it was a four-star, luxury suite in downtown Boston.

Since he had started seeing Tara, she was his first thought in the morning and his last thought before falling asleep at night. As he stood up and stretched, he thought what a waste of a good room. He missed seeing her, and he missed sleeping with her. Evan was now thinking of everything in terms of her: for her, about her, because of her. Never before had he let anything or anyone enter into his conscious mind to this extent except for work. It was all about the drive to succeed, to get ahead, and to establish himself with a

OUT OF MY DREAMS

reputation as the go-to guy. Evan was relentless in his ambition to move up the corporate ladder, and all that sweat was finally paying off. What he hadn't planned at this point was meeting the woman of his fantasies, the one who could turn him on and drive him crazy with just a look, while at the same time go toe-to-toe with him on football and hockey stats and the theory of quantum physics. He hadn't planned to fall in love.

"Jesus Christ, man, you've got it bad," Evan's colleague, a young associate named Jeff Price, informed him one night after work when he wanted to call Tara before heading out for a late dinner.

"Knock if off. This will only take a minute, Jeff," Evan said, annoyed that he had to explain himself to a guy who was five years younger and still trying to go through as many girls as was humanly possible. The fact that they were staying in Boston, in this opulent hotel with its numerous amenities, was not lost on Jeff. Most women were impressed with the fact that they could go back to his room for a great time and be treated to the best in town. Although Evan couldn't care less, Jeff used it to his full advantage.

Evan and Jeff were sitting at a bar after a particularly stressful day, having a couple of drinks. The clients they were trying to entice to sign on with their company were so notable and would bring in so much money and recognition — the two men basically just worked, ate on the run, slept a few hours, and were back in the office.

Evan started to explain some new procedure when two very attractive young women came up next to them to place an order with the bartender. It was a Thursday night, and the bar was a popular hangout for the college crowd as well as for other young professionals.

"Excuse me," a pretty woman with blond hair said as she leaned over Evan's shoulder. "Two margaritas, no salt please."

Standing next to her was another equally alluring brunette who seemed to be very interested in Jeff as his eyes roamed up and down her slender frame.

"Well, hello, ladies! Let me get those for you," he demanded, throwing a twenty dollar-bill on the bar.

"Why, thank you!" said the brunette, moving closer to his barstool.

"Yes, thanks," said the blonde to Jeff, but she turned her full attention to Evan.

"Here ladies, have a seat." Evan stood up and nodded to Jeff. "I'm going to head out anyway."

The blonde's face fell.

"Come on, man. Don't go just yet! One more!" Jeff urged, practically begged.

Evan felt nervous, uncomfortable, and trapped. He was well aware of Jeff's exploits, and now he found himself smack in the middle of the kind of situation he wanted to avoid.

"Yeah, please don't leave yet." The blonde smiled up at Evan, her eyes darting to his left hand to see if he had on a wedding ring. "I'm Marissa, by the way," she said, holding out her French-manicured hand.

Evan shook it quickly. "Nice to meet you." He deliberately didn't give her his name in return.

Jeff stood up and motioned for the girls to sit. "I'm Jeff and my mute friend here is Evan. And you are?" he asked, looking at the lithe brunette.

"Angela. Nice to meet you guys." She smiled while taking his seat at the bar.

The two women were dressed in work clothes, but sexier than usual office attire. Above-the-knee pencil skirts and four-inch heels, with blouses unbuttoned a touch lower than was probably permitted at their offices. Jeff was salivating because a guy can usually tell when a girl was a sure thing, and Angela was falling all over him. Jeff himself was smooth, extremely handsome and fit, and these two were circling each other like a couple of vultures over a carcass.

If Evan wasn't with Tara, it would have actually been fun to stay and watch him run his moves on this girl who also knew how to play this game and win.

Four attractive, young people in a bar, none of them married. Except for Evan, who after only a few months of dating Tara wanted to be married. He wished right now he could hide behind a wedding ring because Marissa was looking at him like she wanted to devour him whole.

Evan agreed to have one more drink and knew he would guzzle it down so he could escape. He realized in that moment how he had outgrown this scene and had no interest in it anymore. Random girls in bars seemed so trivial and unappealing now that he had such an extraordinary girl as Tara.

Jeff, however, was in full prowl mode.

"So, ladies, come here often?" he asked.

"About once or twice a week," Angela answered. "We both work at the same advertising firm across the street. How about you guys?"

"We work for a large investment firm in New York, but we have been coming here regularly to work with some new accounts in the Boston office," Jeff said, sipping his beer.

"So do you live here in the city?" Marissa directed the question at Evan.

"Um, no. New Jersey." He hoped Jeff would keep his mouth shut about possibly moving here. Of course, he didn't.

"But it looks pretty good that we may be here permanently soon." Both women smiled.

After about half an hour of the standard bar chatter, Evan drained his mug and put it down on the bar.

"Sorry ladies, early day tomorrow. It was nice to meet you." He motioned for the bartender to settle his tab. As he did, Marissa reached into her purse and quickly scribbled something on a piece of paper. Evan nodded at Jeff, "Dude I'll see you in the morning, bright and early," reminding him that he needed to be careful with his drinking and everything else.

"Ok, old man, see you in the morning," he laughed.

As Evan turned to leave, Marissa got up to follow him. She gently grabbed his arm, and he turned around.

"I really enjoyed meeting you, Evan. Maybe we could get together sometime?"

He couldn't wait to get out of there. Six months ago he would have stayed and probably would have taken her back to his hotel room. But now there was Tara. She was all he wanted now, no one else.

"I'm sorry, but I'm seeing someone," Evan answered.

"Lucky girl." Marissa smiled sadly.

Not one to give up so easily, however, she reached in to her skirt pocket and pulled out her business card. She slid it in to the breast pocket of Evan's suit jacket.

"If anything changes, give me a call." She then walked back and took her seat at the bar.

Evan basically ran for his life.

The following day, late in the afternoon, Duncan Reed, one of the big bosses in Evan's firm, made an unscheduled visit to the Boston office. After a meeting that lasted over three hours in a large conference room, Duncan, Evan, Jeff, and a few other associates and staff felt confident and ready to proceed with the plans they had laid out for acquiring the new business accounts. As they left the room, everyone shaking hands and smiling, Duncan asked to speak privately with Evan in his office.

"Evan, have a seat. I know it's late, but I won't keep you much longer."

Evan wasn't sure whether to be nervous or excited.

"I want you to know that we are very pleased with the way you have handled everything here, overseeing the new clients in this office. In a relatively short time you have managed what most people would have found impossible. Needless to say, you have impressed us not only with what you have done here in Boston, but with your previous success in New York."

"Thank you, sir. The support and confidence you have given has meant so much, and I have appreciated this opportunity to prove my commitment to the company."

"Well you have more than proven yourself, Evan. Therefore, we would like to make you Managing Director of all Boston operations. How does that sound?" Duncan asked with a huge smile on his face.

Evan stood, intending to shake his hand, but ended up in a hug with a man old enough to be his father.

"That sounds unbelievable! Thank you so much, sir. I am thrilled, and of course I accept your offer!"

"Congratulations, Evan."

He couldn't wait to tell Tara and the rest of his family.

Then Duncan Reed uttered the statement of fact that Evan knew would come next.

"You obviously know you will need to relocate here to Boston. I hope that isn't a problem for you?"

"Not at all." Evan answered. But in his head, he thought: *it could, however, wreak havoc with my personal life, sir.*

"Fine. Great. Now normally, I would take you out to celebrate but unfortunately, I have to get back to New York tonight. Perhaps next Saturday evening you will come to my house for a dinner party hosted by my wife and myself, and we can celebrate your promotion then. And if there is a special lady in your life, we would love for you to bring her also."

"Yes, sir, there is. I'm sure she would love to accompany me, but of course, I will check with her and let you know. Regardless, I will be there. Thank you, sir." Evan prayed Tara would be available, and then he realized they were now living for the weekends to be together and that she wouldn't have scheduled anything that couldn't be easily changed. At least he hoped so.

"Evan, I think it would be appropriate at this point for you to call me Duncan — no more 'sir' — ok?" He laughed at Evan's respectful formality.

"Yes, sir. I mean all right, Duncan. And once again, thank you for this opportunity."

The two men shook hands. Duncan Reed grabbed his jacket and briefcase and left the office.

Evan sat down at his desk and ran his hands through his hair. He couldn't believe it. This was a dream for so long and now it had come true. He let out a huge sigh and thought about how great his life was now. At age thirty, finally in the upper echelon of executives in his company, he would have a salary and bonus that would be staggering, and he could have anything his heart desired as a result. Yet, as he sat there realizing all the things that extreme wealth would allow him from this point on, the only thing he wanted was his girl. He wanted to share all this with only her, and he smiled at his helplessness. Jeff had been right. Evan had it bad, really bad. Instead of wanting to take his entire team out to a restaurant or bar to celebrate and get drunk and have any woman or as many women as he wanted tonight, all he wanted to do was share his news with Tara.

Tara was in bed reading when the phone rang. It was late but she hadn't heard from Evan yet and she was beginning to worry. It had become a habit that when he was away, he would always call to say goodnight. She glanced at the clock on her bedside table: 11:12 p.m.

"Jeeze, again!" She mumbled before she picked up the phone. "Hello?"

"Hey, babe. How are you?"

"Fine now. I was beginning to wonder if you forgot about me."

"Never," he smiled. "So how was your day?"

"Good. Busy. How about you?"

"Oh, not bad. Worked all day. Had lunch. Had dinner. Met with Duncan Reed. Was promoted to Managing Director," all said in a monotone voice.

"Wait a minute! What did you just say?" Tara exclaimed, excitedly.

"Had lunch, had dinner..."

"Shut up — not *that* part!"

"Oh, you mean the part about being promoted?"

"Yes, you jerk!"

"Tara, they promoted me to Managing Director! I can't believe it!"

"Give me all the details right this minute!" Tara demanded.

"Duncan Reed showed up unexpectedly today to review these new accounts and other related business, and afterwards he said he needed to speak with me privately. He sat me down and congratulated me on everything I've been doing for the company and in the Boston office, and then out of the blue, he offered me the promotion. I nearly had a heart attack right then and there!"

"Oh my God, Evan, congratulations! I am so happy for you. You really deserve this, and you have worked so hard for so long!"

"Thanks, sweetheart. I just can't believe it. I'm thrilled, but..."

"But what, Evan? This is everything you've worked for since starting there. Not many people get to live their dream, especially at such a young age."

"Tara, this means I will have to move here. Permanently."

"Well, of course you will! You knew that was a given. And there are worst places you could have been transferred to, you do realize that?" Tara was trying so hard to be positive and supportive for him.

"I know, but you won't be here. Six months ago, I wouldn't have even thought about this, but you are a very real, very important part of my life now. I don't want to lose you."

"In case I haven't said it enough times to you, Evan Kane, I love you, and unless you decide otherwise, I intend to be in your life no matter what. We've discussed this. Please do not worry about us. This is huge news and we need — you need — to focus on the joy of this. No negative thoughts. This is great, great news! Let's just go with that for now. Ok?"

Evan loved her more in that minute than ever before, and he felt so lucky. Most girlfriends would be bitching and moaning right now about the distance thing. Tara could only see how much this meant for him.

"I wish I could celebrate with you right now," he said suggestively.

"Well, then. I intend to show you just how proud I am of you as soon as you get back home. Several times over, in fact."

Evan loved all sides of Tara, but sexy Tara was by far his favorite.

"Oh, I forgot to tell you. My boss invited us to his house next Saturday for dinner. I'll get the particulars this week and let you know. You can go, right?" Evan asked.

"Of course I can! You know how I look forward to spending the weekend with you. That sounds like fun. You just need to let me know about the dress code, ok?"

Evan laughed. "Women! It's always about the clothes, isn't it?"

"You bet your ass it is. Now listen, you've had a big day. You must be exhausted."

"I am," he said as he yawned in to the phone.

"Call me tomorrow. I am so happy for you, honey. Sleep well," Tara said, sweetly.

"Thanks, gorgeous. Can't wait to see you. Be ready for me on Friday. We're ordering take-out and never leaving your apartment until we have to go to this party. Do you understand?"

Tara shivered at the thought of being locked away for twenty-four hours with him. "Oh, I understand, all right. Looking forward to it. I love you."

"Love you too, bye," Evan said.

CHAPTER

19

Tara's doorbell rang early on Saturday evening, and she opened it to a smiling Evan, in his suit, holding a dozen roses. As promised, they had spent Friday night and most of Saturday locked away in her apartment. *He looks so handsome,* thought Tara. She eagerly took the flowers and kissed him lightly on his lips, careful not to get lipstick on him. As she turned to get a vase, he followed her in to her apartment.

He had only gone home to shower, shave, and change into more formal clothes, and buy Tara some flowers after last night. *She deserved them in more ways than one. It was a very good night,* he thought. He whistled as she walked in to the kitchen. Tara was wearing a sleeveless black dress that came up high in the front, so as to not show any cleavage, but had a low, draped back. Evan told her he loved how she looked, that the dress was extremely sexy and classy. Tara's dark hair fell in soft waves around her face and shoulders, and her bright, blue eyes shone sultry against the black dress. Sleek and sophisticated, she would make a striking impression on everyone at the party.

"You like?" She spun around in her kitchen. Then she moved to put the flowers in a vase.

"Very much. You look unbelievably beautiful. Maybe a bit too beautiful," he said as he walked over and took her in his arms. "I may need to have you again before we go."

"Oh no, you don't. I worked hard on this presentation of Tara for your work people, so you can't mess with me right now."

"Whatever you say, Ms. Fitzpatrick. Ready to go?"

"Yes," she answered as she began turning out the lights in her apartment. "I can't wait to meet everyone." Tara was actually looking forward to meeting the people she had heard stories about for months now.

The following morning, Tara was exhausted. It was one of those non-stop weekends and she just kept running from one thing to another. Tara and Evan had gotten home well after midnight and were up early because he had to drive back to Boston and she had to catch a train to Leslie's. The two women had to be at their friend Julia's house by twelve-thirty for the reunion brunch.

"God, there had better be alcohol at this thing," Tara whined, as she fastened her seat belt and slumped in the seat of Leslie's car.

Leslie handed her a large cup of coffee. "My terrific hubby got us these for the drive."

"Bless his heart. I love that man! Does he always know how to anticipate a girl's needs?" Tara asked.

"Only mine, thank God," Leslie answered.

They both giggled. Tara glanced at her phone to see if she had any messages. The time read: 11:12 a.m.

"This is so damn weird, I swear," muttered Tara.

"What?"

"Lately, almost every time I look at the clock it says 11:12. It can be morning or night. What the heck do you make of that?" Tara asked.

"How the hell should I know? You are just so out there sometimes, Tara. I only want to hear about last night. Give me every, juicy detail."

Tara groaned. "I'm tired, so you'll get the abbreviated version. It went great. Evan was like, THE MAN all night, with everyone congratulating him. All of his co-workers were extremely nice, and his boss is a real charmer. The Reed's Park Avenue apartment was elegant and huge! The food was outstanding, the wine was superb, and I almost fell outside when we got there because I was such a spaz in my four-inch heels!"

"Did anyone besides Evan lust after you in that sexy dress?" Leslie grinned while sipping her coffee.

"If they did, I didn't notice because my guy looked so awesome. Les, you should have seen him! It took all my strength to keep my hands off him all night. Besides, everyone there was paired up, so... "

"God, I miss working," Leslie moaned. "What time did Evan leave this morning?"

"Early. He was going to stop by and see his grandfather first before driving back. Charlie hasn't been feeling well lately, and Evan wanted to check on him."

"Is he ok?"

"I think so. He is staying at his place in Harbor Point. Evan's mom went on a cruise with her friends for ten days. At least he has a woman come in to cook and clean a couple of times a week when he is in the city. Otherwise, he would be alone in that big house in Connecticut. As a matter of fact, I'm going to stop in this week and visit him. He is so great; I want you to meet him. And I love him because we have so much in common."

Leslie grinned at her. "Yeah, you two weirdos can have a séance or sacrifice a couple of chickens to the gods or something!"

"Be quiet, Leslie. At least I could talk to him about stuff and not be considered crazy. Some best friend you are."

"Exactly my point. Maybe he would have all the answers to your bizarre questions. Then you wouldn't have to pay for your overpriced shrink," Leslie joked.

Tara looked out the window and thought about that. Even though Leslie was saying this as a joke, maybe she was right. Dr. Saxon was good for helping her understand the psychological and emotional issues in her life, but the other stuff plaguing her seemed too strange for conventional therapy. Tara still had not yet broached the subject of this 11:12 clock nonsense with her therapist. It just was too out there to even mention it, especially to someone who tried to put unexplainable concepts into some semblance of reality. Maybe it would be a good idea to discuss the subject with Charlie, someone who just might have a clue about what it could mean.

Julia Walsh's house was indeed impressive. Sitting on two acres of beautifully landscaped property, her five-bedroom home sat proudly in a development of about twenty-five colonial mini-mansions. Tara looked at Leslie as they pulled on to her street.

"Way to go, Julia," Tara said quietly as she gaped out her side window.

As the two women stepped out of the car, they grabbed the wine and desserts they had purchased for the party and ambled up to the front door.

"Listen, if this ends up being really lame and boring, I'll make up some excuse about Buck being sick and that we have to leave," Leslie said, not entirely sure she was mentally prepared to take this walk down memory lane.

"Or it might end up being a great time and we may not want to leave. Besides, isn't it really bad luck to say your child is sick as an excuse? It's like a self-fulfilling prophecy or bad karma or something?"

"First rule of parenting, Tara: God lets you use your kid as an excuse for *everything.* Just follow my lead and keep your mouth shut."

Tara put her index finger under her nose to simulate a moustache. "Ok, Hitler. Just ring the damn doorbell."

CHAPTER

20

Julia had gone all out to impress everyone. A lavish spread of hot food was set out on her ornate dining room table, as well as platters of fruit, cheese and crackers, cold, boiled shrimp, and of course, cocktail wieners wrapped in pastry.

As Tara was filling her plate with pigs in a blanket, she yelled to Julia who was standing a few feet away. "Thank God you didn't let all this go to your head, Jules. You still remembered to serve the good stuff!" Holding a hot dog up for all to see, everyone applauded Julia, who took a dramatic bow.

There were about twenty-five women who showed up, which was impressive considering everyone's busy schedules. They were a close group in college having lived through the pressures of grades, being away from home, the drama of boyfriends, and the strange phenomenon of being on the same cycle and the raging hormones that happened when living with your fellow sisters. They all helped each other through both good and bad times back then. These girls, women now, most with children of their own, were part of the fabric of Tara's past. She greeted them all fondly, having long forgotten any petty jealousies or differences of opinion. Feeling nostalgic, she tried to have at least a few moments of private conversation with everyone there.

There were women in every room of the downstairs, and a few were out on Julia's back patio, some even enjoying the occasional cigarette that would have been forbidden at home in the presence of their husbands and children. As Tara squeezed through the kitchen, which was naturally the most crowded of all the rooms, she spotted Leslie talking to someone in an alcove off the room who had her back to Tara. She walked up to the two and realized Leslie was deep in conversation with someone she now could not avoid.

Kim Monroe. The wife of Ray Monroe, whose picture Tara had seen on the memorial fence down at the Pitten Building months ago.

This had been Tara's only hesitation in coming to the reunion. She knew there was the possibility that Kim would be here, but she had heard through another friend that Kim had a really rough time dealing with Ray's death and wasn't sure she could deal with being in such a social situation. There were too many questions, too much sympathy from others. Kim was the only one in their group who had lost a loved one on that terrible day, and Tara's heart broke for her.

Leslie's eyes were filled with tears and shot Tara "the look" that meant she had to come and save her.

Kim turned slightly to see Tara approach. A weak smile crossed her sad eyes, and Tara immediately embraced her. While in college, the two had always shared a love of musical theater, which Kim had devoted her extra-curricular life to. Although she was a tech girl, Tara also had an ear for music and loved the great musicals of the '50s and '60s, and would go and watch Kim perform, wishing she herself had the guts to stand on a stage and put it all out there. Tara had been Kim's biggest fan, aside from her family and of course, her boyfriend: Ray.

Tara hugged her and whispered quietly in Kim's ear, "I am so sorry about Ray. I can't imagine the pain you must feel every, single day. I'm just so very sorry."

Kim wiped her eyes and smiled at them both. She had come to learn recently that only those who had suffered their own loss of someone they loved knew the right thing to say. They understood the pain was personal to them alone and to simply acknowledge that it was there was enough.

"I'm so tired of crying," Kim lamented. "As hard as it has been these past few months, I am so happy to see everyone here today. It reminds me of a happy time, a time when we were all so young and crazy with not a care in the world. I need to be reminded of those times. This has been the worst time of my life, and any moment I can escape it now, I do."

"How are your kids doing?" Leslie asked.

"Ok, I guess. You know kids. As long as it doesn't affect their day-to-day existence, they survive just fine," she answered.

Tara remembered this all too well. She had even discussed this not so long ago with her therapist. Kids were resilient, yes, but the scars live on long past childhood itself, she thought.

Kim continued, "My son Alex is six and plays football, and my daughter Emily is five and loves tap dancing. We have a lot of family between Ray and myself, so the support has been great."

"And how about you?" Tara asked. "How have you been getting through this? Unless you don't want to talk about it here. I'm sure you are sick of the same questions, but we genuinely care, you know."

"I know," said Kim. "I haven't seen many of the people here, and everyone is concerned. I get that, and I appreciate it. Having this happen to us means that people will ask questions, and I will need to answer them. All of the victims' families must carry the weight of a burden they never chose. I will always be a *Pitten widow* and my children will be *Pitten kids*. We will never escape that notoriety, just as my husband never escaped from that building."

Tara and Leslie were speechless for a moment, as the gravity of her statement punctured a hole in their hearts for this young woman who had lived through so much and would always continue to do so.

"Were you able to speak with Ray that morning?" Leslie asked, hesitantly.

"No. He kissed me goodbye before he left, as he always did. I tried to call his cell, but he never answered it," she said, with a pained look on her face.

OUT OF MY DREAMS

"What floor was he on?" asked Tara.

"Seventh. I assume he was killed instantly, based on where the bombs went off, but I'll never know for sure."

"That's such bullshit!" Tara blurted out, angrily.

Kim looked at Leslie and smiled. "I miss her colorful language."

"No you don't, Kim. I have to hear it all the time!" Leslie complained. Tara was known to spew a few choice words in their sorority house, especially with the courage of cocktails.

"Well, girls, this is one time where my words are totally appropriate. Look what he did to innocent families!"

"I couldn't agree more, Tara. Ray and I had just celebrated our anniversary. He was too young; they were all too young."

"You won't believe this, Kim, but of all those fliers that were posted down on the fence after, I happened to see the one with Ray's picture. I didn't recognize him at first, until I saw your name on it. It haunted me for a long time," Tara said.

Kim nodded. "My father-in-law posted it on there at my request. I was too upset to go near that place after it happened."

"I know this may be a horrible thing to ask you, but I'm sure you have been asked this a million times before. Did they ever find Ray?" Leslie asked.

Tara shot her a look.

"No, it's ok, Tara. It's so terrible; most people can't comprehend such horrible circumstances surrounding this type of death. It is only natural to be curious, hopeful, that something was found. But the stark reality is that I have nothing. Literally, I mean nothing. Not one single thing. Not his body, not a finger, not a tooth, not a scrap of

186

anything. That lunatic took it all from us. Like Ray never even existed. Like he disappeared into thin air that day. I have nothing of my husband from that day to prove that his precious life was taken by a monster. That madman took him. He took my whole life."

Kim looked up to find Tara and Leslie in tears.

"I'm so sorry, Kim." Leslie choked out the words. The three girls hugged for a few moments. They were huddled together, where no one could hear their conversation. Poor Kim. All the girls at the party obviously, were aware of her loss, and each would express their sympathy and support that day. Tara knew what was needed in that moment, and she pulled away suddenly.

"Don't either of you move. I'll be right back," she instructed.

Leslie pulled a wad of tissues from her purse and handed several to Kim. They both wiped their faces as Tara returned, holding three shot glasses and a bottle of peach flavored Schnapps. She handed both girls a glass and filled them with the sweet, sticky liqueur.

"Oh, God! This stuff sure brings back fond memories!" laughed Kim.

"Exactly." Putting the bottle down, Tara asked them to raise their glasses.

"To fond memories. And this one's for Ray," Tara said.

"To Ray!" The three chimed in unison.

They all smiled and clinked glasses and poured the shot quickly down their throats.

"Thanks, girls," said Kim. "He would have loved that."

CHAPTER

21

T ara and Leslie were unusually quiet on the ride home from Julia's. Both were lost in their thoughts of Kim and Ray and their young children. Leslie finally broke the deafening silence.

"I can't imagine how alone she must feel. I mean raising two little kids all on your own. You have no idea what it's like when one is sick or cranky or both, but at least you can hand off to your husband or at least have someone to bitch to. Kim has no one now." Leslie gripped the steering wheel as she spoke, like she was hanging on to an imaginary Rob for dear life.

"Well at least she has family there to help her," said Tara.

"Yes, but not living there 24/7. It's different, Tara, having your husband there in the house with you to share everything with, to depend on and unload to. It's your own family, just yours and his. Even when he is at work, you know he will be home that night, and it makes it bearable when your kids are unbearable. When you are married and have a child together, it's your life and you share it, warts and all. Kim must be so lonely without Ray. And for him to go in such a horrible, public, tragic way, it just plain sucks. I'll tell you one thing, when we get back to my house, you need to leave soon after because I plan on showing my own husband how much I love and appreciate him."

Tara could not relate to the part about having children. Nor could she totally understand the shared, mutual life between a husband and wife. But listening to Leslie and Kim made her appreciate the complexities, joy, and pain that a couple goes through together. It made her reflect on her life with her own parents and the level of commitment they had to making their family work. The idea of love and eventual loss is evident in death, divorce, or the end of a relationship, but that person is forever a part of your past, for good or bad.

Tara arrived back to her apartment later that evening. She tried calling Evan, but the call went right to voicemail. She left a message that she was home and that he should call back when he could. Of course, when she looked at the clock in her bedroom, the digital numbers displayed 11:12 p.m.

She was now really becoming annoyed with this.

Changing into pajama pants and a tank top, she went to use the bathroom to wash up and brush her teeth. As she splashed water on her face and looked in the mirror, she was immediately overtaken by a realization.

She knew. It was clear as the light of day.

Aunt Noreen was right. Eventually, you figure it out. Today confirmed it. No more doubt.

Tara realized that the man who haunted her dreams all those months ago was, without question, the same person. What Evan had suggested was correct.

It was Ray Monroe.

Leaning on the sink, Tara dried her face and sighed audibly. She actually felt a strange sense of peace, and yet now she had even more questions.

She spoke aloud as though he was standing right in front of her. "Oh, Ray! What are you trying to tell me? Are you trying to tell me something? I'm sorry, I don't understand this! Is it because I saw your grieving wife today who misses you terribly? Is this all my imagination, or is this real? You need to give me more to go on here, Ray. I have no idea what I'm doing or what the hell this all means!"

Tara sat down on the toilet, head in hands. Feeling like she was about to scream, she didn't know who to speak to, if anyone. Her family and Leslie had no answers. Evan was not home, plus she hesitated in revealing too much odd stuff to her boyfriend for fear of scaring him away. This was all too strange and weird. Who could possibly relate to her and to this nonsense?

Slowly standing up, she walked in to her kitchen. She opened the refrigerator and grabbed a bottle of wine and poured herself a glass. Then she reached in the drawer where she kept her address book. Opening it, she scanned down the page with her finger, picked up the phone and dialed the number.

"Hello?" he answered.

"Hi, it's Tara. Sorry to call so late. I hope I didn't wake you."

"Well, hello there, sweetheart. No, it's fine. I was just sitting here reading."

"Can I come see you tomorrow? I really need to speak with you about something. Besides, I want to make sure that you are all right. I'll even bring dinner after work. I can probably be there by 5:30."

"That sounds wonderful. I'll look forward to seeing you then. Bye, dear."

"Thanks, Charlie. See you tomorrow."

Tara arrived at Charlie's apartment and waited while the doorman called to inform him that she was there. He was in an upscale building, and the security was tight, but she had been put on the list of approved visitors.

The doorman directed her to the elevators, and Tara took one to the fifth floor. She hadn't seen Charlie in a while. The last time was with Evan when they met for dinner one night, and Tara missed him. Charlie was her most favorite senior citizen, and she had come to love him. How could she not? Had it not been for Charlie, the Amazing Kane, she and Evan never would have crossed paths. Charlie was her good luck charm.

It took Charlie a few minutes to walk to the door. Most days he felt great and had a lot of energy. Evan said his grandfather hadn't been feeling up to his normal self lately, but he attributed it to his advancing age. He opened the door and beamed at Tara.

"My beautiful Irish lass! You still enchant me!" he said as he embraced her.

Tara kissed him hello but couldn't hug him back because her arms were covered in plastic bags filled with food.

"Hey, you handsome devil! Wait till you see what I brought for us. We are going to clog our arteries and raise our blood pressure and blood sugar tonight!"

"Oh boy! Now you're talkin'!" he said excitedly, as he shut the front door.

"Just don't tell Evan or your daughter that I brought this stuff. I'm still trying to get on their good side and impress them," she said with a wink.

Charlie chuckled with amusement. "Well, I have it on good authority that you are already in my grandson's good graces and that the family likes you, too. So you can relax, sweetheart."

"Thank God for that! Look, Charlie. I got us corned beef on rye, potato salad for me and a knish for you, cream soda, and... cheesecake!"

"Hot damn! Not a green vegetable in sight!" Charlie clapped his hands in delight.

"Au contraire, my good man," Tara smiled, holding up a bag. "Green pickles! The good, crunchy ones. So now you can tell your family I gave you a balanced meal from all, or mostly all, the four food groups!"

"I do so love you, Tara. Let's eat!"

Tara took two plates from the cabinet and got out silverware and glasses. She fixed Charlie's dish and handed it to him.

"My, my, this looks great. Thank you for doing this, sweetie. I was getting sick and tired of cooking my own food and even more sick of my housekeeper's healthy casseroles."

"You are most welcome. Yum, it looks delicious!" Tara smiled, digging in.

Before taking a bite of his sandwich, he asked how things were going between her and Evan.

"Everything is going well. I'm so happy for his promotion. He's worked so hard and deserves to be recognized," Tara replied, happily.

Through a mouthful of food, Charlie laughed. "My grandson is going to make a boatload of money at that place. Just wait and see."

"He seemed to be doing pretty well for himself prior to his promotion," said Tara.

"Yes, but now this puts him in a whole different league. Now he becomes a heavy hitter in the financial world. It's going to require a lot of his time and energies. Also, I understand some international travel. How do you feel about that?"

Tara considered his question as she swallowed a long sip of her soda. Evan hadn't mentioned the travel aspect of the job that Charlie had alluded to just now. That was odd.

"Well, I'm happy he's happy. And I miss him when he's in Boston, but it's kind of out of my control. So we are doing our best now with this imminent long-term relationship."

Now that Tara was actually verbalizing how she felt, she realized that maybe Evan would tire of having his girlfriend so far away and that he would totally immerse himself in his job. Or find closer companionship in Boston. For the second time since Evan had told her the news about his promotion, Tara experienced another pang of insecurity.

"Listen, I'm sure everything will work out. I know he's crazy about you. I've never seen him so happy with a girl as he is with you." Charlie looked at her and smiled.

"Let's hope so, because I am equally fond of him, too. In fact, Charlie, I love him. I really do."

Tara's face lit up whenever she talked about Evan, as his did of her. This was the type of girl Charlie hoped Evan would meet and fall in love with, not some of those floozies he had seen him with in the past. It warmed his heart to know he had a hand in their meeting, but he knew his grandson: When he saw something good, he usually went after it and got it.

"So how's work?" Charlie asked, devouring half his potato knish.

"It's good. The same. Really nothing ever changes at my job. But that's why I like it. It's predictable, steady, unmoving, and I never stop learning. It's so much fun for me to read all these materials every day, stuff I didn't even know existed or mattered. Keeps my mind sharp. And we will be installing some new equipment and software, so I'm really excited about that."

Tara hadn't talked about her job other than to Evan in a while, and it surprised her how she only had good things to say about it. She knew this was rare. Most people hated their jobs.

After they finished their sandwiches, Tara told Charlie to go and sit in the living room while she made coffee. She sliced them each a piece of cheesecake and filled two large mugs. Sitting in wing chairs in front of the fireplace, they looked at each other while tasting the first forkful.

"Is there nothing better in the universe than cheesecake?" he asked as he savored the dessert.

"It's just a little slice of heaven. Yum. By the way, how have you been feeling, Charlie? You look a little pale to me," Tara asked, concerned.

"I'm fine, dear. When you get old, the parts just get a little rusty. I'll be fine."

"Do you see a doctor on a regular basis?"

"Not regularly, but if I need to go, I go. Don't worry yourself about it."

Tara smiled at him but decided to maybe check on him more often, especially since her weekdays would soon get lonely with Evan gone.

"So, my dear. I love that you came here tonight and brought me all my favorite things to eat. And you know I love your company anytime, but you did say when you called that you wanted to speak with me about something. Being the intuitive man that I am, I am guessing it either has to do with my grandson or maybe you want to revisit the unfinished conversation we had the day we first met. So which one is it, my lovely?"

Tara put down her mug and looked at him. "Well, it has nothing to do with Evan."

Charlie placed his empty dish on the coffee table. He folded his hands and rested them on his stomach and smiled. "I wondered how long it would take until you told me."

"Told you what?" Tara asked.

"About the man who has been desperately trying to get messages to his family through you."

CHAPTER

22

"Charlie, what are you talking about?" Tara asked, taken by complete surprise. "Who is trying to send messages?"

"Tara, your voice just shot up about three octaves. Calm down, dear. It's just you and me here. No Evan, nobody but us. And I won't breathe a word of this to anyone, including him. The day we met, I told you there was also a man standing behind you, in addition to your mother. If you recall, we never did discuss who he might be. I imagine now we will."

Tara's mouth was hanging open in shock at his bluntness. She was used to always bringing this subject up first with everyone: Leslie, her father, Aunt Noreen, Evan. It was almost a relief that it was Charlie initiating this bizarre conversation.

"Is *that* what this is, Charlie? I mean I finally know who the man I have seen in my dreams is, but you think he is trying to send messages?" Tara was distraught. She put her head in her hands and covered her face. Looking up at him, she saw that he was still smiling.

"So you think this is funny? Do you have any idea what I have been experiencing over the past few months?"

"Probably. Yes. I do," he said matter-of-factly.

"Jesus Christ, Charlie. What the hell?" she was shaking her head, as he continued to laugh.

"Do you know how many times I have tried to get answers from everyone about what has been happening to me? I have been going crazy! Literally, Charlie — crazy! I even started seeing a shrink for God's sake!" Tara was now pacing around the room.

"I imagine that would be a logical step. The only problem with that is that none of this is remotely logical," he said.

"But you see, this therapist has helped because I've discovered a lot of these issues I've had are tied up with losing my mother when I was a kid."

"I'm sure that's true. Some of it is probably tied to those issues, and I'm sure you've addressed that in your sessions. But there are still more questions than answers at this point; am I correct?" he asked.

"Shit, yes!" Tara yelled. "Sorry, I tend to curse when I'm agitated. Please forgive me."

He chuckled. "I've always believed cursing to be an effective way to release frustration. And I'm sure you have been frustrated over this."

"How do you know?" Tara asked. She was encouraged by the idea that maybe, just maybe, she could finally talk about this with someone who actually believed her, understood this crazy stuff, and could explain why it was happening. She found she was hanging on his every word.

"Because I went through the same thing when I was a teenager. That's when it all started for me."

"Tell me, Charlie. Tell me everything, please," Tara pleaded as she sat back down in the chair.

He looked at her and nodded. "When I was seventeen years old, I was living with my grandmother in Hawaii, and she was employed as a cleaning woman at the naval base at Pearl Harbor. On the morning of December 7, 1941, she was getting ready to go to work. I had just woken up from a dream in a cold sweat. I dreamed of fire, and explosions, and chaos and jumped out of bed, sweat drenching my pajamas. Running into the kitchen, I begged my grandmother not to go to work that day. It was a Sunday morning, and she said she had to go because the staff was limited on a weekend, the pay was higher, and we needed the extra money so we could eat. I told her I didn't need to eat, I only needed her to stay home. I told her something bad would happen if she went to work, that I was certain of this. She laughed at my foolishness and said they would fire her if she didn't go to her job. She kissed me on the head and told me not to worry. "Don't believe in silly dreams," she told me, as she walked out the door.

As soon as she got inside the base, the Japanese planes roared overhead. We could hear it all from our apartment building, just a few miles away. We had no phone in those days, so I sat and waited at the bus stop for her to come home, hoping and praying that she had made it out safely.

She never came home. Almost 2,500 people were killed that day, my grandmother among them. I tried to stop her because I knew that something terrible was going to happen."

"Oh, Charlie, how horrible. I'm so sorry. But it wasn't your fault that she didn't listen to your warning," Tara said sadly.

"That's my point. Who would listen to the incoherent ramblings of a teenage boy to not leave the house? It was ludicrous! She was right to ignore me. I mean, who would believe such a thing?"

"It was weeks or maybe months after that I started to feel strange. Like someone or something was with me all the time. Especially when I was outside in the yard or particularly when I would be swimming in the Pacific Ocean.

Tara swallowed hard.

Charlie continued, "I always had an uneasy feeling after Pearl Harbor and felt unsettled. I couldn't talk to anyone about it. My grandmother was all I had and now I was on my own. I was distraught that I had never said good-bye to her, but resigned myself to the fact that life moves on and so must I. One day, I was cleaning out her clothes and personal belongings because I decided to move back to New York where I could at least live with some distant family members. At the back of her closet, in a hat box that she kept personal and special things, I discovered a small rectangular tin wrapped in one of her scarves. Inside the box was $5,000 in cash, which was a fortune back in those days, with a note attached that read "For Charlie."

Tara looked at him puzzled. "So she had left you money. Who else would she have wanted to have it besides you?" Tara asked.

"Of course it was for me. But the strange part was that the savings withdrawal slip was attached to the cash. It had been dated December 6, 1941. The day before she died."

"Holy crap," Tara uttered.

"Crap, indeed, my dear. So after that incident, a series of things continued to happen to me over the years that led me to understand that I had something unusual going on. I will tell you some other time about those specific incidents, but I think we need to address your things tonight. I just needed you to know that it sometimes comes out of nowhere, but as soon as you open yourself to it, well it doesn't seem to stop. On the other hand, you may have months or even years where nothing happens again. Like a storm that only rolls through periodically. It's awful strange how it seems to work," Charlie remarked.

"Awful, indeed," Tara sighed.

Charlie leaned forward in his chair and looked at Tara. "So, I think you need to tell me what has been happening to you, and I will see if I can clear away some of the cobwebs. Start at the beginning, and we'll try to sort some of this out for you. Coming from one nut job to another." He winked at her.

This was how her conversation had begun with Aunt Noreen. It was eerily familiar, with Charlie asking her to relay the details of her story and him interpreting its psychic meaning.

Smiling back, Tara took a deep breath and began to speak. She talked non-stop, in her normal, run-on sentences. She began to tell him about when she was a child, talking to her imaginary friends on the ceiling. She told him about sensing her own mother's death at eight years old. She talked to him about the visits to the Pitten Building after the explosion, the dreams, the bathroom stuff, the panic attacks, and seeing the picture of Ray on the fence. Charlie sat quietly and listened, mainly without reaction. Occasionally, a small smile of recognition or understanding would appear on his face as if she wasn't telling him anything strange whatsoever. It was the same look her Aunt Noreen had when Tara relayed this exact story to her — a look that said this was nothing out of the ordinary for someone with this gift.

It was after one of those affirmations that Tara felt relieved. Finally, she thought, someone who got it — really got it. Aunt Noreen was right: there were others who experienced similar things. Maybe there was a secret society, a group of normal people capable of some very abnormal things.

"So you think that this is all someone trying to tell me something?" Tara asked.

"Yes. Yes I do," he answered.

"I assumed it was all coming from within me, never really believing it was an outside force trying to break in. Until very recently." Tara remembered her revelation after returning from the reunion and seeing Kim.

"That's how we all feel at first. But as we come to understand and accept it, we stop thinking of ourselves as strange and realize that we are in fact, gifted in a way others are not."

"But Charlie, I have only had these few, isolated instances over the past twenty-eight years. I don't walk around seeing dead people in the subway. I can't read people like you did that day on the street."

"If you remember, I told you I can't read everyone I meet. That is why I would never take money for doing it. I can only read someone who has a person trying to come through."

"How about all those famous psychics? Are they making it up?" Tara asked.

"I don't know. I don't think so because sometimes they hit things right on the nose. I do think some use limited ability to produce unlimited results. Some of these psychics think that once they see they can make money from their gift, well they tend to exploit their ability for profit. That's when they resort to presenting extremely vague images. Some force what really isn't there in order to appear as thought they have a connection to the other side," Charlie surmised.

"I guess it's really easy to tell people what they want or need to hear, especially when you are desperate to hear anything about someone you have loved and lost," Tara said.

"Precisely, my dear." Charlie nodded in agreement. "Would you like to hear my theory on this whole thing?"

"Of course I would! Please!" Tara pleaded.

"All right, then. Here is what I think, not know. Do you hear me, Tara? Because this is completely my opinion, not based in any fact or proof at all. And that is because there is no proof of anything related to what cannot be explained or felt. Pure speculation on the part of Charles Kane."

"I'm listening."

"Scientists have tried to study this field for decades now. Some have come up with plausible theories to explain paranormal activities and even life after death. But the simple truth is this: There is no definitive proof of anything. Some people are either born with it or choose to accept an ability to receive, and for lack of a better word, *messages* from people who physically die or leave this earth."

Tara was confused by what Charlie had just said. "So some are born with it. I get that. Because I've been told that certain members of my family — generations before me — had this thing. As though it was a hereditary characteristic of our family. But what about this choosing to have it? Explain that because I don't understand that. I mean, who would choose this?" Tara laughed.

"Well in my case, I don't know of anyone else in my family, past or present, who has it. I could be wrong because my generation and those before me are not as open as your contemporaries, but I'm sure someone would have said something over the years. Perhaps my grandmother sensed her own impending death, and that's why she had cleaned out her life savings and bequeathed it to me in that tin box. So I think my personality, and many other people like us, just seem to be more open and transparent, accepting, if you will, to that which cannot be explained. Those who have passed over in death, seem to be able to find both types of these mediums and try to send messages through them to their loved ones."

"Okay, that makes some kind of strange sense to me, Charlie. But why are only some deceased people desperate to send messages? Why isn't every man, woman, and child who has ever died waiting on some line in heaven like the ladies restroom at Giant's stadium, to send a message to their loved ones left behind?" Tara questioned.

"Once again, only my opinion here..."

"I understand, Charlie." Tara didn't have to be told again that this was all speculation.

"I think the only ones who try to send messages back after they have died, do it for two reasons, only two possible reasons. This is because I personally believe that what comes after this life, as a Roman Catholic man speaking here, is far better than earth could ever be. That is why for the majority of mankind since the dawn of time, no one who dies comes back to earth. No one wants or needs to. What lies beyond this life is so perfect and beautiful, no one ever wants to come back."

"So what are your two reasons for why people do come back?" Tara asked.

"The first is that the person left behind on earth desperately needs the deceased in order to move on and live life. When the surviving person is in crisis or at a crossroads and cannot move forward, then the spirit of the deceased needs to intervene on that person's behalf. For example, a guy I worked with many years ago had a baby who died of SIDS. The wife was overcome with grief and guilt and ceased to function, and they had another small child at home she needed to care for. But she was inconsolable. This guy had told me all about this one day over lunch. Two days later, I saw the wife sitting on a park bench with her surviving child in a stroller. She was despondent. At that moment, the woman's mother who had died the previous year, overcame my thoughts. I walked over to the grieving woman, and I sat down next to her on the bench. After expressing my condolences, I proceeded to tell her that sometimes I received messages from spirits and that her mother just sent me to her. She looked at me with a blank face. I told her that her mother, Ruth, who everyone in her family called *The General* and who had on a housecoat with clothespins stuffed in the pockets and wore her deceased husband's wedding ring on a chain around her neck, needed to tell her something. With that, she burst into tears, and I told her that her mother would take care of the baby she lost until one day when she could join him. Her mother, through me, wanted her daughter to know the baby was safe and happy with her in the afterlife and that she had to move on with her life and take care of the child she did have and her husband, who was also devastated. They needed her now."

Tara felt a chill run up her back and neck.

"Well, Tara, a look of such joy and peace came over her face and with that she stood up, kissed me on the cheek, thanked me for saving her family and walked off, pushing the baby in the stroller all the way home. It was wonderful, I thought, to be able to do what I did and help someone's hell on earth to end. As a matter of fact, that very couple went on to have three more healthy, beautiful children."

"What made you decide to go and speak to her? Weren't you afraid of what her reaction would be? I mean, how did you know it was for real and not just your imagination?" Tara was stunned at his bravado and curious as well.

"I didn't know, but I took that chance. And you see, it was the right decision. The feeling to approach her was so powerful, I knew it must have been for real. For her to hear what I had to say, and knowing those personal details about her mother, she knew it was for real. We shared that moment together, she and I. It's a gamble sometimes, but I'm glad I told her. It changed their life as a family."

"So in my situation, you think that Ray Monroe is trying to get a message to his family through me?" Tara asked, fearing his reply.

"I think he knew you from college, and spirits seem to find the people who are open to receiving them from beyond and send messages, or symbolic images, although nothing is ever spoken. In my experience, and in the experience of other mediums, spirits rarely, if ever, speak words. It's a conversation that is just understood in the mind of the medium. Between spirit and medium, we simply know what they want to say." Charlie struggled to explain this as best her could, but it wasn't easy.

"Now I'm really confused! What the heck does that mean?" Tara practically cried.

"It's like a sixth sense of knowing what that spirit is trying to convey through you. That's the best I can explain it Tara. I'm sorry."

Tara shook her head, as though to clear it for the next onslaught of information.

"So, Charlie, please explain the second reason why you think people who have died come back into this world to torture people like you and me."

Charlie smiled and walked toward the large front window. "The second reason why I believe they come back is when they have left this world suddenly, or tragically. They are unprepared and go kicking and screaming into death." He turned slowly to face Tara, knowing what her reaction would be.

"Like my friend's husband. Like all those people who died in the Pitten Building."

"Yes."

Now the hairs on the back of Tara's neck stood up. She swallowed hard. "But why haven't they all tried to come through to people like us? Why is it this one person for me, and no one for you? I don't get that, Charlie!"

"Because maybe some of them made peace with themselves at some point before they died or decided the next world was so much better than this one. Who knows, Tara? I told you that I don't have all the answers as to the how and why of this. We can only focus on why this one person is trying to get through to his family through you."

"All right, then. So if the man in my dream is Ray Monroe, what is he trying to say? And why did I have these dreams almost every single night?" she asked.

"I believe a tortured soul takes a longer time to pass over because they are not ready or willing to go. In your friend Ray's case, I imagine he did not want to leave his family until he knew they would be all right without him and be able to cope with his death. Maybe he and his wife had an argument or disagreement and it had not been resolved. Maybe the dreams mean that he was always watching them but couldn't speak to them from beyond."

"Why did the dreams suddenly stop. And why do I now have them only once in a while?" Tara asked.

"I think eventually, the soul has to pass to some next level, but if you didn't respond to his initial messages, usually they will try again."

"Oh, great!" Tara moaned. Then she had a thought.

"Charlie, why do you think in all the years since my mother died, I have never dreamed of her? Not once."

"I assumed she died peacefully in her sleep and felt she could be more of a help to you and your dad over there than here on earth. Were you ever in situations over the past years where you thought I must have someone watching over me, that I just escaped something bad by sheer luck or happenstance?" Charlie asked.

"Hundreds of times," Tara sighed. That horrible day in May came to mind, along with several others.

"Well, there you go. I'm sure she never wanted to die and leave you and your father, but she was happy and settled when she got there and obviously felt she was leaving you in good hands with each other. There is no need for her to come to you because she is happy and knows you are taken care of."

Tara's eyes welled up with tears. "I miss her terribly. To this day."

"Of course you do, sweetheart. Unfortunately, I have no explanation for why God takes us when he does. We only find out when we get there."

"So what does the bathroom stuff mean? That's a real strange thing," Tara questioned.

"That kind of stumps me. I'm sure it has some powerful meaning because of your visceral reaction to it. I just don't know what that is. I would think it just hasn't revealed itself yet," Charlie answered.

"Oh, goody!" Tara said, sarcastically.

"One more thing, Charlie. Then I should probably head home because it's getting late. Plus I have a headache now from all this."

Charlie laughed. He was exhausted, too. It was heavy stuff for both of them.

"Lately, almost every time I look at the clock it reads 11:12. It can be morning or night. It happens almost every day. And it comes up a lot on receipts. What is your take on that?" She challenged him.

Charlie nodded in recognition. "It's funny you say that, dear. I have been experiencing the same phenomenon myself lately, only with the numbers 9 and 11. Once again, I would speculate that Ray is trying to get another message either about the day 11 or the time 11:12. Or maybe he's saying he's always with his wife and his children. I really don't know. Only you can interpret and feel and convey the message. It will eventually come to you. It could be days or weeks, even years." Charlie tried to suppress a yawn.

Aunt Noreen had told her the exact same thing. With a huge sigh, Tara rose from her seat and stretched. She was mentally drained. "So what you are telling me is that this will never leave me until I figure out what he is trying to say to his family?"

"I'm afraid so, Tara."

"So how do I figure that out? Please help me, Charlie!"

"My best advice to you is to stop fighting it and relax. Open your mind and heart and like a mirage in the desert, it will become clear. I promise you."

"I'll try. Listen, thank you so much for this. You have no idea how much you have helped me." Slipping the dessert dishes into the dishwasher and picking up her purse, Tara kissed him goodbye and he walked her down to the lobby. Charlie asked the doorman to get her a cab home and gave him money for her fare.

"Thanks for dinner, honey. I'll see you soon, I hope. Oh, and Tara?"

"Yes?" She smiled before she ducked into the waiting taxi.

He winked. "Welcome to the club."

CHAPTER

23

The following day after work, Tara needed a run. It had always been that running outside was her thinking time, when decisions were made and problems were solved. She never understood why people hated exercise. They just had to use it for a purpose, and then they would actually look forward to that time alone with themselves.

After about two miles, Tara stopped into a small church, tucked between two office high-rise buildings. She had passed by here hundreds of times, yet never entered the tiny, quaint, church, set back from the sidewalk.

Even though Tara was Catholic — and not a very good one of late — she felt that old, familiar pull to just stop inside and say a prayer or two. As she gently opened the heavy front door, she saw it was dimly lit, with only a few people, mainly senior citizens, sitting scattered among the pews. Tara walked up to the front and sat down. As a kid, she always liked sitting in the front pew at church, much to her parents' chagrin. She said she wanted to make sure God saw her there and heard her prayers over the other parishioners.

Kneeling down and blessing herself, she placed her hands in prayer under her chin. After a quick Act of Contrition, Our Father, and Hail Mary (the trifecta of Catholic prayer), she decided the one person she hadn't consulted with about the past year and all its trauma and drama, maybe was waiting right in front of her. After all, this was His domain, wasn't it? The unexplainable, the mysterious, and the belief in something greater than mere human existence? She needed the highest power she knew of to help her move forward. Tara was, frankly, tired of this taking such a central focus in her life. Months ago, she had made a vow to start living her life and fill it with people. But dear Jesus, she meant living, breathing people, not ghosts.

Of course, she had Evan now and all the possibilities of that relationship. But she also had this other man in her life who, it seemed, would not leave her alone.

Tara sat back in the pew and looked at the large cross hanging above the altar. She began a heart-to-heart conversation with God.

"Well, here I am. I know you are thinking, 'It took you long enough!' I'm sure you probably are sick of those who only come to you when they need something. Yes, like me. But you know I love you and try to lead a good life, for the most part. So I apologize if I have offended you in any way, but I really need your help here. You know what's been going on. I mean, you know everything, right? This whole thing with Ray. So, I just want to tell you that I accept whatever this thing is that you have given me, but I need some guidance in how to use it. The signs Ray has sent me are strong and constant, so I think that means I need to do something about it. But here's my question: How do I know for sure that this is real? I feel that Ray wants me to go to his wife and tell her everything I have been experiencing; of that I am convinced. But how do I really know that it won't make things worse for her or hurt her and her children more that they have already been damaged? I just feel as though I have no proof that this is truly what happened and that it is REAL. I mean, who am I to swoop in and unhinge her life again? So what I'm asking is for something from you, to help me know the right thing to do here. Do I go and speak to her about this or just take this to my own grave and chalk it up as a figment of my wild imagination? If I tell Kim, will she tell everyone I am insane, or worse: cruel? Please, I'm asking you God, and Jesus, and the Blessed Mother Mary, and the Holy Spirit, and all the angels and saints (yes, I'm calling in all the troops here) to help me. Send me a sign or something that I should go to Kim Monroe."

Tears began to fall slowly down her face. She wiped her eyes and closed them, continuing her plea.

"So, Father, please help me to do the right thing here. And Mom? I need your guidance, too. I need you to intercede on my behalf and help me make the right decision, the moral decision here. Please, help me."

Tara opened her eyes and slowly blessed herself with the sign of the cross. Taking one last look at the crucifix, she stood and walked down the short aisle to the rear of the church. Once outside, she put her headphones back on her ears and resumed running. Thinking that she had now covered all the bases, she decided to put everything in God's hands and wait and see what materialized. Leave it up to the universe and give it to God. This would be her new mantra.

When she got back to her apartment, Tara decided to check in with Leslie. They hadn't spoken in a couple of days, and Tara debated on whether or not she should tell her about her visit with Charlie. Gauging her mood over the phone would determine the course of their conversation: If Leslie was in a receptive frame of mind, then she would be more supportive of hearing about the decision Tara now knew she was more than likely going to make.

Leslie answered on the first ring, and Tara was surprised. "What are you sitting there with the phone in your hand?" Tara joked.

"No. I'm actually waiting for Rob to call me back from before. What's up? Where have you been?" Leslie asked.

"You know, around. Cleaning my apartment. Running. Working. Same stuff as always."

"Same here. God I miss work! And commuting. And work lunches. And gossip! And going out whenever I just feel like it. And high-heeled, sexy shoes. And flirting." Leslie sighed.

"Wait! You miss commuting? Are you insane?" Tara laughed.

"Not the actual commute part. The stuff after. After work stuff, remember? Drinks and hanging out until all hours! You know, when we commuted into the city with all those cute guys?" Leslie practically moaned.

Tara concluded her friend was delusional. Or she was pregnant.

"Are you *prego*, by any chance?" Tara asked.

"Are you kidding? I'm not ready for another kid yet!" Leslie yelled.

Tara pulled the phone away from her ear. "Calm down, girl! You must be getting your period, then."

"You are absolutely right. I am. And I seem to be taking it out on Rob because he hung up on me. That's why I picked up the phone so quick. I thought he was calling me back."

"You leave your poor husband alone! You know you should just go inhale a pint of ice cream or eat a giant candy bar and leave the men in your house alone, right?"

Leslie proclaimed, "I hope when I do have another baby, which by the way is not happening any time soon, it had better be a girl to even out the scales of justice in this house."

Tara giggled.

"So what else?" Leslie asked, biting into something.

Tara hoped it wasn't Buck's leg. "Well, I'm going to Boston this weekend," Tara answered.

"Good! Let's obsess about what you are going to wear and what you will do and see and..." Leslie said, excitedly.

Tara interrupted her rant. "You know, Les, you have a great life there. You do know that, right?"

"Yeah, I know, but sometimes I just get soo bored! I love hearing about your new exciting life now. It's the life I used to have."

"Oh, for God's sake!" Tara practically screamed at her friend. They both started laughing.

"I need details immediately: when, where, who?"

"So, Evan is hosting a client dinner of about fifteen or twenty people at some restaurant outside of the city. Business casual, he said. What do you think I should wear?" Tara asked.

"I think I would go check out the clothes in that little boutique we love by your apartment. You always have good luck in there. Tell the owner you need sexy business casual, not your usual nerd office dress..."

"Hey!" Tara interjected, insulted.

"Sorry." Leslie continued, "Then go buy a fabulous, new Victoria's Secret push-up bra and matching thong — red, I think. Plus you will need a mani-pedi, and a wax, and a...."

"Whoa, slow down! You do realize they don't pay me all that much, right?" Tara said, annoyed.

"These are investment items, Tara! This is the stage of dating where you need to always impress not only your honey but also his colleagues. Believe me, this is money well spent," Leslie advised.

"Were you always this devious?" Tara asked. "Poor Rob never stood a chance with you."

"You bet your ass he didn't! And he is still happy with me to this day. Except when I'm in a funk, like now. But he's used to it. God had better give me a girl next time so Rob will see in the future that it's not just because I'm a bitch. It's because of these damn hormones."

"Are you sure you're not pregnant? Never mind. Can we change this subject now?" Tara pleaded.

"I guess."

Tara hesitated, but proceeded nonetheless. "So, I realize you are in a mood, but I need you to come down off your broom. I want to talk to you about something."

"Witch," Leslie mumbled. They both laughed. "Ok, what?"

"I went to see Evan's grandfather the other day."

"Is he ok?"

"Yeah, he's fine. I brought him corned beef and cheesecake. He loved it."

"Yum."

Tara told Leslie all about their conversation and how Charlie helped her to interpret everything she had been questioning.

"Jesus, Tara. He could have saved you a small fortune in therapy bills," Leslie said.

"Well, not really. Dr. Saxon has really helped me deal with the stuff related to my Mom's death so I would never consider it a waste of time or money," she said defensively.

Leslie felt terrible. "I didn't mean it to sound that way, Tara. It was a stupid attempt on my part to be funny. I'm sorry. You know I think it was a good thing and that's why I encouraged you to do it. Just a bad joke from a hormonally challenged idiot."

"It's ok. I know," Tara said quietly.

"So what are you going to do now? Or are you going to do anything?"

"I'm not sure, yet." Tara hesitated and then spoke, "If I said to you, I'm considering going to Kim and telling her everything, what would you say?"

There was a deafening silence on the other end for a few moments.

"That you have lost your frigging mind? That you have gone over the deep end? Jeez, Tara, I don't know about doing that. I mean, shit..."

"I know, right? That's how I feel! Like, where would I even begin? Um, excuse me, Kim, but your dead husband has been haunting me, trying to get messages to you and your kids through me. She'll think I'm a raving lunatic, or worse yet, totally insensitive. I mean, who does that? Gets messages from dead people?"

"Well, that psychic on TV swears..."

"Stop, Les! Please be serious! What do you think? What should I do? I am really at a crossroads here. Either I bite the bullet and tell her or drop this once and for all. Never speak of it again or think about it."

"What does Evan think?" Leslie asked.

"You idiot! I don't talk about this to Evan like I talk to you! I only show him so much crazy because his grandfather is that way, too."

"Now who's being the devious one?" Leslie scolded.

"I mean he knows some of it but not all. Plus he's too busy at work to be bothered with all my bizarre junk. I save it all for you. And some for my Dad. Not much though."

"Gee, thanks. Now I feel really special."

"Hey, it's payback for all the years I've had to hear about Rob stuff and your in-laws and Buck's bowel movements and how a penis is so different from a vagina and..."

"Ok, enough! We're even!" Leslie screamed.

"You bet *your* ass, we are. I love it when I leave you speechless, which isn't often," Tara added.

"Listen, Tara. Let me give this a couple of days to think about it, mull it over. Then we can weigh the pros and cons. After your big sex weekend."

"Who said I'm having a big sex weekend?" Tara said, embarrassed.

"Oh, come on! You're two, hot, single, young kids in love, jetting away for the weekend!"

"Um, Leslie, I'm taking the train to Boston, not flying to Tahiti. Get a grip!"

"Don't ruin my fantasy! Do you know what Rob and I are doing this weekend? Having a garage sale! How pathetic is that?"

They both burst out laughing. Tara was not concerned, though. She knew Leslie talked a good game, but she loved her life with Rob and Buck and wouldn't change a single thing about it.

Tara's train arrived on time. Evan was still in his suit as he walked up to greet her, picking her up while hugging her. Then he whispered something in her ear that made her melt into a puddle of nothing.

"My girl. My girl is here."

Tara hugged him and put her face in his neck to smell him, to gather everything about him in her arms, wondering if it would ever get old. After years with the same person, did you ever stop loving all the things that attracted you to that person in the first place? She knew how special this beginning part was and never wanted it to end.

Evan grabbed her bag. "Is this it? Small bag for a whole weekend."

"Well, I am a very resourceful packer. And the dress I'm wearing for the dinner could be folded a million times and not wrinkle, it's that kind of material," Tara answered.

"Can't wait to see you in it." He smiled confidently. "Then out of it."

Tara blushed. The thought of him, the actual being with him now, then later, aroused and excited her. She smiled remembering Leslie's description for this weekend. Sex for her had always been a good thing. Sex, with love, with this man, put her over the moon.

"You realize that if you stare at that long enough, she might reach out and grab you," a man's voice startled Tara.

She was standing in an adjoining room to where the dinner would take place. The restaurant was an old Victorian home, just outside the city limits, which had been turned into a fine dining establishment in the 1980s. It was designed to be a sitting room, complete with gaudy, mauve-colored antique furniture and heavy, ornate draperies. Tara was looking intently at an oil painting hanging over the fireplace of a woman. Tara turned and smiled at the young guy who was watching her. It must be a work colleague or client of Evan's, she thought, because his firm had reserved the entire place for the evening.

"She is a little scary!" Tara laughed.

"Well, I imagine if you lived in this spooky old house, you wouldn't be happy either," he smiled. "But I heard the food here is four-star." Extending his hand, he said, "Hello, I'm Ryan Kelley."

"Tara Fitzpatrick," she smiled, shaking his hand.

"A fellow Irishman, or woman, I presume?"

"You presume correctly. Both sides of the family. And you?" Tara asked.

"Same. My mother was a McGonegal," Ryan answered.

"My mother was an O'Connell. Just once, wouldn't you like to give a name like, oh, I don't know, John Smith or Mary Jones, and have no one know what the heck your heritage is?" Tara joked.

"And I have the added burden of two Irish first names!" he laughed.

"But the luxury of free drinks on St. Patrick's Day!" Tara shot back.

Ryan smiled. He found this girl extremely attractive and charming as hell. And, there was no ring on her left hand. *Perfect.*

Evan happened to look up from the adjoining room where he was entertaining a small group of clients. Tara had slipped away briefly to use the ladies room, and he was waiting for her to return.

When he noticed she was in the next room, laughing and talking to Ryan Kelley, Evan was suddenly gripped with anger. *What the hell?*

Evan couldn't walk away from the conversation, because these were important clients and they were discussing some very urgent business concerns. Yet he wondered: *It's all very innocent, polite conversation in there, right?* He was confident in Tara's feelings for him, but was he imagining it or was she flirting with Ryan Kelley? *Sure, he had a way with the ladies, but couldn't Tara see through that? My Tara. She's mine.*

Evan was convinced Ryan was handing her one of his standard pick-up lines right now. *What an ass!* Evan was overcome with jealousy, and that really surprised him. He and Tara had been growing their relationship in somewhat of a bubble, only going out with their families or close friends like Leslie and Rob. This was the first time he noticed how attractive Tara was to other men and it scared him and pissed him off. He hated the thought of anyone looking at Tara in the way that he did. This is how easy it is to go all caveman for your woman, Evan thought, the woman you loved and desired. It was primal, and it didn't feel so good.

Tara looked away from Ryan to try and find Evan. She had just run to the ladies room and on her way back had become fascinated with some of the antiques in the house and with the stern woman in the painting. She spotted Evan still talking to the group in the next room, but she saw him looking directly at her. And he did not look happy, either. *Is he jealous that I'm talking to Ryan?* Tara smiled at the idea of Evan being jealous.

Ryan assumed Tara was smiling at something he had just said.

Evan thought: *Why are they smiling at each other so much?*

Frustrated, Evan signaled the headwaiter and asked him to start getting the group seated for dinner. He needed to let Ryan know just whom Tara was really with. Immediately.

Finally breaking free, Evan walked over to Tara, kissing her lightly on the cheek and placing a possessive arm around her waist.

Ryan tried to hide the look of surprise and disappointment on his face.

Evan's eyes peered at Ryan with a triumphant look on his face.

Tara felt like she was the grand prize in a male pissing contest.

"Babe, I see you've met Ryan. But they are seating us for dinner now, and I came to get you."

"Oh, all right. Great. Well, it was very nice to meet you, Ryan." Tara smiled at him, enjoying these last few minutes of Evan's jealousy.

"The pleasure was all mine, Ms. Tara Fitzpatrick. I should have guessed a captivating girl such as you wasn't without an escort tonight. Enjoy your evening."

Later, as everyone was leaving, while Tara was speaking to some of the other women, Ryan grabbed Evan by the arm.

"Dude, if I were you, I would put a ring on her finger. And fast. She's really something special."

Evan felt particularly foolish. "I know."

CHAPTER

24

As Evan lay there with a sleeping Tara in his arms, he had come to a few conclusions. He realized they had only been together for a short time, yet he also realized it was long enough for him to know she was *the* one. Tara was beautiful, intelligent, well educated, from a great family, affectionate toward kids and animals, etc. She made him feel like he was the most important person in the world, and he thought about her almost every waking minute of the day. She made him laugh and look at the world differently. He had become less cynical and more empathetic. Their intimacy existed on many different levels, not just a sexual one. Evan told her things he would have never shared with anyone else, and they were comfortable with each other without being predictable. All the boxes were checked on this girl, his girl.

Other men were definitely looking at Tara in the same way he did. Evan suddenly became afraid that Tara saw this, and he feared she would think he was afraid to commit to her and would realize she could have any guy she wanted. Like Ryan *Fucking* Kelley. In a conversation one particular evening when they had been discussing past relationships, Tara confessed that her teens and twenties were like a blur, dating sporadically, never giving any one guy a chance. She felt she was never really ready for a serious relationship, that work was her whole life. But since she had begun therapy, she was able to sort out some of the stumbling blocks she had put in the way of getting involved with someone on a long-term basis.

Evan also realized that Tara might not want to wait around much longer for him and that she might tire of their long-distance situation and all the strain that came with it. Hell, there were a million guys in Harbor Point and New York City that she could date who would be more than willing to take his place. Last night had been the fire he needed to be lit under him, the push to make the next logical move. It made Evan see that he needed her with him all the time, for the rest of his life. The idea of losing her, for any reason, made him physically ill. He loved her, he wanted her, but above all, he knew she was the other half of him he had been waiting for, without ever being aware of it.

Evan decided this was the week he would start the process of finding the perfect ring for her. An engagement ring. His grandfather had a friend who owned a jewelry store in Manhattan. Evan would get his number and give him a call on Monday. Once he made this decision, Evan began to get excited about the details, and his mind was racing in a million different directions. Getting the ring and designing the perfect proposal worthy of this woman he adored — it had to be memorable and special. Just like her.

On Sunday morning, Tara and Evan woke up and decided to go to breakfast before she would catch an early train back to Jersey.

"Join me in the shower?" he asked.

"No, you go first. You wore me out last night. I can't take any more," she uttered, pulling the sheet over her head, giggling.

"Lightweight," he responded, stepping in to the large, hotel walk-in shower.

Minutes later, Tara stuck her head in the bathroom. "Hey, Evan? What was the name and do you have the number of that guy from work who does the DJ stuff on the side? My cousin needs it for her wedding, and I told her I would get it from you this weekend."

Evan yelled from the shower. "Go in my address book in the nightstand drawer. Last name is Allesio. Joey Allesio."

Tara opened the drawer and found the book. It had become Evan's junk drawer, and it was filled with random items: screwdriver, calculator, rubber bands, and tons of take-out menus.

She picked up the book and a bunch of business cards and slips of paper came spilling out.

"Oh, shit!" Tara mumbled, picking up a few of the cards from the floor. Evan was too busy to actually enter the names and numbers into the address book where they belonged. It was easier to just throw them in to the book and do it at a later time. Except that would probably never happen, she thought. Typical guy.

It was then that she noticed one card in particular. It had handwriting on the back in large, obviously feminine penmanship. On the card, it read: *Evan — Loved hanging out with you tonight! Let's do it again real soon, but next time we'll skip the bar and come right to my place!*

Tara turned the card over.

Marissa Massaro

Account Representative

A & J Advertising

Boston, MA

It listed her office phone and cell phone and in that curvy cursive, she had also scribbled down her home phone number.

Tara felt anger and panic simultaneously.

"What the hell is this!" she said loudly. Then her brain went into overdrive. *When did he get this card? It had to be fairly recent, since he hadn't been in Boston that long. What did it mean that she loved hanging out with him tonight? When was he hanging out with another girl? Was he hanging out in bars during the week with other women while he saw her on the weekends? Would he hang up the phone with her at night while another girl waited for him downstairs in the hotel bar? And what was that shit about skipping the bar and going right to her place? Had he already been to her place? And how many times? This woman obviously meant something to him for him to have saved her business card in his home address book!*

Tara felt like such a fool. She had innocently found this card by mistake. *What if I purposely looked? Would I find further evidence of cheating with this girl or with other women? After all, he was thirty and not married. Was he actually just another player? Had I had been too stupid or naive to see it — too caught up in the romance?* She felt like a complete idiot.

Tara had to get out of there. She pulled on her jeans, a sweatshirt, and shoes and threw everything she could find of hers in her bag. Grabbing her coat, purse, and overnight bag, she ran out of the suite just as Evan turned off the water in the shower.

Wrapping the large, fluffy, white towel around his waist, he walked out of the bathroom. Tara was not lying on the bed, naked, as he had hoped. In fact, she was nowhere in the suite at all.

"Tara?" He called as he walked through the bedroom to the living room area.

"Babe? Where are you?" He called, jokingly.

Thinking she probably ran downstairs to the lobby to get them a quick coffee and the newspaper, he sat down, propping some pillows against the king-sized headboard and began to read through his emails. After about ten minutes or so, he looked up.

"Where the hell did she go?" he wondered.

It was then that he noticed his address book on the floor with business cards strewn all over, like it had been dropped. On the nightstand, he saw a single card. It must have been the one Tara was looking for. As he picked it up and looked at it, his face turned white.

"Holy shit!" he said, gritting his teeth. "Fuck!"

He dressed quickly and grabbed his cell phone, calling Tara's number.

It went straight to her voicemail. Four times.

Evan felt sick to his stomach. He sat down on the bed and just stared at the wall. Why the hell did he keep the card that girl gave him the night he and Jeff went out? He honestly didn't remember putting it in his address book. Then he recalled why. He thought maybe the advertising firm she worked for could become a potential client he would pursue in the future. He didn't care about some girl named Marissa. He meant to bring the card into the office and have his secretary file it under potential contacts. He never imagined Tara would see it. Come to think of it, he never even read the back, he just looked at the front and stuck it in the drawer.

Jesus, what did Tara think when she read this? That I had slept with this girl? Could she really think I would do something like that to her? Did she really think I could be that much of an asshole? And why did she just run out of here without asking me about it?

Suddenly, an even sicker feeling came over him. Here he thought they had the perfect relationship, that they trusted each other, that they were rock solid. Maybe he had it all wrong.

But then he thought about last night and how jealous he had become when Tara was talking and laughing with Ryan. Evan had the advantage of being there to see that Ryan meant nothing to Tara, that nothing happened between the two. Tara didn't have that luxury in this situation. Her jealousy, her running out today was based on a damaging note left in Evan's personal, private belongings. It was suggestive enough to point the finger of suspicion in Evan's face, and for Tara it left a whole lot of questions. She was understandably hurt and confused.

Evan felt like such an idiot.

He knew he had to get to her. She would most likely be on her way to the train station, or already be on a train headed home, so he grabbed his car keys and headed down to the hotel garage.

Tara was lucky enough to find a taxi waiting in front of the hotel. She slid in quickly and asked the driver to take her to South Station, where the Amtrak was just about to leave for New York. The only problem was that it wasn't an express train, so it would take a longer time to get home. But Tara didn't care. At least she was out of there and didn't have to see him.

The hurt she felt was overwhelming. As she sat on the train, looking out the window, a wave of guilt and regret overtook her. Maybe she shouldn't have run out of Evan's room like she had. Maybe she should have given him a chance to explain. Perhaps it was a huge misunderstanding and Tara had jumped to unfair conclusions. Evan was a handsome, successful guy. He probably had women throwing themselves at him all the time, including leaving suggestive notes and phone messages. Hell, Tara thought, I now had men interested in me more than ever before: that guy Ryan last night, a friend of Rob's she had met once before at their house had seen her in the city and asked her out just last week, and recently a software salesman from work asked her out but she told him she was seeing someone. Tara was convinced that once you didn't care about meeting someone anymore, that's when men appeared in droves.

Apparently, the "I couldn't care less" vibe was very attractive to the opposite sex.

By the time her train arrived at Penn Station, Tara had resigned herself to the fact that she had done the wrong thing in leaving so abruptly. She was afraid that she had blown everything and feared that Evan would think of her as irrational, unstable, immature, and impulsive. Tara pulled out her cell and dialed his number, but it went directly to his voicemail. She decided to try him again when she got back to her apartment in Harbor Point, where she could ask for forgiveness in private.

On the other hand, Tara was happy with one thing she had not done. For the first time, she didn't immediately call Leslie for her usual lifeline or her father for answers. She realized she had made a mistake, reacting like she had, and she had to try and make amends. Tara decided that if Evan accepted her apology, she would never jump to conclusions without speaking to him first. If he didn't, then he really wasn't the man she thought he was and all that stuff she feared would, indeed, have been true. It was as simple as that.

Evan had roughly four hours before he would get to Harbor Point, hoping this was plenty of time to put his plan in to action. He was at his best right now: multi-tasking, using his cell phone to weave through people like he was weaving his car through traffic on Interstate 95. It was a rush, making things happen to his satisfaction.

The first call was to his grandfather.

"Grandpa, it's me, Evan."

"Hello son, what's up?"

"I need your help."

"You got it. What?"

"Well, I did sort of a bad thing. But I want to fix it with a good thing. A great thing."

"You lost me, boy."

"It's about Tara. And me. Grandpa, I want to propose to her. Today. Later today."

"Congratulations!" Charlie exclaimed. "You know how happy that makes me! I think she is terrific, beautiful, and the two of you are perfect for each other."

"I couldn't agree more." Evan was really getting excited over this whole plan.

"So, I take it that is the good thing, correct?" Charlie asked.

"Yes. That's the good thing."

"Um, what's the bad thing, Evan?"

"She left me."

"WHAT!"

"Here's the deal. Tara came up this weekend because I had a work function. This morning she accidentally found a business card that some girl in a bar wrote on and got the wrong idea and bolted while I was in the shower."

"Must have been some note for her to just up and leave like that." Charlie said, annoyed with his grandson.

"The note made it seem as if we were on a date and that I had been to her place but I swear, I had just met her that night. God, this is embarrassing talking to your grandfather about," Evan groaned.

"So this floozy tried to get her hooks in you?"

"Sort of. But I ran out of there as soon as I could. She slipped her business card in my pocket."

"Why on earth did you keep it?"

"Because, being the capitalist that I am, I saw a possible business opportunity with the advertising firm she worked for. I had no interest in her. Why would I when I have Tara, Grandpa?"

"I believe you need to tell Tara that, son. Not me."

"I'm going to. So listen, the night before this happened, I had decided I was going to propose to her anyway. Tara is on a train right now headed back to the city. I'm driving there now, but I need a huge favor from you."

"Okey, dokey. This is going to be fun!" Charlie laughed.

"I need you to call your buddy, the jeweler in the diamond district. What's his name?"

"Irving Fleischer," Charlie answered.

"So, I need you to call him. Oh, shoot, wait! I forgot it's Sunday! Do you think he's there on a Sunday?" Evan became frantic at this possible wrench in his plan.

"Evan, Irv Fleischer is my dear friend, and I have his home number. Even if his shop is closed, I'll ask if he could do us this special favor."

"Thank God. Ok, so can you call him and tell him I'm on my way and ask if I can meet him later at his store? Also, tell him I will call him in about twenty minutes. I have to make a few other phone calls first," Evan instructed.

"No problem."

"Tell him I will be buying a ring today, and will be spending a lot of money for it. But I know exactly what I want; he just has to get it ready for me to pick up later."

"I'm sure Irv will be able to help us out. Not only is he a good businessman, but he is also a true romantic at heart."

"Great. Then later today, I will need you to play a pivotal role in getting Tara where I need her so that I can propose. Are you sure you're up to this, Grandpa?" Evan needed to be certain everything went according to his plan.

"You can count on me. Let's hang up now so I can call Irv. Call me back in a few minutes."

"Thanks, Grandpa. You are the best."

Evan then called Information in New Jersey for Jimmy Fitzpatrick's phone number.

"Hello, Mr. Fitzpatrick? It's Evan Kane." He now realized how nervous he was. Evan had met Tara's father the weekend after they had first gone to Leslie and Rob's house. Since then, Evan had taken Tara and Jimmy to a couple of ball games and dinners, and he had gone with Tara to New Jersey to visit her dad.

"Hey, Evan. Please call me Jim."

"Thank you, sir. Listen, I know this may sound strange, and I apologize for doing this over the phone and not in person. But I'm driving to Harbor Point to see Tara and well, with your permission, and I hope your blessing as well, I would like to ask for your daughter's hand in marriage. I love her with all my heart, and I promise you I will take care of her for the rest of my life."

"Wow, Evan. I sure didn't expect this phone call today! Talk about quick! But then again, you both aren't teenagers. You're old enough to know that when it's right, it's right. I know I did when I got engaged. Are you sure you want in on this crazy family here, Evan?" he laughed.

"As long as Tara is in it then, yes. I'm sure."

"Well then, my boy, you have both my permission and my blessing. I know how she feels about you and how much she cares for you. When do you plan on asking her?"

"Later today. But it's obviously a surprise so if she happens to call you..."

"Don't worry, my lips are sealed."

"Thanks, Mr. Fitz...Jim. Thank you so much!"

"You are most welcome. I know you two will be very happy."

"Thank you. I couldn't agree more."

"By the way, Evan?"

"Yes, sir?"

"Her mother would have loved you."

The next call was to Leslie.

"Hello?" She answered.

"Leslie, hi. It's Evan."

"Hey, man. What's up?"

"Listen, it's a really long story...By the way, have you spoken to Tara today?" he asked.

"No. Why? Should I have?" she asked, suspiciously.

"No. Just surprised, I guess. So listen, I'm sure your best friend will give you all the gory details eventually, but here it is in a nutshell..."

"Wait. Isn't Tara *there*? With you?"

"No, she isn't."

"Where the hell is she, then?" Leslie questioned.

"She's on a train headed to Harbor Point. We had a misunderstanding this morning." Evan proceeded to tell her the same story he had told Charlie.

"So, I'm driving my car back to Harbor Point to see Tara. To apologize."

"That's so romantic!" She then yelled to her husband, "Rob, Evan is so romantic! Why can't you be like Evan? Wait until you hear this!"

"Leslie. I need you to be calm when I tell you this next part, ok?"

"Ok. What?"

"I am coming back because I want to propose to Tara. Today."

Shrieking was a mild adjective to describe Leslie's reaction.

"OH MY GOD! OH MY GOD! OH MY GOD!" She screamed in the phone. "She is going to go postal! OH MY GOD!"

Confused, Evan asked, "Is that a good or a bad thing?"

"Good, you jerk! Oh my freakin' God!"

"Leslie, please put Rob on the phone."

"Rob! Talk to Evan! I'm hyperventilating here, and I need to get tissues!" she wailed.

"Rob, it's Evan. Listen, could you please keep Leslie quiet if Tara calls her? I'm proposing tonight, and I want it to be a surprise."

"Dude, you got it. I'll lock her in the closet and gag her if I have to. Go forth and get engaged, young man!" Rob laughed.

"Thanks, Rob. Now can you put your wife back on the phone, please?"

"Sure." He handed it back to Leslie, and she blew her nose loudly in to the phone.

Evan pulled the phone away from his ear and grimaced.

"Listen, Leslie. I'm on my way to get the ring now."

Leslie howled again.

"But I need to know her ring size. Any idea?"

"Of course, I know! Girls talk about weddings and stuff nonstop after they hit puberty. It's the same size as mine. And I know because she has tried mine on many times. Size six."

"Thanks. Leslie. You're the best. And I'm sure you will hear from her later. I gotta hang up now." Evan had already been on the phone with her too long.

"Wait! Don't you want my input on the kind of ring she would like?" Leslie yelled.

"No, Leslie, but thank you. I have something very specific in mind, and I'm not telling anyone but the jeweler. Sorry."

"Ok, then. Good luck! And tell her if she doesn't call me right after you ask her, then I'm not coming to her wedding!"

"Yeah, right."

The next call was to Irving Fleischer.

"Hello, Mr. Fleischer? This is Evan Kane, Charlie's grandson. I hope he spoke with you."

"Hello, Evan. Yes, you're grandfather just called. He said you need an engagement ring, today. Is that correct?"

"Yes, sir, I do. Is that possible? And would I be able to pick it up later today?"

"I believe so, if it's not too complicated a request. Exactly what did you have in mind?"

"What I would like is a two-carat ring, and I'm willing to spend whatever that takes. I assume around $10,000. Am I right?"

"We can do that!" The businessman replied enthusiastically to this effortless sale.

"Great. So here's what I want: a cushion cut diamond in a platinum setting, with small diamonds all around the band. Can you do that in my time frame?"

"I know exactly what you are looking for, young man. And I can absolutely do that. If need be, can you be a little bit flexible on the price? It will all depend on the diamonds and their quality."

"Yes, Mr. Fleischer, I will pay whatever I need to, and I only want top-quality diamonds. For a top-quality girl, you understand."

"I understand perfectly. Listen, Evan, you can trust me. I've known your grandfather for a long time, and he was very good to me and my family. I will take care of you and your young lady just as your granddad has taken care of my loved ones with some special housing needs. You can count on that!"

"Perfect!" Evan smiled.

"Do you know the lady's ring size by chance?"

"Yes. She's a size six."

"Wonderful! I'll get right to work. I can have it ready for you to pick up at four. Will that time work for you?"

"That would be great. Thank you so much, Mr. Fleischer. I trust that you will make the perfect ring and select the finest diamonds," Evan instructed.

"I certainly will. See you this afternoon!"

Evan called Charlie back to update him on all the latest developments and to give him his final instructions.

"Now, Grandpa, I need you to call Tara's answering machine and leave a message. I'm sure she will check it as soon as she walks in the door at around two. Ask her to call you as soon as she gets in. When she does, I want you to tell her that you would like to take her out to dinner tonight. Don't take no for an answer. Tell her to meet you at my buddy Jake's restaurant at 6:00 p.m. It's where we went on our first date. I'll call Jake and have him set everything up there."

"That's it? That's all you need me to do?" Charlie sounded disappointed. He hoped he would be able to be there in person to witness Evan's proposal and to watch Tara's reaction.

"Grandpa, you will have helped me out more than you know. I couldn't have done all this without you. And if she says yes, it will have been because you were instrumental in this whole scheme. Hell, you are the reason we met in the first place, remember?"

Charlie did remember. It was ironic that he was responsible for their meeting on the street that day, and now Tara was connected to both Kane men, just in very different ways.

"Very well, Evan. Keep me posted. Think of a really nice proposal. Women love this sort of thing and the story of how you do it will have to stand the test of time. Got that?"

"Yes, Grandpa. I will try to make it memorable. God, this is a lot of pressure!" he laughed.

"Not if you want to make her happy. Give her a good story to tell your grandchildren some day."

Wow, thought Evan. This was really happening. Tara and he would be a family. She would be his wife, and he would be her husband. A wave of emotion engulfed him with a feeling of being right where he needed to be: with her, forever.

Evan made all the final arrangements with Jake. Although he complained that it was smack in the middle of a football Sunday, Jake told Evan he was a sucker for love and would make sure they had the private room in the back and not to worry.

The last call was to his former secretary in the New York office, Denise. She had worked for Evan for a few years and treated him more like a son than her boss. She was with her daughter who also lived in Harbor Point, and they all happened to be at her house having lunch when Evan called.

Denise was so happy to hear from him and when Evan said he had a huge favor to ask, she didn't even blink an eye. Evan always called Denise *Mohammed* because in his opinion, she could move mountains and get the impossible accomplished.

Evan asked if she could call in some favors from her friends who were event planners. Then he told her about his plans for the proposal and Denise suggested a few romantic touches, things that would make it more special for Tara.

Now all he had to do was wait for Tara and pray she didn't hate him. And that she would say *YES.*

CHAPTER
25

Tara had been trying to get in touch with Evan, but he wasn't answering his cell or the room phone. When she had first checked her own cell after arriving at the train station in Boston, she listened to the message he had left.

"Tara, where the HELL are you?" That message was followed by three hang-ups.

Unlocking her apartment door, she stepped in and threw her bags on the couch. The light was flashing on her answering machine. The first was a hang-up. The second was from Charlie asking if she would meet him for dinner tonight. Tara groaned. She was in no mood to socialize with anyone. She was distraught that she wasn't able to reach him. He was probably really pissed at her for running out on him. But wasn't he even curious to find out the reason why? Did he care so little about her? She could have been kidnapped for Christ's sake! Pushing these thoughts aside, she had to call Charlie back and politely decline his dinner invitation.

"Hi, Charlie. It's Tara."

"Are you alright? You sound strange," he said, concerned.

"No, I'm fine. Just a little tired." She didn't have the energy to tell Charlie what really happened.

"So let me buy you dinner tonight. Then you won't have to cook. Besides, I owe you after our wonderful deli night."

"Thank you, Charlie, but I'm not up to going out tonight. Could we make it for another time?"

He decided a little white lie was needed in this situation.

"Well, you see, today is my birthday. And since none of my family is around, I thought you would be willing to celebrate it with me." Charlie was laying the guilt trip on thick, knowing Tara couldn't, or wouldn't, ignore his birthday.

"Oh, jeez, Charlie — Happy Birthday! Um, ok — but where is your daughter and the rest of your family today?" Tara was puzzled that everyone, especially Evan's mother and brother would abandon him on his birthday. She thought it was strange that Evan hadn't mentioned it this weekend, but she assumed he had simply forgotten to tell her.

Charlie prayed God would forgive him if he told one more lie because it was all in the name of love. "They came in to the city last night and we went out because they all had commitments today. You know how Sundays are. The kids had soccer games." Evan's brother

Dan had two boys, and they were always on the move. "So how about it? You wouldn't refuse an old man on his birthday, would you? Not sure how many I have left!"

Tara caved. "No, of course not. What do you have in mind?" If she wasn't so fond of Charlie she would have pressed to get out of it, but she was not the kind of person who put herself first. She knew what it felt like to be alone in the city. Not good, especially on your birthday.

"I would love to go to Jake's Place. Do you know where that is? Evan's friend owns it. It's a great sports bar. That way we can eat and watch the game."

Great, thought Tara. *Now I have to return to the place Evan and I had our first date. Where we sat for hours getting to know each other. Where we sat until Jake had to throw us out because we didn't want to part from each other. Where I fell in love.* It felt like yesterday, and yet it felt like a million years ago.

"Yes, I know the place," Tara answered. "What time?"

"Is six all right?"

"Yes, that's fine. I'll see you there later."

"Thank you, sweetie. It means a lot to me."

"Anything for you, Charlie."

Before Tara left to meet Charlie, she decided to try Evan's cell one last time. When it went to voicemail again, she debated leaving a message but instead, just hung up. She figured: What was the point?

They were probably finished now. In fact, with her luck, it was probably doomed from the start.

Hailing a cab, she thought about how life can change in an instant. Here she thought she was going to spend a great weekend in Boston with her boyfriend and instead, their whole relationship had imploded. She thought about her mother's sudden, unexpected death and then she thought about Ray and Kim. But then she scolded herself. You couldn't even compare death to a break-up, even though she mourned the probable loss of Evan in her life. Tara told herself to stop being so melodramatic. After all, hadn't therapy taught her better coping skills?

As she sat in the cab, she looked out the window and watched the people on the street. Sunday in Harbor Point was slower, less frenetic, and it made her relax a bit. Tara decided that she would go have a nice dinner with Charlie and attempt to call Evan again tonight when she got home. She was going to try fix whatever had broken down this morning, no matter what it would take. He was worth it; they were worth it. Love, like they had found, wasn't just disregarded because of a stupid misunderstanding. *Time to put my big girl pants on and act like a grown woman, not a jealous adolescent,* she decided.

Tara had the driver drop her off a couple of blocks before the restaurant. There was a great cupcake bakery she wanted to stop into first so she could pick up a dozen mini assorted for Charlie. He had a real sweet tooth, and it would also double as a last-minute gift and birthday cake.

Opening the door to Jake's, she saw it was very crowded on a Sunday. He obviously drew a nice crowd during football season. Spotting the young hostess, Tara walked over carrying a cake box.

"Hi. I'm here to meet a friend," Tara said to the hostess, just as Jake intercepted her.

"Tara! Remember me?"

"Of course I do! How are you, Jake?" She gave him a quick, hello hug.

"What brings you here? Football fan, I take it? Where's Evan?"

"Well, as a matter of fact, I am a huge Giants fan. And I'm not with Evan tonight (Ugh, she cringed). Actually, I'm meeting his grandfather here. Do you know him?" Tara asked.

"Sure, I know the old man! But listen, it's so crowded and loud in here, I'm going to put you guys in my back party room so you can hear each other talk. Is that ok?" Jake asked.

"As long as there is a TV, that would be great. I know he wanted to watch the game," Tara answered.

"Do you want me to take that?" Jake motioned to the box she was holding.

"Oh, yeah, please. If you could stick it in the refrigerator — they're cupcakes. Today is his birthday, and this is a little surprise for him."

Jake grinned a sly smile. "Oh, we *love* surprises, here." Taking the box from her, he said, "Follow me this way."

Tara walked behind Jake, squeezing through the crowd of people in the bar area. Just when she thought he was leading her to a table in his back room, Jake stopped at a closed door and opened it.

He gestured for Tara to enter before him, with a dramatic sweep of his arm.

Tara stopped dead in her tracks. As she slowly walked through the doorway, she saw a room lined with balloons of every color in the rainbow. There had to be hundreds of them! The entire floor was covered with small, colorful balloons and several large, helium filled balloons with ribbon streamers hung from the ceiling. It looked like something out of a movie.

Tara looked perplexed. "Wow, Jake! Did you know it was Charlie's birthday, too? Because..." When she turned to address her question to Jake, it was *Evan* who was now standing in the doorway.

"Evan?" Tara was stunned. "What are you doing here? I thought, I thought..." She couldn't get a coherent word out. "Wait...Where's Charlie? What's going on?"

Evan walked up to Tara and took both of her hands in his.

"Tara, I'm afraid I'm guilty of deception here, but certainly not the kind you've been imagining since this morning."

She couldn't believe he was standing here before her. *He came back for me!* Evan followed her all the way home to New Jersey. *He really did care!*

Tara quickly slid in to his arms and buried her face in his chest, breathing him in. "I've been trying to call you, to apologize for my stupidity and for jumping to all kinds of crazy conclusions, but you didn't pick up your phone! I assumed things were over between us and that you wanted nothing to do with me after I ran out like I did. I thought all kinds of horrible things! I acted like an idiot. I'm so sorry!"

Evan pulled her closer and kissed the top of her head. "When I discovered you must have left after seeing that stupid, damn business card, I figured you were probably already on a train back home. So I jumped in my car and started driving here to explain."

"Oh, Evan!" Tara sighed. "I'm sorry you had to drive four hours to deal with my asinine behavior! I should have never left like I did. I should have given you a chance to explain. It's just that I was so jealous, hurt, and angry. It felt like my whole world had collapsed."

"No, it's my fault. I should have thrown that card away when I got it. You see, Jeff and I went out for a quick dinner one night, not too long after we started the job in Boston. These two girls came up to us, and I wanted to leave immediately, but Jeff, well he was trying to get lucky and begged me to stay. I had one more quick drink and tried to hightail it out of there. This girl followed me and wrote that on the back of her business card while I was paying my bar tab. She stuck it in my pocket as I was leaving the three of them in the bar. I knew I would never call her for a date, but I thought the advertising agency she worked for could be a potential client. That is why I kept that damn card. I swear, Tara, that's the truth. I never saw her before that night, and I promise you, I never saw her after that."

Tara grabbed him and kissed him. "I do believe you, Evan. And I'm sorry I ran out on you and acted like a two-year old. But the thought of you being with someone else after what I believed we meant to each other just wrecked me. I have never loved anyone as deeply as I love you."

He pulled away from her embrace so he could see her face. "I feel the same way about you; I hope you truly know that by now.

This was just a huge misunderstanding, and we need to put it behind us."

They were laughing, hugging, and kissing, like no one else existed on earth except for the two of them.

Once Tara came up for air, she realized how strange it was not only that Evan was here, but that they were standing in a room filled with balloons. Looking around, she had a confused look on her face.

"Evan?"

"Yes, baby."

"Did *you* arrange this for Charlie?"

"I did not. No."

"Um, did Jake?"

"I don't think so. Let me ask." Evan yelled over his shoulder. "Hey, Jake! Did you do this for my Grandpa?"

"Hell, no!" Jake answered.

Then Evan asked Tara, "Why would I do this for my grandfather?"

"Because it's his birthday?" she questioned, barely in a whisper now.

"It is *not* his birthday."

Tara swallowed. "It's not?"

"No, it isn't. This is not for my grandfather."

"No?" She barely got the word out.

"No, Tara. This is for you. All of this is for *you*. That's what I meant when I said I deceived you. I got that poor old man to lie to you. For me. For a very good reason."

"Really?"

"Oh, yes. A *very* good reason. Because, you see, I needed him to get you here. For me."

"Really?" Tara was barely squeaking out a response at this point.

"Yes. And I had Jake help me out also."

"You did?"

"Yes. Because I needed some privacy." Evan was smiling that million-dollar smile of his.

"Privacy?"

"Yes. And I needed a room that would scream CELEBRATION. So I enlisted the help of my former secretary and friend Denise, who brought her daughter and son-in-law and several well-compensated balloon merchants to come and get this room ready, in the place where we had our first date. Because it's a special place. It's where I first fell in love with you. It only took one night. And so I'm here to ask for all the rest of your nights. I want you to spend the rest of your nights with me, as well as your days. Because, Tara, I can't really live another day without you."

Tears were streaming down her face.

"I love you with all my heart, and I promise to be the man you deserve for the rest of your life. I will always be grateful to whatever power in the universe brought you to me because I know I have found the missing piece of me that I have been waiting for. And that is you. It will always be you."

"Oh, Evan."

Slowly, Evan got down on one knee and holding her hand, looked up at her. "And so, Tara Fitzpatrick, will you marry me and make me the happiest man on earth by becoming my wife?" With that, a little black box appeared, and Evan opened it. Nestled inside the soft, white satin, was the most magnificent diamond ring Tara had ever seen. She gasped when she saw it.

"Yes, Evan! I will absolutely marry you!" She was crying and laughing and couldn't believe it was happening.

He stood up and took her hand and gently slipped the ring on her finger. Leslie was right when she told Evan Tara's size. The ring was a perfect fit, and Evan was also right. The ring he selected was perfect for Tara.

All of a sudden, Tara and Evan were surrounded by people congratulating them. Jake ordered a free round of drinks for the entire place, Denise and her daughter wanted to fuss over Tara's ring, and guys from the bar were slapping Evan on his back and shaking his hand.

At one point during all this excitement, Tara looked up and found Evan just smiling at her. She mouthed "I love you," and he winked and said, "I love you, too."

The day that had started out to be so wrought with confusion, hurt, and misunderstanding had ended up being the best day of their lives so far.

Tara and Evan both called their families, and Tara, of course, called Leslie. Rob finally had to extricate the phone from Leslie's hand so Tara could hang up and go celebrate with her new fiancé. Finally, at around nine, Evan whispered in Tara's ear. "Let's get out of here and go home and really celebrate this engagement." When she quickly stood up, Evan laughed.

"What?" She looked at him with a straight face.

"A bit anxious there, aren't you, Miss Fitzpatrick?" She leaned down and now was the one whispering in his ear. "As a matter of fact, I am. I would like to show you just how happy you've made me, Evan Kane. And all I want to be wearing when I do so is my gorgeous, new engagement ring."

"Ok, we're out of here!" Evan proclaimed, quickly.

Tara took some of the helium balloons and told Jake to let his employees and customers take the rest home. She hated to see all that beauty go to waste. Evan also had Denise's son-in-law take plenty of pictures to document the big night for their relatives. And Leslie, of course.

The happy couple thanked Jake for his duplicity and everything else as they hugged goodbye at the door. As they were leaving, the hostess handed Tara the box of cupcakes that had been intended for Charlie.

"Don't forget these! Gee, I hope someday I get proposed to like you did!" she said enviously to Tara.

Tara smiled up at her new fiancé. "Yeah, it was pretty wonderful."

Jake yelled as they walked out the door, arms around each other. "Just make sure I get an invite to the wedding, guys. I'm sure it's gonna be a blast!"

Tara and Evan decided to spend the night at her apartment where she did, in fact, thank him properly for her ring. Several times. As they held each other in the dark, neither one could sleep.

"You never did tell me — how did Leslie react when you told her we were engaged?" Evan asked.

"Pure hysterics. I think she was more excited than when she got engaged! She told me you called her for my ring size."

Evan held up her hand, and they both looked at the beautiful ring, using the light from the full moon outside.

"And Leslie was right. I would have hated it if it hadn't been a perfect fit."

Tara sat up and looked at him. "It is perfect, all of it. I can't believe how happy you've made me and how excited I am about our future." She lay back down and snuggled into his arms.

"Me, too. I didn't realize how great getting engaged to you would feel. It just seems so natural, even necessary. I don't want to wait, Tara. I want to get married as soon as we can — no long engagement. The thought of going back to Boston without you, especially now, depresses the hell out of me."

"I feel the same way. Being separated from you before was hard; now it will just be torture."

"Listen, I will need to get back to Boston sometime tomorrow. I'll call Jeff and let him know I'm out of the office for the day, so let's try to start putting some plans into place for us."

Tara smiled. "As a matter of fact, I don't have to be back at work until Thursday because they are renovating my office. So I plan on driving back to Boston with my fiancé until then. That is *so* cool to say *my fiancé!*"

Evan sat up this time. "Are you kidding? That's so great!"

"I was going to surprise you Sunday morning and tell you, but — oh well — you know," she said, embarrassed.

"This is perfect! We'll have four hours in the car, plus this week to start making some decisions. I'm thinking that between now and Wednesday, we could contact a realtor and start looking for a place for us to live. Oh, shit, Tara! Will you be ok with moving to Boston? I never even factored it in that you will have to relocate and find a new job. Everything will change for you, and nothing for me."

"Evan, my love. I will go wherever you are. The only requirement I have for a place to live is that you are there in it. Kind of easy, see?"

He smiled. "I don't know how you feel about it, but I would like us to look for a house outside of the city. The idea of having to move twice in a couple of years doesn't thrill me, and I don't think we should be in the city when we decide to start our family."

"Our family! Just think, Evan — you and I are going to be a family! First, just you and me, Evan and Tara Kane: Mr. and Mrs. Evan Kane. Then we'll have our first baby, and we'll be the Kane family. Oh, my God, I can't believe this is really happening! I love you so much!"

Tara pushed Evan on his back and climbed on top of him. In the moonlight, Evan thought, she looked more beautiful and sexy than ever before. Maybe it was the magic of the night or the excitement of the engagement, Evan wasn't quite sure. But he did know that his life would never be the same, and that he had given over his heart to the one person in the world who would always safeguard it and fill it with more love than he ever hoped to find.

CHAPTER

26

Tara made the most of those few days in Boston. She and
Evan knew it would be so much harder to separate from
one another now that they were engaged to be married
and had the luxury of the week together in a four-star hotel. Having
met with a realtor right away, Tara was able to preview a few homes
in the suburbs that would suit their needs, and she narrowed it down
to two for Evan to see. Having called her boss asking for the rest of
the week off for personal reasons, Tara took Evan to tour the houses
on Friday afternoon.

They both fell in love with a four-bedroom colonial that was
only five-years old, complete with a swimming pool. It was in a great
school district, in a neighborhood that consisted of mainly young

families and newly married couples so they would be able to make friends with people their own age. The best part was that the seller needed to stay in the house until the end of April. This would provide Tara and Evan the time they needed to put together their wedding back home. Evan would have just gone down to City Hall and been done with it, but Tara wanted a meaningful ceremony and reception, and Evan wasn't about to deny her. Knowing how difficult that day would be for a girl without her mother to share it with, well, Evan simply agreed to her every wish.

After a tearful goodbye at the train station on Sunday, Tara settled back in her seat and closed her eyes. The past week had been a whirlwind of activity, planning and just being completely happy. Her world had changed so drastically, and now she had this brand new life to look forward to with the person she loved more than anything or anyone in the world.

Now that Tara was moving to Boston, she made the decision to finalize some business in her life in Harbor Point. As she began to make a mental checklist in her head, she realized that one of the things she needed to do was make an appointment with Dr. Saxon and terminate her therapy sessions. They had mutually agreed in their last meeting that Tara had met all her initial goals, and she was ready to move on and out of therapeutic care. Tara was anxious to tell her about her engagement and see her reaction. She would call this week to schedule a final appointment.

On Tuesday, Tara went for a run after work. She would miss being a city runner; she loved so many things about this city, but she loved Evan more. Being with him, making a life together was all that mattered now. She also decided to wait until about a month before the wedding to tell work that she was leaving. Tara had always kept her personal life private at her job, and since she worked with all men, they weren't interested in hearing about weddings and showers and what she would do after she got married. It wasn't that they didn't care about her; they just had their own agendas that mainly consisted of computers, data, and research. When she did return to her office that week, none of the guys even noticed her engagement ring, and it was pretty hard to miss. Only the secretary in the department noticed, and she told Tara that it was beautiful and wished her well.

Leslie was driving Tara crazy with wedding details. Since Tara didn't have her mother to help, Leslie and her mom had stepped in to guide Tara through all the minutiae of showers, rehearsal dinners, dresses, flowers, favors, music, photographer, videographer, seating arrangements, and, of course, the bachelorette party, which Tara refused to attend.

"Oh, come *onnnn!*" begged Leslie.

"No. Absolutely not. Why would I want to look at some half-naked guy in a G-string when I have Evan?" Tara asked.

"OK, so do it for me, then. I have no problem with some jacked, half-naked dude giving me a lap dance in a G-string! Come on — it'll be fun!" Leslie begged.

"No. I draw the line there," Tara warned.

Other decisions Tara made were easy and drama-free. Like informing her landlord that she would be moving out in May. *Done.*

Tara's runs were becoming longer and faster, since she wanted, like every bride, to be in the best shape possible for her wedding day. After a shower, she made herself a turkey cutlet over a huge salad. Getting away with "single" dinners such as soup, cereal, a salad, would soon be a thing of the past, unless Evan was traveling. Soon she would have to start cooking real meals for her new husband. Tara giggled. This was probably the only time in a modern-day marriage when a new bride easily reverted back to the mindset of the old days, when trying to please and impress her spouse would have been her sole purpose in life.

If Evan didn't have to work late, they would spend at least an hour on the phone at night. Their lives consisted of making plans, going over details for the wedding, and making decisions on the house they had put a deposit down for. Life was all about when their life would start, and they couldn't have been happier.

Tara hung up with Evan and looked at the clock: 11:12 p.m.

It had been a couple of weeks since those familiar numbers had come up.

"Ok, Ray," she said, loudly. Tara had decided whenever this happened now, she would acknowledge that it was Ray doing it. "I need more of a sign that this is you trying to say something! Do you understand that your wife will think I'm insane? Do you get that?"

Tara decided, as she lay in bed, staring at the ceiling, that once she and Evan were married and living under the same roof, she couldn't continue to have these episodes in her life. Evan was used to weird stuff because of his grandfather, but Tara didn't want to begin her married life with a ghost in their house. Like closure in therapy, she needed to get some type of closure with Ray Monroe. Tara wanted her relationship with Evan to be all about them, not something or someone from her past. As she had with Evan, Tara had only shared a small amount of information about Ray with Dr. Saxon. She knew she wanted to discuss this subject in her final session. The whole issue of Ray Monroe needed to stay behind in Harbor Point and not follow her to Boston.

CHAPTER

27

"Tara, so good to see you. How have you been?" Dr. Saxon asked as she guided Tara to the familiar chair opposite her own.

"Well, I have some wonderful, exciting news to share with you. I'm getting married and moving to the Boston area in May!"

"Tara, congratulations! My, this is very good news! I am so happy for you!" Dr. Saxon was thrilled. One look at Tara's face and it didn't take a genius or a psychologist to see that she was radiant.

"At the risk of sounding unprofessional but completely curious — let's see the ring!" she laughed.

Tara extended her left hand and Dr. Saxon took it gently in both of hers.

"Oh, Tara! It's exquisite! Your fiancé must love you so much to select such a beautiful expression of his feelings for you."

"You have the nicest way of saying things, Dr. Saxon. Thank you so much."

In an age where feminism was a given, it was amazing how three things could still reduce women to near hysterics: engagement rings, weddings, and babies.

"Tara, please come and sit. So, this is our final session. I would like to begin by saying it has been a pleasure meeting you and sharing this journey with you. Tara Fitzpatrick is a remarkable young woman! I know you will leave here and take what you have learned about yourself and have a wonderful, fulfilling life."

Tara nodded in agreement. "For so long, I kept myself insulated, thinking the bubble I had created around my life would protect me from the outside world when all it did was prevent me from living in the real world. Looking back on it now, I feel like I wasted so much time!"

"No time in this life is ever wasted, Tara. Every experience, or nonevent as you mention, has to be viewed as all part of the learning process. The key is to recognize it, take what you can from it, and use it to better your life. I believe you have come to realize that there is no value in looking to the past and having regrets. As human beings, we often cannot control most of the events, both small and monumental, that will happen. Every day will not be a perfect day; some will come close. Hopefully, your wedding day." Dr. Saxon smiled, and Tara returned the smile, knowing her wedding day would be a perfect day.

"But some days will test you to your very core. Your goal will be to look at problems and hard times for what they are and acknowledge them while learning from them. All the while, you will be able to gain some positive perspective. Now Tara, I would like you to tell me, what will you take away from this therapeutic experience?"

Tara paused for a moment. She wanted to carefully gather her thoughts before she answered. "I think I have finally learned that who I am, and what I am, exists in both the past and present. My early experiences, especially my mother's death, affected me in profound ways. But until I began this process of exploration, I didn't really face my life and what was happening, or not happening in it. I hid from everything — people and the emotions I should have been feeling. I buried everything along with my mother because I thought that would be the easy way out. Rather than feel anything, I wanted to feel nothing. But in doing that, I was not living at all. I was slowly dying myself." Tara put her head down and softly cried. What a revelation, and what a release it was to finally say it for Dr. Saxon and for herself.

Looking up to the ceiling, she smiled slightly. "So, in answer to your question, Dr. Saxon, I will try to be present in my present. I will deal with what happens today, whether it is good or bad, and not fear the future. I am actually, looking forward to see what my destiny holds. I will try not to think, or hope that life is perfect, because that isn't realistic."

"Living a human life is never perfect, and to have that expectation is most people's downfall," Dr. Saxon interjected.

"Exactly. I will embrace the good times realizing that I will need those memories to shield me when the bad times hit. I've learned that life, in all its complexities, is a mix of the two, and no one is immune to tragedy."

"As was evidenced by the horrific events at the Pitten Building," Dr. Saxon added.

"Yes," Tara agreed, deciding this was the perfect segue into her dilemma regarding Raymond Monroe. "Before we end today, I would like to get your perspective on one final issue, if I may," Tara asked.

"Of course."

"Remember when we discussed dreams and their meaning, especially the ones I had after first seeing the explosion site?"

"Yes, and through our sessions we concluded that those dreams and seeing all that was buried underneath the rubble represented and reflected the feelings and emotions you had hidden after your mother's untimely death. That those events paralleled your own experiences," she affirmed.

"Correct and I completely agree with that conclusion. But remember the man I told you about, the one in the dream? The one I thought may have been my friend's husband?"

"Yes. The one who died in the Pitten Building. What about him?"

Here goes nothing, she thought. "If I told you I think he is trying to come through to me, to get a message to his wife *through* me, would you honestly believe I was crazy? Please, Doctor, don't call Bellevue!"

Dr. Saxon laughed. "We never did fully explore that issue, did we?"

"No, we didn't," Tara answered. "But I need to. And there are a couple of other, well, odd things that have been going on that I have no explanation for."

"All right, then, let's try to figure them out in the time we have left here. You relay the things that have been troubling you, and I will try to give them a plausible theoretical explanation, if I can. Because, Tara, if you remember, I did admit that there are certain things in the universe that cannot be explained. As a clinician, I do recognize this fact. However, I will give it my best shot to interpret whatever you ask me to."

"Ok. Just remember — no judgments."

"No problem, Tara."

"Here goes. I'm going to start at the beginning."

Dr. Saxon nodded in agreement.

"My father told me that when I was a little girl, before my mother died, I would come downstairs in the middle of the night and check on my mother — I mentioned this once before — to see if she was still breathing. Like I sensed she was going to die. And then she did. Was this a premonition? How, at that age, could I have sensed that she would have a heart attack?"

"Many young children are fearful that their mothers will die and leave them. Worries are common at this stage of development. Nightmares, fears of accidents, night terrors — these are issues young children have and therefore, not unusual at all. Actually, more common than you would think."

"My father also told me I would speak in gibberish before I could even talk to imaginary people on the ceiling or floating above me. I would just carry on conversations with them." Tara laid down the gauntlet once more for her.

"Again, young children have vivid imaginations and curiosity. Particularly if the parents of a child are not openly affectionate or demonstrative in their feelings, the child will create imaginary playmates who will fill this need."

Tara thought about her parent's mantra: "Never wear your heart on your sleeve; keep your emotions to yourself; never let them see you cry; no public displays of affection." Although her parent's love for her was fierce and unwavering, the physicality of that love was more heard and seen than given.

"Ok, Doc. Good analysis on that one. Now about the dreams specifically. Why have I never dreamed of my mother, but yet I had continuous dreams of a man I barely knew?"

"Children who experience the death of a parent at a young age often don't have an initial gut reaction because they believe the parent will come back, in some way. If the death has not been discussed and mourned, and the child does not grieve properly or sufficiently, then it becomes difficult for the child to get on with life. You didn't dream of your mother because, in your mind, you really never chose to think about her. It was too painful. So you continually pushed those thoughts and feelings away. This unconscious choice not to grieve manifested itself in self-denial and avoidance."

Tara just stared at her as she continued.

"With the more recent dreams, now as a mature adult, you experienced a profound sadness at seeing the horrific death of your friend's husband who has left her and his children, and you understand what that loss will mean to them. It haunts you and occupies your thoughts because, in essence, it parallels your own personal feeling of loss regarding your mother. Here you are now, feeling and expressing it — grieving for them. Back when it was happening to you, Tara Fitzpatrick would not, could not, and did not."

Tara shook her head. "Wow, you're good. You are really good."

"Why, thank you," Dr. Saxon said, proudly.

"Ok, two more things. First, lately almost every time I look at the clock, it reads 11:12. It can be morning or night. Like, almost every day. I happen to glance at the clock and there it is: 11:12. And sometimes I'll pay for things in stores and the total comes to eleven dollars and twelve cents. Why is that? This never happened before the bombing of the Pitten Building and the dreams, so why now?"

"My guess is that it may be one of two things, or, more likely, a combination of both. To begin with, the events of that day are now a part of our everyday life, especially those of us who experienced it all directly, first hand and up close, here in the city. I personally, will always live with the images of that day and after in my head. The sounds, the smells, the sight of utter chaos, human suffering and physical destruction that are forever ingrained into our memories that day. Those images will remain forever. So you see, Tara, that is not unusual. You are not alone in your sadness, anger, and grief. We all feel that. Repeatedly seeing 11:12 on the clock may be your brain's internal clock, making you look at that particular time of day because that time and those numbers now have a very real significance in our lives. And you remember our discussion on the complexities of that amazing human miracle between your ears. So much in our brain cannot be explained, so we shouldn't even try."

Tara nodded in agreement.

"The other thing seeing the numbers may represent is the idea of time and how it relates to your life. Perhaps after seeing the devastation at the Pitten Building, it represents the idea that 11:12 is linked with time itself, that time is precious, or that it is time make certain changes in your life. This is all highly speculative, I know, but it could be a plausible explanation."

"Well, then, I'll take it, because it makes perfect sense when explained by you." Tara was pleased; she was finally getting actual, reasonable, explanations for these oddities that had plagued her life.

"Now, last thing," Tara said.

"Good! I feel like I'm back in graduate school being quizzed on theoretical explanations for the unknown!" she laughed.

"This is the strangest, so get ready. My bathroom."

"You did touch briefly on this also, if I remember."

"Yes. So many times over the past months, I would go in to the bathroom in my apartment and become, well, overwhelmed is the only way I can describe it. Like panic attacks and sweating and feeling overcome with dread and a feeling of desperation. I have no explanation at all for this, and if you come up with something on this one, I'll be really impressed, Doctor."

Dr. Saxon appeared puzzled, thinking, and then spoke. "My initial thoughts are that you are using or seeing your bathroom as a symbol."

"A symbol of what?" Tara asked.

"A symbol of what it is: a place to clean up; to cleanse oneself; to wash away the dirt of the day. To step in a shower and cleanse from head to toe. Wash everything away, down the drain, and eliminate all that is undesirable and uncleanly. Wishing to clean up one's life. Dealing with things that are painful and difficult. See where I'm going here with this, Tara? Perhaps this is why it caused you so much stress when you went in to your bathroom. Because the idea of confronting your unresolved issues, to clean up your life, to rise up out of the piles of emotional rubble were overwhelming to you."

Silence as they looked at one another.

"So...? Did I answer all your questions?" Dr. Saxon asked her dumbfounded client.

"You must have gotten straight A's in school. That was the most brilliant analysis I have ever heard, because I think you are spot on with all of it. It all makes sense to me now. I just want you to know something, Doctor. In this one session, you have lifted a huge, huge burden off my shoulders. And for that, and so much more, I will be eternally grateful." Tara felt, finally, an explanation for the unexplainable, which had finally been explained.

This satisfied her mind, but she still felt pulled in a different direction.

"Well, thank you for that enthusiastic vote of confidence," Dr. Saxon said, pleased with herself, also.

The intercom buzzer went off, and the receptionist announced the arrival of Dr. Saxon's next patient. She walked over to her desk and pressed a button, letting the receptionist know she had gotten the signal.

Walking back over to Tara, she looked at her and smiled. "You have accomplished so much here. I want you to continue as you move ahead with your life, to make positive changes and just be happy. Tara, you have so much good to look forward to. Please send me a note or email and let me know how you are doing. Boston is a great place. I'm sure you and your fiancé will make a wonderful life there."

Tara reached out and gave Dr. Saxon a firm hug. In a soft, quiet voice, she spoke. "Thank you. Thank you for all you have done for me. I will never forget how you helped me open my mind and my heart. You have been incredible, and this has been one of the best experiences of my life."

Dr. Saxon loved this; when she could terminate a therapeutic relationship with someone she truly cared about and send them back into the world with positive, successful closure. The nature of a client/therapist relationship is a close and personal one; the loss or ending of it comes with a certain degree of sadness.

"You are so welcome, Tara. Now go and live a happy life."

Tara answered. "I will. I finally will."

CHAPTER

28

Evan was spending just about every weekend back in Harbor Point. Tara was trying to get her fill of both the beloved town and New York City before she had to move to Boston by dragging Evan to every tourist attraction, museum, play, and restaurant she could think of.

"Are you sure you're ok with moving?" Evan asked her one Sunday afternoon as they walked through Central Park.

"Too late now, mister. Did you forget we put a deposit down on a huge house that is waiting for us in Massachusetts? No turning back now!" Tara looked at him, like he had forgotten.

"No, I mean I know we do. But if you are having second thoughts about any of this, well I want to know," he said, concerned.

Tara stopped walking and turned to face him.

"Are you kidding me? I'm so excited about our new life there and how much fun it's going to be making new friends, fixing our house, learning about the area. Having you every single night in the same bed as me..."

A look of relief came over his face.

"Evan, why would you even ask me that?"

"I don't know. Sometimes I think maybe I'm asking too much of you. Because of me, because of my job, we, you, have to leave everything here and move to a new state. It's a lot to ask someone — to leave their job, their parent, their family and friends..."

Tara grabbed his jacket, pulling him into her, silencing him with a kiss.

"I told you before, when you asked me to marry you — which by the way has been the best day of my entire life so far — that I would follow you anywhere. We can make a home any place in this world, as long as we are together. I'm not sorry we are leaving Harbor Point and New York City, just a little sad sometimes. I love this place, but Evan, I love you so much more. Please sweetheart, don't concern yourself with the idea that I'm not happy. All I can think about is our wedding, the new house, and all the things that have to be done with both. My mind is constantly racing with details and lists." She let out a huge sigh.

As they resumed walking, Evan slipped his arm around her waist. "What do you think you want to do about work after we move there?"

"Not sure yet. I haven't thought that far ahead. I just assumed I would start looking for something after we were settled in the new house. Why?"

"Actually, my mom asked the other day when I spoke to her. She told me she doesn't think you should get a job after we get married." He said it with a chuckle, waiting for her reaction.

Once again, she stopped dead in her tracks. "Oh? And what does she suggest I do with my time all day? This is not the 1950s! I've worked since I was fifteen years old. I'm surprised she made that suggestion. I took her for being more progressive than that."

Tara was annoyed at her soon to be mother-in-law. She liked Evan's mother, and she hoped that she could continue to like her in the future.

"She didn't mean it in an anti-feminist way. Remember, my mom is a product of the '70s. She just feels that we're at the age to start thinking about having a family. Give her a break, Tara. My mother is desperate for more grandchildren, I guess," he laughed.

Tara got the feeling that Evan was relaying this conversation with his mother in an effort to gauge her reaction on the subject.

"I know we talked about kids and believe me, they are in the near future. And I realize that you make a lot of money and could easily support us without me working. But I will always need to keep one foot in the job market."

"Can we make it a toe rather than the entire foot?" Evan asked, half laughing, half serious.

"Tell me what's going on in that handsome head of yours," she said.

"It's just that setting up the house when we finally move in will take up a lot of your time. Also, my job will involve a lot of entertaining clients, both in our home and out at restaurants, and I would like you to be a central part of that. I'm proud of you, Tara. I'm proud to show off your beauty and intelligence and confidence as a person. Besides, kids will be a reality in the near future, like you said. I'm just letting you know — you won't have to work outside of our home. You will have plenty to keep you busy." He waited for her reaction.

"Evan. My dearest, sweet, fiancé," Tara said, slowly.

Oh shit, here it comes, he thought.

"When you asked me to be your wife, I assumed that meant *partner*. As partners, we have an equal stake in this relationship. I have no problem with the fact that you will need me to help with certain aspects of your career. I get that you are a big shot now, and I accept the responsibilities that come with it. But the role of following you around like a puppy dog is not my idea of equality, and I can't make that my only purpose in life."

"That's not what I meant and I think you know that, Tara. All I'm trying to do is ease the burden of you thinking you have to work…"

"I want to work, dammit!" Tara said it so loudly, people were staring at them.

"I realize that! But what I'm trying to explain is that because of my job, our solid financial situation, you can do whatever you want, even if it means working from home or even something part-time. I want you to have endless opportunities to do whatever you want now. That's all I'm trying to say. I'm not trying to turn you into a Stepford wife, for Christ's sake!"

She turned to look at him. "Listen, sweetheart. I know you mean well and want to take care of me. I love you for that. Just let me figure out that part of my life on my own, ok? I promise I will be the perfect, corporate wife when you need me to be, and no other aspect of our life will suffer because I have the need to do something with my brain and my education. But I will need to carve out some niche for myself that doesn't include you or our future children. I just haven't figured it out yet. I hope you can understand that."

"I get it. I just want you to know that we don't need you to bring in a paycheck right away, that's all."

"Thank you. I know you mean that in the best way possible. Let's just play a lot of this marriage stuff by ear, ok? I'm sure we will need to make tons of compromises along the way, and I'm willing to say nothing is written in stone. I think every situation just has too many variables."

"Now you sound like the techie you are. Such a pretty nerd."

"Just kiss me now and shut up, you jerk."

Evan kissed her and then they started walking, holding hands.

"Now listen," he said, "I won't be coming back here next weekend because I have a huge project I'm working on, and I need to be in the office. Will you be ok with that? I mean, you are welcome to come up and hang out and do stuff, but I won't be able to keep you company."

"No thanks, I'll pass. The bridal place called to say Leslie's dress is in, so I'll have her come in to the city. Maybe she'll agree to spend the weekend with me."

"Good plan," he answered. "Just stay out of trouble."

"Can't promise anything when Leslie's involved," she laughed. Tara was thinking lately how the move would put her so much further away from her best friend, and she decided she would make her stay the whole weekend after all. Surely, Rob would understand.

"I'm starving — how about you?" Evan asked.

"I could eat," she answered, realizing she wanted something on a real, New York bagel. God, she would miss the bagels here. And the pizza. Because no other city in the world could even compare to New York for those two specific favorite food items for Tara.

Oh, wait, she thought. Don't forget: New York-style cheesecake; corned beef sandwiches on real, rye bread; New York State apples; and soft, baked, giant pretzels. And the diners of New Jersey, Jersey corn and tomatoes, salt water taffy, custard ice cream at the boardwalk, pork roll...

I have to stop! She laughed to herself, thinking that maybe she would lose a few pounds when she left the city.

Settling in a booth, Evan looked at the menu while Tara sat with her chin resting in her hand.

"I take it you know what you want?" he asked.

"Yes. Pork roll, egg, and cheese on an everything bagel," she answered, staring into space.

"I feel like a huge omelet," he said, still reading the menu.

"Funny, you don't look like one."

Evan peered over the top of his menu and raised an eyebrow. "Do you think that joke from like, first grade, is even the least bit funny?"

"Yes, I do," she answered with a straight face.

The waitress took their order and brought their coffee.

Sipping loudly from his mug, Evan looked at Tara who was back to staring into space.

"What's up with you? You're a million miles way."

Turning her eyes to him, she said, "Just thinking."

"Dangerous."

"Now who's in first grade?"

They laughed.

"Evan, I need to have a discussion with you. More like get your opinion on something that has been in my head for a long time now."

"Is it about the wedding?"

"No, nothing as simple as that, unfortunately."

"So what, then?"

Tara slowly stirred her coffee. This was something she felt like she had to share with her future husband. He would take her, warts and all. Of this, she was positive.

"I feel this need to clean up everything before I move to Boston, tie up all loose ends and stuff," she said.

"What stuff are you referring to specifically?" Evan asked.

"Remember when I told you the stories of all that weirdness related to the Pitten Building explosion, especially seeing that guy I knew from Rutgers who died in the building?"

He nodded. "So?"

"Well, in addition to dreams and other nonsense I won't get into, I'm experiencing this thing where for the past few months, the numbers "11/12" come up constantly — like when I pay for things, the total is eleven dollars and twelve cents, or most often, I look at the clock and the time is 11:12. I talked to Charlie about it, and my therapist. They both have different interpretations, but I need to go with my gut here. I've concluded, after taking in all the strange signs and happenings in totality, that this guy, Ray Monroe, is trying to come through to me in order to get a message to his wife."

"What kind of message? I mean, how would the numbers "11/12" signify a message? I'm confused."

"Your grandfather interprets it as Ray trying to tell his wife something through me, like he hasn't fully passed over into the next life because his death was so sudden and tragic and chaotic. That he wants his wife, Kim, to know that he didn't go willingly or easily. That he fought to stay with her and his kids, but it was out of his control."

Evan continued his questioning and was puzzled. "So what are you proposing to do? Are you seriously thinking about going to this poor woman and telling her something you don't even know is really true?" He looked dumbfounded at his fiancé.

Tara was afraid he would have this reaction. "Evan, it's not only the dreams and the clock. Remember I told you I have also had these sensations, almost like brief panic attacks when I would go into the bathroom? I know that has some significant meaning, also. I just haven't figured it out yet. But it must relate to him, too."

He just looked at her.

Tara hated that look. "Listen, don't you look at me like that. Like you think I'm nuts. I'm only telling you this whole crazy story because I know you *KNOW* this kind of thing exists. Your own grandfather is living proof of it. So stop looking at me like I should be institutionalized or that you want to pull this ring off my finger and run for the hills. You, above everyone, Evan Kane, know that this is real in some strange way and that I am perfectly sane."

Evan rubbed his eyes then ran his hands through his hair.

"Jesus, Tara. All I can think about is our poor kids and what they may inherit someday! It's bad enough this shit is on my side of the family. Now they'll get hit with both barrels from your genes, too! They are going to hate us, you realize that, right?"

Tara giggled, taking a sip of her coffee, relieved that he wasn't rejecting her, after all.

"In some force of the universe, we were destined to find one another, my darling Evan."

"I guess. So what are you planning to do with this information, Kreskin?" he asked.

"I'm convinced that if I don't finish this, if I don't relay what I think I know to be true regarding what he is trying to say through me, it will literally haunt me the rest of my life. I need to go and tell his wife what has been happening since the day I saw his picture on that fence. Only then, will all this stop."

"So, an exorcism, of sorts?" Evan asked.

"Yes. I guess — an exorcism of thoughts: my thoughts of Ray's thoughts. God, that's *soo* out there! But I hope that once I rid myself of this burden, and that's what this psychic stuff is, Evan, a burden, well then it will never ever, happen again. I just don't have the stomach for all this," Tara said, happy she had finally hashed this out with the one person's opinion that mattered most to her now.

Evan reached over, took her hand, and fingered the stones around the band of her engagement ring. "You do realize, she may think you are crazy, right? I mean, you will sound certifiable, Tara. I think you have to prepare for that reaction. She may throw you right out of her house."

"Or," Tara contemplated, lifting the coffee mug slowly to her lips, "I may be the answer to her prayers."

CHAPTER

29

"After we finish with all this dress nonsense, I need a serious drink, and later, let's hit some bars!" Leslie whispered in Tara's ear, as the saleswoman hung the matron of honor's gown on a hook in the large, dressing room.

"Did you bring your shoes with you?" The plump, serious seamstress asked, carefully taking the dress out from under the plastic wrapping.

"Sure did," Leslie answered, holding up the pair of silver, barely there sandals that complemented the soft, tiffany-blue sheath Tara and Leslie had selected.

As Leslie stood before the floor length mirrors, she could see three sides of herself in the gorgeous gown.

"Your husband is gonna want to make another baby when he sees you in this dress! You look so hot!" Tara said, admiring how Leslie had banished the last of the Buck baby weight from her body.

"I do look good, if I say so myself!" Leslie said, turning back and forth in front of the mirror. It was elegant and fitted her form beautifully, as though it was made just for her.

"All we need to do is hem it, and we should be good to go." The seamstress pinned a perfect hem in seconds. "You can go and take it off, now."

Leslie went to change and bounded out of the dressing room. "Let's get out of here! I'm a free woman for the entire weekend, and I want to make the most of it! Shake your ass, Tara Fitzpatrick, and let's go have some real fun!" she said, excitedly.

Tara rolled her eyes. "I'm only doing this because I pity you, you know. You don't get out much anymore."

"Oh, shut up, Tara. Pretty soon you'll be in the same boat, and you will live for any excuse to let loose every once in a blue moon."

"We need to stop back at my apartment and drop these shoes off, then we can head out and grab an early dinner," Tara instructed.

"Ok, but tonight we are going out to a club. I want to dance and drink and flirt with cute guys. What?" she asked, when Tara looked at her like she was possessed.

"You do remember you are happily married, right? And are responsible for a small child, right?" Tara questioned.

"Oh, please, lighten up! Since when are you Miss Goody Two Shoes? I'm not actually going to *do* anything. It's just girl's night out — harmless." Leslie winked. "And you did refuse a bachelorette party, remember?"

The girls settled into the booth at a small Irish pub a few blocks from Tara's apartment. After ordering their drinks and food, Leslie sat back and stretched. "So what else is on your list of things to get done before the wedding? Seems like most of it is covered, right?"

"Yeah, I think I'm in good shape," she answered. With just about two months to go before the big day, Tara was organized and calm.

"My father has been a little weepy lately, though. I think it finally sunk in this past week that his only child is finally grown up. Because you are not really an adult until you get married, you know." They both laughed.

"Ole Jimmy Fitzpatrick will now get his wish. And just wait until you get pregnant! Your father will bust a gut," Leslie added.

"Hey, listen to this. Evan's mom thinks I should try to get pregnant, like right after we get married, and not even try to find a job!" Tara said, exasperated.

"See! I told you that you would be living my life soon! What did you say to him? I mean, you know that you don't have to work, Tara. Evan makes more than enough to support the two of you plus a small country. It's nice not to have that pressure. You could do anything you ever wanted to do," Leslie remarked, after sipping her wine.

Tara made a face. "I don't know. It seems all too perfect and weird. I've always worked: when we were teens through college, until now. I can't imagine not having a job, not making my own salary. The idea of being dependent on Evan for money is not appealing to me. I guess I never pictured myself as just a stay-at-home type."

Leslie became annoyed at her friend. "You know, Tara, being *just* a stay-at-home wife and mother used to be respected, honored, even desirable. Now, it is looked down on by other women who would actually love to be in your shoes but can't. Some women who work try to make stay-at-home moms feel inadequate and inferior, when in reality it is the hardest job in the world. Sure, you don't have to pull on pantyhose every morning and can leave your bras in the drawer all day if you want, but you also get no recognition, no pay, it's 24/7/365 with no days off, no fabulous wardrobe to wear outside of the house, no fun lunches with co-workers, and no gossip around the water cooler. You have to deal with repair people and contractors coming in and out of your house and running your husband's errands because, of course, you are home and have nothing to do all day. And then there's laundry and house cleaning and food shopping and making three meals a day, then cleaning up when those meals are finished. Then, there are diapers, poop, and vomit..."

"Enough!" Tara put her hands up for Leslie to stop. "Jesus, you make it sound like it's the worst job on earth!"

Leslie put her glass down and her face softened from the angry tirade. "But that's the thing, Tara. It's the best job on earth. Because in reality, being a wife and mother means you are the one in charge. You really are the boss, the head honcho, the one who steers the mother ship. Everyone's happiness and sanity revolve around you. If it weren't for you, everything would fall apart. You are the nucleus, the catalyst for everyone's success. If you look at it in the right way, it is a total power trip. I am the rock, in control of my family's emotional, spiritual, and physical well-being. I am the one they want and need, and without me, nothing gets done. No one's ego gets bolstered; no one gets told everything will be all right; no one gets nursed back to health. I move them forward, even if to everyone else in the world, I appear to be stagnant and unfulfilled. We stay at home mothers and wives don't get monetary compensation, but what we do receive is the knowledge that were it not for us, our families would be totally destitute. The bonuses don't come with dollar signs but with hugs from a toddler who takes your face in his tiny little hands and says, "I love you, Mommy," and when your husband walks into his house at night after work and looks at you and sees his oasis in the long dry spell of his day in the outside world where no one appreciated *him*, either. Those are my rewards, and for now, they are plenty. I could not be any happier, and I wouldn't trade it for anything. Because, at the end of my life, I can say that I was the center of my family. When all is said and done, that is what will have really mattered for me, personally — not how far I progressed in a career. And one day, I'll go back to work outside my house, but for now, this is where I *want* to be. Some feminist I have become, right?"

Tara gazed at her best friend. Since they were little girls, Leslie always had the gift to get to the heart of the matter and say exactly the right thing when it needed to be said. Everyone should be lucky enough to have such a person who is part of his or her inner circle. Tara pondered that maybe a true feminist was a woman who was totally in control of her life in the way she chooses to live it, whether that was a CEO or a housewife.

Tara raised her glass to Leslie in a toast. Nothing more needed to be said or heard on the subject. She was right; we all make our lives in our own world.

"Les, I need to ask you for a huge, huge, colossal favor."

"Sure. Shoot." Leslie assumed it had something to do with the wedding. Since they were kids, they were always taking turns saving each other from all sorts of melodramas and potentially hazardous situations. Like the time Tara took the fall for Leslie when she stole makeup from the drugstore when they were twelve. If Mr. Mancino found out, he would have grounded Leslie for a month, and she would have missed Dean Montgomery's birthday party where Leslie was planning on scoring her first French kiss. Tara didn't care; she *hated* boys at that age and didn't want to go to the party anyway. Or the time Tara begged Leslie to go with her into the woods by the railroad tracks where a bunch of kids from school had some pot and were going to let anyone try it who was willing, and Tara was willing, but Leslie was petrified that her father would smell it on her. They both ended up going and no parent was the wiser for it that night. Their lives were a series of push and pull for each other, a modern-day Lucy and Ethel, Laverne and Shirley, Sponge Bob and Patrick.

"I've given this a lot of thought and even some prayer. I've spoken to Evan about it, and I feel comfortable and at peace with myself that I'm making the right decision here," Tara said slowly, confidently.

Now Leslie looked puzzled. She almost thought Tara was going to tell her she was calling off the wedding or something ridiculous like that. She was about to find out just how strange it really was.

"Ok, now you are scaring me, Tara. What's this all about?" Leslie said, holding tightly on to the stem of her wine glass.

Tara looked right in to her questioning eyes. "I've made a decision that I would tie-up all the loose ends of my life before I move to Boston and begin a new life there." Tara waited for her response.

"Ok, good plan. And?" Leslie asked.

"And one of those loose ends is Ray Monroe." Tara looked at Leslie to see if she understood what she meant. After a few seconds, Leslie's expression registered that she did.

"Oh. *Oh.* Jesus, Tara, really? Really? Are you sure you want to do that? I mean, really, really sure?"

"Yes. I'm positive."

"Wow!" said Leslie, looking stunned, surprised, and frankly, afraid for Tara.

"As I said, I've given this a great deal of thought. I don't think I could live with myself if I don't tell her what I know. What he wants her to know."

"What you think you know, Tara! You can't be sure if all that stuff is even real! I mean, a few dreams, some odd happenings, some events you assume are related to Ray's death. It's one thing to think about something you feel is true. It's a whole other thing to drag innocent people who have been destroyed by it in with you! Are you absolutely sure you want to do this?"

"No, Leslie. I don't want to do it. I feel as though I *have* to do it. Something, some force is compelling me to go to her, and it's getting stronger as I get closer to my wedding date. I can't describe it; it almost feels like a gravitational pull toward Kim Monroe. And now that I've made the decision to actually do it, it feels right, really right. Please try to understand and support me with this. It's a huge gamble, I know. But its just one that, in my heart, I am sure I have to take. This has been an endless journey I have taken with Ray. It's time for me to bring it to a conclusion; no more fighting it. That means telling Kim everything that's happened since his death and what I believe it means in regard to her and her kids."

"Wow. Ok, then. I guess." Leslie said, defeated. "So what is the favor you need from me?" She appeared to be totally confused.

Tara reached across the table and put her hand on Leslie's arm. "I want you to come with me when I tell her."

"Oh, Jesus Christ, Tara! NO WAY! No way, no how — no can do!"

"Yes, you can."

"NO!"

"Please?"

"NO. WAY. NO!"

"Listen, Les. If I go by myself, I think it will frighten Kim too much. With you there, I think it makes it look less, well, ominous. Me alone — looks like I'm nuts. You there with me, makes it seem more legitimate. I mean, the both of us can't be insane. Right?"

"Yeah, but I have absolutely nothing to do with this shit. This is all your gig, Tara. Not mine!"

"I will make it perfectly clear to Kim that you have no part in it whatsoever, that you simply came with me for moral support. I promise! Please, I need you there with me. I don't think I can do this alone. Please, Leslie, I need to do this."

Leslie looked at Tara's face. She knew there was no choice here.

"Damn it," Leslie mouthed the words silently while gritting her teeth.

Tara smiled. She knew she had her. They had too much history together for Leslie to refuse her plea for help.

Leslie gave her a dirty look. "You really suck, Tara Fitzpatrick. And you will owe me SO HUGE after this! You will spend the rest of your days repaying me for this. No matter what I ask, you will have to say yes. I hope you realize that."

Tara leaned over the table and kissed Leslie right on her head. Then they started giggling when the people at the next table made faces at them.

"Thank you, Les. I don't know what I did to deserve getting such a great best friend. You are the best, the *bestest* friend ever, and no sister could be any better than you," Tara said, with tears in her eyes.

"Cut the sappy shit, Tara. I said I'd do it."

"Yes. Yes you did, didn't you!" said Tara.

"Actually, this won't be so bad after all," said Leslie, thinking, with an evil smirk.

"How's that?" Tara asked, as she reached in her bag to check her phone for messages.

"Because now you can't possibly refuse any of my outrageous plans for this weekend!" Leslie roared with laughter, smacking the table.

"Oh, God," groaned Tara.

"That's right, Ms. Fitzy! So let's go back to your apartment, get dressed appropriately for what I have in mind, and hit every club in New York City, baby!" Leslie yelled so loud the entire restaurant heard them.

"Paybacks are a bitch, girl!" Leslie sang victoriously.

"Paybacks *are* a bitch," Tara muttered, defeated.

CHAPTER

30

Tara and Leslie said very little to each other in the car as they drove to the Monroe's house. Each woman was wrapped up in her own concerns regarding what would happen today. *What would the fallout be as a result of this?* As Leslie turned into the street, she said quietly, "This is it." Tara nodded at her prophetic comment. The neighborhood Kim lived in was fairly affluent, with well manicured lawns and mature trees. If you lived here in this place, Tara decided, you had made it; you were accomplished, settled, and happy. The perfect, suburban existence.

After Leslie had left the city on Sunday afternoon, Tara had carefully composed an email to Kim. In it, Tara expressed how good it was to see her at Julia's, and that she was finally following up on her promise that they would get together and really catch up on each other's lives. Tara offered for her and Leslie to go to Kim's house, so she wouldn't have to worry about getting a babysitter. Kim emailed back that she was thrilled to hear from them, and that as it turned out, her in-laws had the kids all day the following Saturday, if they wanted to come then. She said she would have lunch ready and that way they could just lounge around in her house and talk uninterrupted.

Tara and Leslie loaded up on wine, desserts, gifts for Kim's children, and a large bouquet of pink tulips for Kim. As they pulled up in front of the house, Leslie turned off the engine and they sat there for a few moments looking at the beautiful home that Ray never got to come back to on that horrible day. This realization sent a chill through her.

"Are you absolutely sure you still want to do this? Because we can just go in and have a normal visit and try to make her laugh and not have any other drama except what she decides to share with us about her husband." Leslie was practically pleading with Tara to change her mind.

Tara glanced up at the second floor windows of the house and had two words pop in to her brain: *no windows. No windows.*

"No windows," Tara said as she turned to face Leslie.

"What?"

"No windows. He died in a place with no windows. I just know that. I just felt that," Tara said, in a whisper.

"Um, ok. Now you are starting to freak me out. Is being here in this house going to catapult you into the twilight zone today, Tara? Because if is, I'm leaving right now. I'll call Kim from the road and tell her I had car trouble or that Buck threw up or anything just to get out of here!"

Tara put her hand on Leslie's arm to calm her. "Relax. Everything will be fine. Come on, let's go get the stuff out of the trunk."

They grabbed the items they had brought and slowly walked to the front door. Before pressing the bell, Leslie looked over again at her best friend. Tara nodded, as if to say "I'm sure, let's do this." Leslie took a deep breath and pushed the small, white button.

"Here we go. God help us," Leslie muttered.

Through the frosted glass panels on the front door, they could see a shadow approaching from down the hallway. Kim opened the door and let out a delighted squeal to see them.

"Hey, guys! I'm so happy to see you! Come on in!"

The three girls hugged, and Kim took their jackets and hung them in the hall closet.

Tara glanced at the grandfather clock as she turned around. Then she had another jarring revelation.

Ok, Ray. Now I get it. I got it. I promise I will tell her...

"Did you have any trouble finding our street?" she asked, interrupting Tara's train of thought, as they followed her into the kitchen. Kim took all the boxes and bags from them and set them down on the island. Tara handed her the flowers, and Kim immediately put her face into the bouquet to smell them.

"Not at all. I MapQuested it, and the directions were perfect," Leslie answered. "Oh my gosh, Kim — your house is so beautiful!"

"Want the tour?" she asked, obviously proud to show off her lovely home.

"Yes!" Tara and Leslie answered at the same time.

As they walked from room to room, Tara saw a beautifully appointed house with custom draperies and dark, hardwood floors. When Leslie complimented the continuous wood and tile throughout, Kim explained that she and her son suffered from asthma and that carpet aggravated their condition. Still, everything was warm and inviting.

As they climbed to the second floor, Tara and Leslie paused to look at the framed photographs that lined the wall leading up the stairs. Baby pictures, wedding pictures, vacation pictures: portraits of a family and the moments and events they shared together. It was a visual pictorial that told their history, a story that had been tragically cut short.

The children's rooms were gender-appropriate with football and other sports-related items in her son's room and princess and dance themes in her daughter's room. Tara noticed several pictures of them with their father were displayed in each of their bedrooms.

The master bedroom was painted in a soft gray and white and a large wedding portrait of Kim and Ray hung on the far wall. It was probably the first thing Kim saw every morning when she woke up.

Tara immediately sensed him in the room. Yet, never having experienced anything like this before, she didn't trust that it was real. Was she just imagining it because she was there in Ray's house? To her, it felt like an energy was in the room, an awareness of being in a moment. Tara found it hard to describe, even to herself. It was just there, and she knew it.

"Gee, I'm sorry girls — did either of you need to use the bathroom? I forgot to offer!" Kim apologized.

"I will, if you don't mind. Leslie's husband always gets me an extra large coffee when I show up at their house. I love him for it, but it kills my bladder!" laughed Tara.

"Wait till she has a kid, right Kim?" Leslie warned.

"That's for sure. And it really disintegrates with each pregnancy, Tara!" Kim and Leslie were in a club that Tara wasn't.

"Right through there, Tara," Kim pointed.

While Tara walked away toward the master suite bathroom, Kim and Leslie continued their mommy discussion about kids and sleeping issues and how to get rid of a binky habit.

"Meet us back downstairs when you're done, Tara," Kim called to her.

"Ok." Tara walked into the bathroom and shut the door. When she turned around, she was hit with a barrage of sensations and disturbing images. Leaning against a low vanity, Tara closed her eyes. She felt dizzy and disoriented. It felt like the scene in *The Wizard of Oz* when the tornado hits Kansas and everything is swirling around Dorothy's house. While Tara's eyes were closed, she saw what she thought was — steam? From the shower? No. Wait. *It was smoke.* Thick, white smoke all around her. Then she heard what sounded like a hair dryer. Or was it just something blowing? No, it had a definite sound to it, a buzzing, blowing, high-pitched sound. It was all too bizarre but suddenly she knew. She just knew it, she felt it.

Ray was in a bathroom when he died.

A bathroom. A windowless bathroom.

Of course.

Now I understand.

Tara was absolutely certain of this, and these other new things were coming at her all at once. It was as if Ray knew he had to use Tara for the short time she would be there, and he wanted to make the most of it. Tara had no idea that coming into Ray Monroe's house would elicit such powerful connections for her. All she wanted to do was share her information from the past months with Kim, and now she had all this new stuff to contend with. More convinced than ever that she was doing the right thing in coming here, Tara took a few deep breaths and walked over to the sink. She splashed some water on her face and then remembered that she had to empty her bladder. Just like when it would happen in her own bathroom, Tara knew she had to get out of there. She quickly did her business, washed her hands and walked out to join the girls who were laughing downstairs.

When she entered the kitchen, Tara gave Leslie that look. The look that said something strange had just happened to her. The look that said "Don't leave me alone, because I'm in his house and it's like he's poking me on the shoulder to say something."

Leslie gave a quick shake of her head when Kim's back was turned to them. Like *not now, Tara!*

Annoyed at Leslie's dismissal of her, Tara turned her attention to Kim. Grabbing a handful of peanuts from a dish on the counter, she asked, "How long have you been here? Looks like a great neighborhood."

Kim spoke as she opened the first bottle of wine. "We moved in the year after we got married. I have great neighbors here. They have been a godsend since Ray was murdered."

Tara and Leslie looked at each other.

"That's how I describe my husband's death. That he was murdered." Kim spoke with a combination of sadness and anger as she looked up from what she was doing.

Leslie picked up her glass of wine. "Listen, Kim. We haven't seen each other in a long time, and we have three lives to catch up on. You don't have to talk about anything that makes you uncomfortable or sad if you don't want to. We'll understand."

Then Tara interjected, "Or, you can tell us everything about that day and the days after and what it's like for you now and we will listen. Because when you love someone and they die and leave you, it changes you forever. I know."

As much as Tara loved Leslie, she hadn't lost anyone close to her yet, and couldn't possibly understand how long lasting and devastating the effects could be.

Kim looked at Tara and gave her a weak smile. "I had forgotten you lost your mother when you were little. I used to feel so bad for you in college when we had those stupid mother-daughter things in our sorority. I mean, looking back, how insensitive it was for kids who didn't have a parent to come to those events. Now I see it. I live it. And I know it must have sucked for you."

"Sucked you know what, girl!" Tara said, as the three of them laughed. She looked at Leslie and smiled. "But my buddy here and her mom saved me from a lot of those awkward moments, thank God."

Kim handed Tara a glass. "You know what, girls? I will tell you all about these past few months because I realize everyone has questions, about all of it. But first, I want to drink lots of alcohol with two crazy chicks I spent a lot happy times with many years ago and hear about all the happenings in both of their lives, every good and bad detail. Then, I'll talk, ok?"

They clinked glasses, drank wine, and ate chicken salad with red grapes and walnuts on flaky croissants from Kim's local bakery and spinach salad with strawberries. They laughed over Leslie's stories about Buck's antics and her early married years. They excitedly discussed Tara's wedding plans and fussed over her engagement ring. Leslie and Kim doled out marriage and in-law advice, and how to get your new husband to do anything and everything you ask. Kim had, unfortunately, declined Tara's invitation to the wedding. She said it was still too hard for her to be in bigger social situations without Ray, especially weddings. Kim told them all about her own wedding to Ray, and the three women lamented the fact that they had lost touch with one another after graduation. It was good to be able to resume their friendship again, but to see Kim enduring such pain made talking about weddings and happy times extremely difficult and awkward.

After two bottles of wine, mostly consumed by Tara and Kim because Leslie was the designated driver, Kim made a full pot of coffee, and they cleaned up the mess in the kitchen. Then they took the coffee and two large platters filled with cupcakes, brownies, cookies, and pastries into Kim's family room. They sunk into her large, sectional couch after leaving their shoes scattered all over the floor.

"God, I love this room! I would never come off this couch!" Tara snuggled against the soft, deep cushions.

"I know, isn't it great? Unfortunately, I spend way too much time on it," Kim said, sadly.

Leslie took her hand. "I'm so sorry we lost touch after graduating. Life just seemed to take us all away from each other, in different directions. But I feel so bad that I wasn't around to help you after losing Ray. I can't imagine the hell you've been through."

"It was hell. I still feel numb. All the emotions of the day never leave, at least not for me. If I ever do have an hour when I'm not thinking about it, I'll instantly be reminded by something on the news or a form will come home from school that will ask for both parents' names. Now I am a single parent. Before I was a couple; now it's just me. I was a wife; now I'm a widow. And it all happened when I least expected it to. I wasn't ready. I'm still not ready."

"Have you talked to a counselor?" Tara asked.

"Yes, and the kids have been, also. It helped some, especially for them. I'm the one who is having so much difficulty moving on. I'm stuck. Stuck in the memories of the past, before all this. And the worst part of it all is that the night before he was killed, we had an argument. It was because of my selfish stupidity. We both went to bed angry, and when he left for work that morning, I had my back to him while he dressed to go to work, and I pretended I was asleep. Because I was mad at him. I was pissed at my husband who was about to walk into hell and be murdered. Nice wife, right?" A tear fell down her cheek.

"Kim, you had no idea what would happen that day," Leslie said, trying to imagine how it would feel fighting with Rob and then never being able to apologize because you would never see him again.

"I realize that, but it doesn't make me feel any better that my last words to my husband, the man I loved, my best friend, were from the mouth of a bitchy, spoiled brat. I wanted to go away for the weekend with a group of girls from town to celebrate someone's thirtieth birthday. Big girls' weekend away. Ray complained and asked who would take care of the kids and house and all I wanted was a weekend away from my life here, to act single again. Well, I got my wish in a huge way, didn't I? Karma is a real bitch." Then Kim began to sob.

Tara went over and hugged her. "Stop beating yourself up over it. All couples fight. I'm sure he understood where you were coming from."

"But I'll never know, will I? That's what's been so damn hard! That's the main reason why I can't seem to move on with my life. There is so much I'll never know because he left here that morning and I wasn't able to even speak to him! I don't have the slightest idea what happened to him, how he died, when he died, what he was thinking or feeling. I have no grave to visit, nothing of his body was ever recovered. All the unknowns, that is the absolute worst part."

Tara felt a shiver run through her. She glanced up from hugging Kim and saw Leslie looking at her. Leslie nodded, crying, and Tara nodded in return.

Standing up, Tara walked over to get a box of tissues from a side table and handed them to Kim. Glancing at a clock on the table, she was reminded of her earlier, sudden revelation.

"Kim, I need to share something with you. Something that has been with me since that horrible day, that I have struggled with," Tara began.

Kim looked up at Tara with absolute panic on her face.

Leslie saw this. "Jesus Christ, Tara! You are making it sound like you are about to tell her you had been having an affair with her husband! Would you please clarify what you are talking about?"

"Oh, shit, Kim — no! No, that's not it at all! This is something that has to do with me, and how it relates to you and Ray…"

Leslie shot her another dirty look.

"Oh, hell. I'm not very good at this. I have no experience in how to talk about this. Can I just start at the beginning and you just listen to the crazy, insane, makes-no-sense story I am about to tell you? I promise, there is no affair in any part of what I am about to tell you."

Kim sat there, still puzzled and confused as to what she was talking about.

"Here goes." Tara took a deep breath, then released it. "Not long ago, I came to discover that as a young child, I experienced certain things in my life that were, well, unusual. Without going into specifics, they involved incidents of a psychic nature where I seemed to have some kind of ability or connection to things and people beyond this world. I hadn't remembered them, until my father explained it to me after telling him what I am about to share with you. But I always had remembered having this sort of out-of-body experience while sitting in class one day when I was in the sixth grade, which I knew was out of the ordinary.

Leslie gave Tara a questioning look.

"Yeah, Les. I never told you about that weird incident. At the time, I didn't want you to think I was a complete lunatic sitting in Sister George's class."

"Well if it was Sister George's class, then I understand. She was so incredibly boring, Kim. Most of the class probably had an out-of-body experience just to mentally escape her class!" Leslie joked. She was hoping to break some of the tension.

Kim wasn't laughing, however. Obviously, she was in no mood to joke right now. Leslie quickly shut up.

Tara continued, "Nothing really ever happened in regards to this kind of stuff all through high school or college. Then, a few days after the explosion at the Pitten Building, I decided to go down there to see for myself what it all looked like. I realize now that I felt pulled, compelled to go down there. As I walked along the area they were letting people go to, I came upon that part of the fence that was covered with fliers and posters that victim's families had put up. Out of all the pictures there, I looked up to see the one that had been posted with your husband's picture on it."

Kim nodded, remembering that Tara had briefly mentioned this when they were at Julia's house. "My father-in-law put that up there at my request. We were all frantic. We thought that maybe, possibly, he was badly injured in a hospital somewhere. There was so much confusion that day. We hoped..." she whispered quietly.

"He looked familiar to me, but it had been so long since I had seen him. It wasn't until I saw your name on the flyer that I knew it was Ray. I called Leslie to tell her. We were both devastated for you and your kids."

Kim shook her head at the memory of it.

"So, Kim. Here is what happened next." Tara sat on the floor, directly in front of her. "I'm about to explain a series of things that happened, related to that visit. But I need to preface this by saying first of all, I don't really know if what I am about to tell you is actually real or imagined. I have no scientific proof whatsoever. I am not a psychic, fortuneteller, medium — whatever you may choose to call it. I consider myself to be perfectly sane, intelligent, not crazy, and would never do anything to hurt you, your children, or malign the memory of your husband. I have struggled with coming to you with this because I have no fact that it is true or real, but I feel as if I have to do this, that I am morally obligated to tell you. It has also been my own personal journey since this happened, to come to terms with what this is and what I would do about it. As I told you, I will be moving to Boston, and I couldn't leave without telling you this story, Kim. *His story.* I think, *I know,* that Ray is the one who wants me here with you today. This really is not my choice to stir up these emotions and memories for you again. But I know now, I'm doing the right thing, and I'm sorry I didn't come to you sooner. It's just that I was trying to figure it out myself, and I think I finally have. Does any of this make the least bit of sense to you?"

Kim looked at Tara. In her eyes, Tara saw a woman who was grasping at any bit of information that she was willing to give her. "I'm still listening. If I've learned anything from all this, it's that nothing in this life makes any sense to me now, so my mind is open to whatever you have to tell me. Please, go on."

Tara got up and sat on the couch next to her. "Just to backtrack for a minute, I had discovered that I am not the only one in my family who is weird like this. My father conveniently neglected to tell me that on my mother's side of the family, certain members also have this gift. Which is, as I came to find out, more of a curse than a gift because having it only makes you appear insane to those outside your gifted family."

Leslie smiled at this remark while Kim hung on her every word.

"After speaking to my aunt who also has this ability, I realized it is more of a sixth sense of the world, an awareness that you are in tune with stuff that most people are not. Yet, you would be surprised how many people do have this. Evan's grandfather has it, and he was the one who helped me connect things that were happening to me with Ray."

"What things?" Kim asked.

"The day after I saw Ray's picture on the fence, I began to have continuous, alternating dreams. There were two different dreams that I would have every, single night for months: one or the other — exactly the same images. The first dream was a faceless man who was standing on the sidelines of some kind of ball field, like football or soccer, just watching a group of children play. In the second dream, I believe it was the same man because his height and build matched those in the first one. Now, he is standing in the back of a theater or auditorium watching some activity take place on a stage. In both dreams, he never speaks, and although I cannot make out a face, I am sure he is smiling as he watches."

Kim put her hands over her face and began to weep. She knew what Tara had seen all those months.

"Kim, I have come to believe that the man in my dreams was Ray and that it was him watching your children, his children. After we saw you at Julia's party and you told us your son played PeeWee football and your daughter took dance lessons, I knew it was Ray and that he is always watching them. It means that he will forever watch over them in the place he is now. They won't know he's there, but he will always be there."

Kim looked up with tears streaming down her face. "Tara, my daughter said she saw her Daddy at her recital back in June, and he waved to her! I told her that it wasn't possible, that she had mistaken him for someone else's father, and that her Daddy was in heaven. She screamed at me and said, "NO! It was my Daddy and I saw him and he wouldn't miss my recital!" I didn't believe her! I thought it was wishful thinking on the part of a bereaved child!"

The hair stood up on the back of Leslie's neck.

"What I've learned," Tara continued, "Is that when someone is taken suddenly or tragically from this life, they do not pass over easily or immediately. I sensed that due to the circumstances of Ray's death, he was not ready to leave this world. I always had the feeling that he literally went kicking and screaming, and it took him a long time before he was ready to pass and would accept his own death.

That's when the dreams stopped. Once again, Kim, I have no proof that this is what happened, only a gut feeling. Your husband did not want to leave you and his children. He was a tortured soul, one who was in constant turmoil over his death."

Tara put her hand over Kim's. It was cold as ice.

"Should I continue? There's more, but it's harder to tell."

"Yes, please. I want to know. Whatever you can tell me."

Tara spoke, "In addition to the dreams, I would also have these overwhelming sensations of doom and dread when I would enter the bathroom of my apartment: I would feel a sense of chaos and despair, even full-blown panic attacks. And just a while ago when I used your bathroom upstairs, I sensed something new where I was surrounded by fog or smoke. It reaffirmed my belief that Ray died in a bathroom at his office in the building. A windowless bathroom where he was able to survive for a short time because at least he could breathe in there."

Kim's eyes glazed over. "His office was near the bathroom, and it annoyed him. We used to joke about the fact that he held an executive position in the company, and that he had to take enough shit all day. It made us both laugh." She stared at Tara, now in a completely different light.

"I sensed he was trapped in there. He tried to get out but something prevented him from doing so," Tara added.

"From what they told us, the bomb that was planted on his floor was the one that didn't go off initially at 11:00 a.m. It was the one that went off an hour later, at noon. We just assumed everyone in his office was killed instantly from either the first bomb, or definitely by the second one," Kim reported.

Tara had another chill run through her. *Noon. May 11. 11:12. Oh, God, Ray. Now I understand.*

Tara spoke quietly. "That would explain my sense of chaos. But I truly believe Ray survived the initial explosion."

"You said you never spoke to him that day, right?" Leslie asked.

"No. I know when he would get to work, he always left his cell phone on his desk. So if he were in the bathroom when the first bombs went off, he would not have had his phone with him. I always told him he should get a clip so he could carry it around with him. He would laugh and tell me he already looked like enough of a nerd because he had his email device clipped to his belt and kept two pens, one black and one red, in his dress shirt pocket. The man was always writing stuff down, and he always carried a pen. He probably still had a damn pen but no phone with him. If he was still alive for a time, he had no way of contacting me. He must have been terrified." She shuddered.

"There is one more thing that I wanted to tell you." Tara stood up again and walked over to take a sip of her now-cold coffee.

Kim once again looked to Tara for the answers she was finally getting to her agonizing questions since Ray's death. Leslie watched and for the first time realized Tara had made the right decision in telling Kim what she had feared would be taken in the wrong way. It was, in fact, giving her so much comfort and peace. It was the absolute right decision.

"You told us that they never recovered any part of Ray's body. But I am certain that you will, at least, receive something that belonged to him. Something will be found and returned to you. Something that Ray wants you to have, because it meant so much to him."

"But Tara..." Kim tried to interrupt her.

"Kim, please let me just finish this last thing. I have been haunted by the concept of time. I have seen the numbers 11/12 on clocks constantly, and I know this represents the day and time he died, the time you spent together in the past, and that he will love you and his children for all time. And out of all of the things that he had in his possession, his wristwatch meant the most, right?" This was the other revelation that had just come to Tara since entering Ray's home, his sanctuary. It had come to Tara when they entered Kim's house and she saw the grandfather clock in the foyer.

Tara knew. She knew they had found it.

I finally get it, Ray. All of it.

Kim closed her eyes and began to sob loudly. Then she leaned forward and let out a moan that shook Tara and Leslie to their cores. It was the kind of emotional response you never want to hear come from another human being.

They both rushed to Kim's side as she rocked back and forth on the edge of the sofa, and they tried to console her. Leslie gave Tara a look. Now she was not happy they had come here after all. Look how this poor woman was suffering, and they were responsible.

Suddenly, Kim sat up and let out a slow, deep breath, trying to compose herself. She stood and walked out of the family room toward the kitchen. Tara and Leslie just sat there and looked at each other, not knowing how to act or what to say. Was it their cue to leave or follow her or what?

Then, Kim came back into the room and walked up to Tara. In that instant, Tara knew what she was about to say.

Two lives were about to be changed forever.

CHAPTER

31

Ray Monroe forced his eyes open at five-thirty in the morning and turned to look at his wife who was lying asleep next to him. Still facing in the opposite direction, she seemed as if she hadn't moved at all last night. The silent treatment would be guaranteed today, but he wasn't sure he deserved it. After all, had she really thought through this crazy request of hers?

After shaving and showering, Ray dressed in the walk-in closet with the door closed so the light wouldn't wake Kim. Picking up his shoes from the floor, he glanced at his reflection in the mirror before shutting off the light. He walked over to the bed and kissed his wife goodbye, hoping that she wouldn't still be mad at him later when he got home.

Heading downstairs to the kitchen, he tried not to step on the stair he knew would creak, causing the dog to bark and wake up his children and the entire neighborhood. Ray's kids had just started swim lessons the day before and were wiped out. The sun was just beginning to come up as he let the dog outside into the fenced backyard. Ray walked to the front door to get his newspaper. He loved the new delivery person who got his *New York Times* there at the house before he left for work. It saved precious minutes in the life of a commuter — no waiting in line at the train station newsstand.

Ray noticed some papers that were left on the kitchen island as he slipped his suit jacket on. One was left lying on top of his wallet and cellphone. "For my Daddy, Love Emily" was scrawled across the bottom of a crayon drawing of two stick figures holding hands. Ray smiled, folded the sheet, and slipped it into his pants pocket. He may need to look at it later if his day sucked or if something annoyed him at work. It would remind him of the reason he actually went to work every day.

Opening the back door he let the dog back in and gave him some fresh water. Kim would feed him when she got up in a couple of hours, and he could wait until then.

As he pulled the car out of the driveway, he realized it was garbage day and that he forgot to put the pails out at the curb. "Shit!" he cursed under his breath, threw his car in park, and hurriedly dragged the cans out. Kim always put the garbage out from the house, but it was his job to put the cans in the street. This was a ritual that had started when they first married and had never changed over the years. The Monroes had a definite division of labor in their household, which made most stuff run smoothly. Each spouse had his or her routine tasks with Kim in charge of the inner sanctum and Ray handling the yard and outside maintenance.

That's why when she had mentioned she was thinking of going away for an entire weekend with her girlfriends for some thirtieth birthday party next month he had protested vehemently. Who would get the kids to soccer and Sunday religious education class? Who would make breakfast, lunch, and dinner? Do laundry and make beds and run the vacuum and feed the dog? Besides, Ray really wanted to play as much golf as he could now. The weather was perfect, and he needed to work on his swing before the summer started. And weren't weekends family time for Christ's sake? Who did she think she was — a teenager or some chick back in college where you could just go and party whenever you wanted? She was almost thirty years old with a husband and two young children, a dog, and a house that she was in charge of. Jesus, what was she thinking?

Kim had brought the subject up after they had gone to bed last night. She said that she never asks for anything and had never left the kids since they were born. Couldn't he give her this one time? Surely he could manage things for one single weekend! It would recharge her batteries, she had said.

I didn't realize they were dead, he had said. It would just be a huge inconvenience for everyone in the family, he had told her.

She called him selfish and unsupportive. He said she was selfish and immature. She slammed the bathroom door. He slammed the closet door. She fell asleep, back to him, whimpering. He fell asleep, back to her, seething.

As he drove to the train station, Ray thought about his family. He loved his wife and kids. He was lucky. They lived in a great neighborhood in the suburbs of New Jersey, with easy access to the beaches, boardwalks, and the city. They had terrific friends and neighbors, all of them raising their families and working hard to provide for them. He had no right to complain about anything in his life.

Ray was hit with a rush of regret and guilt. So what if his wife wanted one measly weekend with her girlfriends? She never asked for anything; she was low-maintenance and always made sure his needs — all of them — were met. Some of the wives he knew demanded jewelry, luxury cars, vacation homes, and designer clothes. Kim didn't care about any of those things. In fact, she always put herself last.

As he sat in his seat on the train, Ray realized what an ass he had been the night before. He decided he would call Kim during lunch and apologize. He could sacrifice one weekend if that's all she needed. Hell, she had done that and more for him in the past.

As the elevator doors opened, Ray stepped out onto the floor of his office. He made it a habit to arrive before everyone else at around 8:00 a.m. so that he could rifle through the endless emails from clients and colleagues. No distractions; no interruptions.

He had grabbed a coffee and bagel at his usual place after he got off the train. As the guy handed Ray his breakfast, he actually told him to have a nice day, which was unusual. Normally, he never said a word.

Everyone seemed to be in a good mood for a Tuesday: Blue sky, warm, spring air after a cold winter, and a rainy April brought a welcome change. Even the most disgruntled of people had to feel good on a day like today.

Due to a dentist appointment, Ray's secretary wouldn't be in until later in the morning, and he needed to double-check a report before it went out. He took off his suit jacket and hung it on the back of his chair, put his cell phone on his desk, and took a sip of his extremely hot coffee. Taking the lid off so it would cool, he took a large bite of the bagel and with a red pen in hand, began to read.

Raymond Monroe had been working at Federal Trust since he graduated from college. A mid-size insurance firm, the company had been impressed with his work and promoted him to a management position early on in his career. In the beginning, Ray worked really long hours so he could establish himself and was rewarded for his efforts. Ray and Kim were married after graduating from Rutgers University, and their first baby came soon after. Wanting to be young parents, they had back-to-back pregnancies and had gotten their wish. It was hard sometimes with two babies and being so young themselves, but they managed easily with Kim staying home full-time and doing freelance writing and Ray making a decent salary.

Ray liked working here, and he loved the people. The commute each day was sometimes an inconvenience, but there was no better place to be than in beautiful Harbor Point, in the historic Pitten Building. It was the right place to be.

By the time Janet arrived at 10:45, he was finished with the changes to the report and had gone through most of his emails.

"Hey Ray, what's up?" she called as she moved about her cubicle. A fifty-six-year-old grandmother, Janet had worked for Ray for the past three years. They were a good fit; she got his sense of humor and understood his compulsive quirks. He in turn was flexible when she needed time off and was patient and fought to get her decent yearly pay raises. Ray liked her, but above all his wife liked her. All was well with the world.

"I'm done with the revisions on that report that has to go out today. Whenever you're ready, it's yours," he said.

"Give me a sec and I'll be right there," she said as she sat down at her desk to change from her sneakers to proper heels.

The phone rang. "Ray Monroe's office — may I help you?" Janet answered. She looked up as she made eye contact with Ray. "No, I'm sorry but he's not available at this minute. May I take a message?" She gave him a smile as he mouthed, "Thank you."

"Ok — whatcha got for me?" she said walking into his office.

As she reached for the report, she accidentally knocked over his now cold, half-full coffee cup, missing the paper but soaking the right cuff of his shirtsleeve. Ray jumped out of his chair.

"Oh shit, Ray! I'm so sorry!" she said, embarrassed by her clumsiness.

Janet exclaimed, "I'm wound so tight today; I don't know what's wrong with me! This morning I dropped cereal all over the floor and then burned myself with the curling iron — now this! Jesus, Ray! I'm so sorry!"

"It's ok. Accidents happen. Believe me, it's fine. At least I don't have any important meetings today." He looked at her and smiled. There was never a day where Ray didn't have his calendar filled with meetings.

"We're all entitled to a bad day once in a while, even you Superwoman."

As Janet tried to clean up the mess on his desk, she mumbled under her breath. "Menopause sucks." He laughed while she silently hoped this day would end better than it had started.

Ray needed to go to the restroom to try and remove some of the coffee from his cuff and get the stickiness off his hands before the staff meeting that was scheduled at eleven. He slipped the watch off his wrist and laid it gently on the desk. It was his most prized material possession, a wedding anniversary gift from Kim.

He had always loved antique watches and had his eye on a 1928 Omega Regulateur wristwatch. To the average eye, it wouldn't appear to be as valuable or rare as it was. Ray's grandfather had a similar one, and he had always admired it. His grandfather would have probably left it to Ray one day, but he was mugged in a parking lot and the thief stole both his wallet and the coveted watch. Ray spent years trying to hunt down a similar one, searching jewelry stores and the Internet. His wonderful wife finally found it in a gallery in New York City and surprised him on their fifth anniversary.

Ray felt his gift to her — a trip to the Cayman Islands — paled in comparison. Kim was amazing, and after all these years he couldn't believe how lucky he was. Once again, the guilt over the night before troubled him. He decided then that rather than waiting until noon to call and apologize, he would do so before his staff meeting.

She had written *THE GIFT OF TIME* on the card that was attached to the box when she presented it to him. It was so appropriate; she loved giving something that symbolized their past, present, and future. Kim really tried to make everything so special and meaningful; most times Ray just felt so inept in the romance department.

After washing his hands, he wet some paper towels and attempted to work on removing the large coffee stain. Punching the hand dryer mounted securely on the wall, he angrily tried to dry his shirt cuff. Not sure if the white shirt could ever be saved at this point, he glanced in the mirror and straightened his tie. He had about five minutes before his meeting. He could probably get another cup of coffee if he hurried. Also, he wanted to try and call Kim. As he opened the bathroom door, the world exploded.

Breaking glass, flashes of light and darkness.
Plumes of smoke and fire. Hot fire.
The excruciating sound of bending metal.
More explosions of something. Intense heat.
The smell of gas.
The ceiling and walls caving in.
Papers flying. Furniture flying.

My colleagues. My friends.

Unimaginable screams coming from those friends.

Hell on earth in an office building.

An antique Omega watch falling quietly to the floor.

CHAPTER

32

Standing a few feet from Tara, Kim held a sheet of white paper and a small, thick, gray plastic bag. She handed the letter to Tara.

"Four days ago, I received this by certified mail."

Tara looked at the paper. It was some sort of an official letter, evidenced by the bold lettering in the heading. The title read: "Notification of Recovered Property."

Glancing up, Tara looked back at Kim, then Leslie who remained on the couch with a perplexed expression.

"What is it?" Leslie asked, directing her question more to Kim.

"It's a form letter sent out by the Harbor Point Police Department regarding the personal possessions that have been found either in the wreckage at the Pitten Building or from the debris that was taken to an empty hanger at Newark airport. After almost ten months, with hundreds of people sifting and searching through tons of rubble and dust, thousands of items were recovered. Very few families were able to claim loved one's remains due to the explosion itself, or the fire that ultimately, brought down the rest of the building. Did you know that less than sixty intact bodies were recovered? And for many of us, those we loved and cherished completely disappeared that day. But for some, a tiny piece was left behind. A driver's license, a work ID, a cell phone or pager, a credit card. Some were lucky enough to recover a wedding or engagement ring. The Police Department set up a Jewelry Recovery website, where they cataloged and described items that had been found."

Now the tears were rolling down Tara's cheeks. She *knew* what was coming, whether it was from her gift or from pure, human instinct.

Leslie, still in the dark, asked, "What does all this mean, Kim?"

Not breaking eye contact with Tara, Kim continued to speak. "The transfer of personal property takes place at Police Department headquarters in Harbor City, in a windowless, small room in the basement. Out of the thousands of items that were recovered, 164 of them were watches. Wristwatches."

Leslie's hand slowly covered her mouth. No sound would have come out, even if she could have formed any words.

Tara closed her tear-stained eyes, breaking contact with Kim's.

"Some of the watches were still working, others had stopped; frozen in time."

Kim reached into the silver bag. "My husband's watch, however, is still keeping perfect time."

Leslie gasped in disbelief at the sight of Kim holding out Ray's watch, part of the leather band still attached to one side.

Tara and Kim's anguished eyes locked together, as if Kim was staring into the face of her husband.

"I saw a photograph of the watch that had been posted on the website. The police required me to bring some form of verification to claim it, so I brought the receipt from when I purchased it for our anniversary. It was an antique Omega Regulateur wristwatch from 1928, and the receipt proved that it was Ray's. I picked it up yesterday."

"Oh, my God, Tara," Leslie whispered.

Tara stood and walked over to Kim and they embraced. Quietly crying, Kim hung onto Tara, eyes closed, imagining she was holding on to her husband. Both knew that Ray was there, with Kim, inside of Tara, for a fleeting instant in time.

For Tara, it was vindication, a final culmination of the intense emotional roller coaster of the past year. It felt better than a breakthrough in therapy, drinking water when parched, eating when ravenous. It was final, it was closure, hopefully, for both women.

Leslie still remained frozen on the sofa, observing what she knew could never leave this room. It was all too powerful, and no one aside from the three of them could ever explain to anyone what had just taken place. It was a moment solely for Kim and Tara, for Kim and Ray, and for Ray and Tara.

Raymond Monroe could finally rest in peace, his message clearly delivered to his grieving wife. A part of him was returned to her, and because of Tara, Kim knew he would always be with them. Knowing how he died and that he had survived for a short time after the first explosions, had settled some of the mystery surrounding his death. Kim would have to let go of the lingering guilt over the argument they had the night before he died and whether or not he had forgiven her for her behavior. He loved her and her children and that would have to be enough: enough for her to begin to move on with her life without him in it.

Tara reached out and Kim handed her the watch. Except for a few scratches and half of the leather band missing, it was in remarkably good condition. She turned it over in her hands, feeling a powerful link to the sturdy timepiece. As she read the inscription on the back, she smiled. It was all so clear to her now. All the signs were evident; all the connections were unclouded. Pay attention to the signs. They were there all along, waiting for her to see them.

"For all time," Tara read. "How fitting, how perfect."

"In the card I had given him that day, I said that I wanted to give him the gift of time for our fifth anniversary. I had no idea how symbolic that would be, given how little time we had left."

"It seems to me that time is the most precious gift we have as human beings," Tara said. "We have to cherish it and not squander it and make the most of being here. I think that getting Ray's watch back after all this is his way of telling you that he wants you to move on now, for you and the kids. My time with Ray is finished. I have done what he needed me to do for him. Now it is *your* turn, Kim. He wants you to go and live the rest of your life. It's time.

Kim nodded and gave a reluctant smile.

Leslie stood up. "Tara, I think we need to get a move on here, it's getting late. This has been the most emotional day since I gave birth to my son, and I need to go home and get drunk."

All three laughed. "Bet you wish you weren't the designated driver after today, right?" Kim said. The poor girl was absolutely worn out from this entire ordeal, but she seemed to be at peace with all that had taken place.

"You got that right! But listen, Kim. I want you to know that I am here for you if you ever need me. We need to stay in touch from now on." The two hugged for several, long seconds.

"Thank you so much. I do know how much people care about us, and I really appreciate it. I think I'll try to come up with a plan, a new plan for our future. Leslie, could I have a few minutes alone with Tara before you guys head out?"

"Sure. I'll just use the ladies room before we go," she answered. There was a small bathroom off the kitchen.

Kim turned to face Tara who had started trying to gather up the coffee mugs and dessert dishes.

"Tara put that stuff down, I'll deal with it after you girls leave. Listen, I want to say something to you. Words cannot describe how I feel right now. I realize it took a lot of guts to come here today and reveal what you did. You took a huge gamble, but I want you to know it may have just changed my life. I will never completely get over his death, but maybe now I can live with the pain a little bit better. I'm going to make a serious effort to move forward from this day on because I know that is what he would have wanted. If the reverse were true, I would want him to. I wish I could have known that he had forgiven me for being such an ass the night before, but I'll have to live with that. Knowing that he fought so hard not to leave us, but was powerless to do so, is what I will hold on to. I would have never known all this if it hadn't been for you. Thank you, from the bottom of my heart, for telling me what you did today. It was the right thing to do, Tara. Both you and Ray can rest easily, now. The message has been received and accepted."

Kim was exhausted, and she just wanted to be alone to absorb everything.

"We both found closure today. The weight of this knowledge has been lifted off my shoulders, and I finally feel peace. Peace for all of us. Whatever lingering doubts or guilt you may have need to be put aside. Ray loved you until the minute he died. I'm certain that argument was forgiven. He loves you and his children wherever he is now. He wants you to go on." Tara hugged her tightly.

"Hey, Kim. I'd like to ask one small favor. If you ever feel the need to tell this story, especially to the kids when they are older, please leave my name out of it. Just tell them some crazy woman told you. I want to go and live a quiet life with Evan and be invisible. I've had enough drama in the past year to last me a lifetime!"

"Don't worry, Tara. This is too personal, and I think I want to keep this just for me. I'm not even sure I will tell the kids. I don't think they will need this as much as I do. But I assure you, this can stay between the three of us."

With that, Leslie emerged from the bathroom while Tara went in. The girls cleaned up the remaining mess while eating from the plate of desserts that had been overlooked in all the emotional unfolding of Tara's revelations.

As they walked to the front door to say goodbye, Tara glanced at the grandfather clock in the foyer. The time read: 4:15 p.m.

Tara smiled. It was time for everyone to move on and have life get back to normal.

Sliding into the driver's seat, Leslie turned to stare at Tara.

"What?"

"I have to admit it, Tara. I'm more than a little afraid of you right now."

Tara laughed.

"No. I mean it, seriously. I am in total awe of you. I really had no idea that that thing of yours was that profound. What you did in there, for her, well, it was...amazing. I'm really, really proud of you."

"Gee, thanks Mom!" Tara laughed. "I'm just happy this whole ordeal is over. Now we can all move on with our lives — all of us. I am hoping there will be no more dreams or visions. I did what he needed me to do so now I'm done. So get us back to your house so I can go home and get married. Ok?"

"Whatever you want, boss. Like I said, I'm afraid of you."

"Be quiet and drive, Les. I want to go home. To Evan."

One Year Later

Boston, Massachusetts

"The doctor will be with you in a few minutes, Mrs. Kane," the technician said, enthusiastically.

"Thank you." Tara was laying on the exam table, her growing belly exposed as Evan put his palm over it.

"This is the big day, honey. Are you excited?" he asked. It was raining hard outside, but nothing could put a damper on this day for them.

"God, I can't wait! So what do you think, Evan? Will it be true?"

"Knowing you? Knowing *our* history? Probably."

Tara was twenty weeks pregnant, and today they would find out if she was having a boy or girl. When they had decided the time was right to try for a baby, Tara got pregnant immediately. She attributed it to answered prayers; Evan, of course, boasted it was from his super stud sperm.

The door opened. "Good morning, guys! How are you feeling, Tara?" Dr. Addison breezed into the room.

"Pretty good. The morning sickness is almost over, thank God," Tara answered.

"Great!" Dr. Addison said, as she squeezed the warm jelly over Tara's stomach.

"Ok, let's see what we have here." She began to move the wand in broad circles over her skin, instructing, "Watch the monitor right over there."

The couple stared in awe as their baby floated around in Tara's belly. Evan squeezed her hand as the emotion flowed over them.

"Everything looks terrific. All is progressing nicely. Exactly as it should be at this stage," Dr. Addison confirmed. "Do we want to know the sex of this little person or are we waiting to be surprised?"

"We want to know, please," Tara answered excitedly.

As the doctor made one final pass with the wand, Evan held his breath.

"It's a girl!" Dr. Addison announced. "A healthy, strong baby girl!"

Tara turned to Evan. He had tears in his eyes. The love they felt for each other was now sealed forever by the creation of a child.

Evan looked at his wife and nodded, as if to say, "Yeah, I know. This is the new best day of our lives." Then, he leaned down and kissed her lightly on her lips as he whispered, "Told you."

Dr. Addison printed several pictures for them to take home and then she cleaned the gel from Tara's stomach. Helping her sit up, she said everything looked great and she would see them next month.

Walking out of the medical building, they noticed the pouring rain had stopped and the sun had come out.

"Look — a rainbow!" Evan said, pointing to the sky over the buildings. "That's good luck, isn't it?"

Tara smiled, watching it stretch over a wide expanse of sky. "No, Evan. That's my mother." She thought about how blessed her life was and that all her dreams had come true, including the one dream she never expected to have.

A week before the scheduled ultrasound, Tara finally had a dream about her mother. She appeared clear as day and unlike she had been told, her mother spoke directly to her. Ann Fitzpatrick looked happy and was smiling. She told Tara, "You will have a beautiful, little girl, just like I did," and then she was gone. Tara woke Evan to tell him about the dream and asked if he thought it was real.

"Are you seriously going to ask that, Tara?" He laughed and pulled her into his arms.

Since they had been married, Tara was "spook free" and resumed a normal, drama-free life. But then, out of the blue, was this dream. If she hadn't experienced all those things over her lifetime, she would have simply said it was pregnancy hormones to blame.

Gazing again at the pictures of this tiny miracle inside her, Tara glanced up to see Evan smiling at her.

"Keep your eyes on the road there, Daddy: precious cargo on board."

"I know what you are thinking, Tara," he laughed.

"What? No, you don't. You are not the psychic one in this family."

"My point exactly! You are wondering if the baby will inherit what you have!"

Now she smiled at Evan. Maybe he had, in fact, gotten a small part of his grandfather's gift, too. And maybe their children and their children's kids would keep passing it on through the generations.

Or maybe it was simply a husband and wife who would always be on the same wavelength.

Only time would tell.

Harbor Point, New Jersey

Detective Jerry Toller looked up from his desk when he heard a knock on his door. Standing in the open doorway was Bobby O'Shea, who had been in charge of the Pitten Building debris cleanup project in Harbor Point.

Jerry looked surprised to see him. "What brings you here? Slow day at work?" The two men had worked closely since that fateful day on May 11,1999, and shared many sights no human ever needed to see.

"At least I have a real job. All you do is sit in this cushy office and push papers all day," Bobby teased. Both men had a healthy respect for each other's responsibilities. Bobby found all the pieces of lives that were left in the rubble of the Pitten Building; Jerry, who handled the recovery operation at the Police Department in Harbor Point, helped the families to identify those pieces of lives lost that day. It was a hard thing for both men, and they took the task seriously.

"You are not going to believe this one, man. Just when I think we are done and have seen everything there is to see, we find some obscure thing, and it all comes flooding back," Bobby said, shaking his head.

"What is it?" Jerry asked, now very curious.

"I had my boys trying to finish up the last of the scrap metal debris, and one of the guys spotted a flash of color in the pile. When he turned over a flattened chunk of steel beam, he found this."

Bobby took a piece of metal from an evidence bag he was carrying. It was about two-feet-long, twisted and mangled beyond recognition.

"After he and another guy extracted it from the steel, they examined it to see what it was. Turns out it is one of the wall hand dryers they had in the bathrooms in the building. As you can see," he turned the flattened metal over on its side, "The nozzle got tucked up against the box and partially melted into this piece of steel."

Jerry took the object and studied it. "Ok, this is the first one we've seen of these dryers, but what is it that you find so fascinating?" he asked, still curious.

"No, it's not the dryer that interested us, it's what we found barely sticking out of it that caught our attention."

With that, Bobby pulled a plastic bag out of his pocket. Inside the bag was a piece of paper, with what appeared to be a drawing by a child. Jerry put on his glasses to examine the picture. It was a rendering of two stick figures, one larger than the other, holding hands. The background of the drawing was in a vivid blue, obviously representing a blue sky. It was this vibrant blue that had caught the worker's eye amid all the dull, gray and brown steel. The picture read, "For my Daddy, Love Emily" scrawled in crayon in what was a very young child's novice handwriting.

"This was jammed all the way up in the arm of the dryer. And on the back, some guy left a note to his wife. His last words to his wife," Bobby explained.

Jerry turned the sheet of paper over. On the back of the drawing was a handwritten letter from a man to his wife, written with a red, ballpoint pen.

"Jesus Christ," whistled Jerry, as he read over the letter.

"The poor bastard must have been trapped in one of the bathrooms on the upper floors and penned this final farewell to his family," Bobby said.

"Yeah, and then shoved it in the nozzle of the dryer so it wouldn't burn in the fire that was probably raging outside that bathroom door. He must have had the picture in his pocket and brought it to work that day. A gift from his little girl."

"I guess — you're the detective. But it sounds as though something like that would explain this. He had no fucking clue what was going on outside the door because there were no windows in there. Shit. Anyway, I can't believe this letter survived the explosion, and the fire, and that we actually recovered it."

Jerry was somber. "Another voice from the dead. After all this time, they seem to still pop up at the strangest moments and even stranger places. I mean, Bobby, a bathroom hand dryer? Who would have ever thought to stick it in there, and who would have thought we would ever find the damn thing? Just incredible!" Jerry said, shaking his head in disbelief.

"So, what will you do with it, Detective?"

"Cross reference the names in our database and find a match. Then I'll call the widow to come in and identify the handwriting and drawing. These poor people! When will it ever stop for them?" Jerry asked with anger in his voice.

"Hey, it sounds from the note that he was apologizing to her for a fight they had, so maybe it will actually help her, you know, make her feel better. Maybe it's a good thing," Bobby decided.

"Do you really think, after all this time, it will help or hurt her?"

"I think," Bobby said thoughtfully, "After everything she's been through, he would want her to read this and she will find that this letter could not have come at a better time."

Both men nodded in agreement. Detective Gerald Toller wrote the three names on a slip of paper: *Kim, Emily, and Ray.* Then he sat down to search for them on his computer.

Meanwhile, Bobby O'Shea sat back in his chair to once again, read the love letter a man had written to his wife, on the last day of his life, on the worst day in Harbor Point, New Jersey. A man who was about to die, trapped in a windowless bathroom, hoping to get a final message to his family.

My Dearest Kim,

I don't know what is going on, but I think they set off a huge bomb somewhere on my floor. I was in the bathroom, and now I'm trapped in here. I can't move the door open because there is something blocking it. I wet my shirt and put it along the floor by the door, but the smoke is coming through the top. I don't know how much time I have until the firemen get here, and it's getting harder to breathe. If I don't get out of here I want you to know how much I love you and the kids and how happy you have made me all these years. I'm sorry I was such a jerk about your trip. I was the one being selfish. You take such good care of all of us and you deserve a break sometimes. I love you more today than I ever have and thank you for our two amazing kids, for our life. I'm writing this on the back of a picture Emily left for me in the kitchen this morning. I love them both so damn much! If I don't make it out of here, I want you to go on without me, baby. Someday I want you to find someone else who will love you and take care of you and our kids. Just make sure he is worthy of you and will treat you good. I love you, Kim. I will always love you. Please kiss and hug our kids for me every day and tell them how much Daddy loved them. How they were wanted and cherished. And tell them that their Daddy loved their Mommy and that the last thing I wanted to do was to leave them and you. I just want to scream! I am so pissed this is happening! Who the hell would do this? And I'm scared. God, Kim — I'm so afraid right now. I just wish I could talk to you, hear your voice. I don't think I'm getting out of here alive. Please, my darling wife, remember I will love you always. For all time.

    Ray

The End

Acknowledgments

Thank you to my friends and family who supported me through this long process.

To my sisters Jayne and Patti for always being there for me.

A huge thank you to my literary mentors and friends Beth Ferry and Mike Farragher for all of your help.

Special thanks to my editor, Laura Ginsberg. Your insight and guidance enabled me to better tell this story.

To my daughters, Katie and Maria, thanks for your patience. It meant so much.

To my husband, Rick who encouraged me to have a dream.

And to my parents who are always in my heart.

About the Author

Mary Lou Irace is a former college administrator who earned a B.S. in Sociology at Rosemont College and an M.S. in Education/Student Personnel Services at Monmouth University. She lives in New Jersey with her husband and two daughters. This is her first novel.

54494138R00203

Made in the USA
Charleston, SC
05 April 2016